I0647394

POPULAR PUBLICATIONS   FACSIMILE EDITIONS

Terror Tales #1
(September 1934)

Starting in 1934, editor (and publisher) Harry Steeger unveiled *Terror Tales*: perhaps the flagship magazine in Popular Publications' so-called "Weird Menace" lineup of titles. Running for almost 50 issues, *Terror Tales* showcased some of the best suspense, mystery and terror stories to see print in the pulps. This premiere issue contains stories by Arthur Leo Zagat, G.T. Fleming-Roberts, Wyatt Blassingame, and Hugh B. Cave, among others.

Authors:

Arthur Leo Zagat, G.T. Fleming-Roberts, Wyatt Blassingame, John Flanders, Henry Treat Sperry, Hugh B. Cave

Illustrators:

Rudolph Zirm, Amos Sewell

If we told you return of this coupon would

GUARANTEE YOU $50 A WEEK,

WOULD YOU MARK AND MAIL IT?

But we don't tell you that! It's not true. Too much depends on you

WE DO say this — and can prove it: Thousands of men all over the country today are making $50 a week and over, and are emphatic in the conviction home-study training through I. C. S. Courses is the greatest single factor in shaping their careers! If you have just a vague wish for more money, don't trouble yourself or us with the coupon. But if you mean business, so do we!

EVERY TIME YOU SEE A COUPON LIKE THIS, OPPORTUNITY IS KNOCKING AT YOUR DOOR

Volume One   September, 1934   Number One

FEATURE-LENGTH MYSTERY NOVEL

House of Living Death............................By Arthur Leo Zagat   **8**

Harold Armour, deserted by his friends, forgotten by society, fought creeping madness through long days of mounting terror—while nightmare horrors came to life, and evil, mindless creatures lived with him in the dark house where fear dwelt always. . . .

THREE MYSTERY-TERROR NOVELETTES

Dead Man's Bride............................By Wyatt Blassingame   **60**

The Undead should long before have abandoned all fleshly fancies. Yet Eve Wingard, vibrant with life, was needed in that noisome realm where the dead walk always.

Hands Beyond the Grave....................By Henry Treat Sperry   **84**

A plain tale, simply told, by a man who lived two lives—and suffered much in both!

Terror Island ....By Hugh B. Cave   **102**

It was a grim gathering to begin with . . . but before the first night of their strange reunion was ended it had become a nightmare of shrieking fear and ugly passion.

SHORT TERROR TALES

Blood Magic............................By G. T. Fleming-Roberts   **50**

Her ancient fingers worked on tiny, needled figures—and her neighbors died one by one!

A Night In Camberwell....................By John Flanders   **80**

A tale of one dark night's adventure that you will not soon forget. . . .

— AND —

The Black Chapel............................A Department   **126**

Cover Painting by Rudolph W. Zirm

Story Illustrations by Amos Sewell

Published every month by Popular Publications, Inc., 2256 Grove Street, Chicago, Illinois. Editorial and executive offices, 205 East Forty-second Street, New York City. Harry Steeger, President and Secretary, Harold S. Goldsmith, Vice President and Treasurer. Entry as second-class matter pending at the post office at Chicago, Ill., under the Act of March 3, 1879. Title registration pending at U. S. Patent Office. Copyright, 1934, by Popular Publications, Inc. Single copy price 10c. Yearly subscriptions in U. S. A. $1.00. For advertising rates address Sam J. Perry, 205 E. 42nd St., New York, N. Y. When submitting manuscripts kindly enclose stamped self-addressed envelope for their return if found unavailable. The publishers cannot accept responsibility for return of unsolicited manuscripts, although care will be exercised in handling them.

4

The Cream of the Crop!

Magazines bearing this seal give you extra value
in thrilling fiction!

10c DIME DETECTIVE MAGAZINE

NOW 144 PAGES!—Features in the current August 15th issue a Cardigan Novelette by Frederick Nebel, NOT SO TOUGH—novelettes by Fred MacIsaac, J. Paul Suter, and John Lawrence—plus three great detective short stories. 7 smashing mysteries in all with danger-action on every page!

10c DIME MYSTERY MAGAZINE

The weirdest stories ever told! Featuring HONEYMOON IN HELL, by Wyatt Blassingame, and many other blood-chilling mystery novelettes and short stories written by masters of eerie fiction. Out August 15th!

The SPIDER

Offers you another great full-length exploit of Richard Wentworth, the Master of Men, in REIGN OF THE SILVER TERROR. Plus thrilling short stories of crime detection. Out August 3rd!

DARE-DEVIL ACES

Smashing flying stories of the Western Front. Read DIVING DYNAMITE by O. B. Myers, THE BATHTUB ACE by C. M. Miller . . . other great yarns.

MAVERICKS

Great new stories of the dim owlhoot trails, featuring FIVE AGAINST THE LAW, full-length novel by Kent Thorn, ONE MAN POSSE by Max Brand, Walt Coburn's BUTCH CASSIDY—SHERIFF MAKER, and others. A new, glamorous thrill in Western fiction! Out Now!

STAR WESTERN

THE BIG 160 PAGE MAGAZINE

GUNLESS GUNMAN, feature novel, by Max Brand, rides point in this great issue. Other salty tales of cattle-trail and range by Walt Coburn, Ray Nafziger, William F. Bragg, Art Lawson, Robert E. Mahaffey and others. Out Now!

G-8 and His BATTLE ACES

Follow G-8 as he battles the most ghastly squadron that ever flew—a staffel of man-beasts! A complete novel—THE PANTHER SQUADRON.

SECRET SERVICE Operator #5

America's Undercover Ace

Jimmy Christopher meets his supreme courage test in MASTER OF BROKEN MEN! Also thrilling Secret Agent shorts. Out Now!

10c DIME WESTERN MAGAZINE

Walt Coburn's great new novel, RIMROCK RENEGADES; Harry F. Olmsted; Ray Nafziger; Cliff Farrell and other top-hand Western writers wait for you in this great issue. Out August 15th!

DUSTY AYRES And His BATTLE BIRDS

An amazing account of the next great war. If you want to know what is going to happen when America fights again, read THE CRIMSON DOOM!

Big grin, big fist—swashbuckling Captain Bill and his gold doubloons set the South Seas aboil in Gordon Young's complete novel of a new character who will be famous.

A Taste for Terror

DID you ever as a child watch, fascinated by fear, as the shadows in your night-darkened room took on shape and form and furtive, blood-chilling motion? Have you ever choked back a scream of blind, unreasoning terror at the sudden sharp crunch of a footfall behind you on some deserted walk? If you've undergone either of these experiences, you'll remember the quickened beating of your heart, the swifter, tingling flow of blood through your veins. And you'll remember, too, the sudden, all-embodying sense of terrific suspense which held you breathless and palpitant for the fleeting fraction of one swiftly passing second.

That quickened beating of the heart that is always brought on by fear or fright, with its resultant speeding up of the blood flow, the bodily tension, the peculiarly breathless feeling of unusual awareness, all are part of nature's defensive machinery inbred in man since the earliest danger days of the race. In primeval times those reflexes, occurring when danger threatened, enabled the human animal to prolong his life and conquer his natural enemies. Stimulated by them, he could retreat with greater speed and agility or fight more fiercely than those other animals whose hearts and nerve centers were not so greatly affected by the fear emotion.

But today, in a generation protected and coddled by the artificial safeguards of civilization, the average citizen finds scant play for those tonic bodily reflexes which are so largely caused by primitive fear. The thrill of sport brings about a similar, though very much milder, form of stimulation. But sport is a poor substitute at best for the lusty dangers and conflicts of a day and period that is forever gone.

Is there any wonder then that we of today have been called a generation of thrill seekers? There's the tonic quality of rare old wine in a real thrill honestly felt—a stimulation, a toning up of all bodily functions that helps us to throw off, for a while at least, the accumulated virus of too-easy living.

Thrills, we believe, fill an important, necessary function in any normal, healthy human life. It is the hope and aim of this magazine to counteract to some extent—vicariously but none the less poignantly—the regrettable lack of this age-old stimulus in present-day life. In this, the first issue of TERROR TALES, and in the issues to follow, you shall be stripped of those safeguards which protect you from physical danger, spiritual menace and quick, heart-rending terror. You shall live alone with murderers and walk with maniacs. You shall witness strange midnight rites and taste of terror beneath some wan nocturnal moon. You shall battle mystery and menace and evil unbelievable in man. You shall learn much of witchery, werewolfery and those mystic blood cults which spring full blown into noxious life.

TERROR TALES is no magazine for the weak, the sickly or for those who suffer from high blood pressure. But if your heart is strong and your circulation normal we know that you'll enjoy its robust fiction fare. . . .

THE EDITOR

House of

By Arthur Leo Zagat

Have you ever asked yourself the grim question: "Am I going mad?" Harold Armour, deserted by his friends, forgotten by society, fought that ghastly conjecture through long nights and days of panicked, mounting terror— while nightmare horrors came to life and evil, mindless creatures lived forever with him in the dark house where fear dwelt always. . . . A masterfully told tale of dark, impenetrable mystery and black passions, written against an eerie background that will thrill you and shock you!

Complete Mystery-Terror Novel

ARE *you* sane?

Are you *certain* there is no taint in your blood, no lurking bomb of madness in your heritage that may not explode under sudden stress and make of you a staring-eyed lunatic— seething, perhaps, with the passion to see red blood spurting from arteries severed by your knife?

Not long ago a red bubble of rage exploded within your skull and you wanted to smash a leering, grinning face before you; smash it to a gory pulp. Temper, you say. Temper? Are you sure? Dead sure?

Remember: a madman believes himself normal, is convinced it is those others who are insane; those others who do not see the evil faces he envisions, who do not hear the shuddersome, compelling voices whispering in his ears the command to kill, *kill, KILL!*

Think. Think of the time you woke to deadly stillness in the night and knew,

knew beyond doubt that someone was in the room, *something* that in the next horrible moment would be at your throat, ripping the life from your quivering

Living Death

breast with sharp, unhuman claws. You
tried to scream for help and could not;
you could not stir a limb, a finger; and
the clammy-cold sweat on your brow was
like an icy touch from Outer Darkness

. . . After an eternity you managed
somehow to switch on your bed lamp
. . . and nothing was there, nothing at
all. "A bad dream," you muttered, still
shaking with abysmal fear. *But was it a*

dream? Were you not awake; acutely, fearfully awake as you plumbed that hell of causeless terror?

The fear of death is nothing, the fear of being buried alive a pale, wan thing, to the uttermost horror man can face: the fear of going insane, the fear that one *is* insane!

I know!

I HELD on to the rail as puffing little tugs bunted and hauled the *San Pedro* into its dock at Bush Terminal. My legs still buckled at the knees, a triphammer still pounded at the base of my skull though it was three weeks since I had come to aboard the freighter and known that I was homeward bound. Before that, I could dimly remember a parade of reptilian horror through my cabin, dim, vasty shapes moving through the mists that alcohol had evoked within my soul. But I had not touched a drop aboard ship, and my head was clear. I swear that it was.

Not that I was thinking. I was trying not to think. I was trying not to remember the terse cablegram that had come to me on the saltpeter *estancia* in the hinterland behind Iquique, the yellow slip carrying the news of my father's sudden death, the message that had rocked me back on my heels and set me guzzling *pulque* to deaden the week of waiting before I could get a boat for home. I was trying not to realize that the big house on Fifth Avenue would be cold, and empty; that dad would not be there to engulf my hand in his and say—as he always said on my return from one of the earth's far places—"Hello Hal! I've missed you. Come in and have a drink."

I suppose they let me guzzle to sottishness and insensibility as the kindest way to help me through that infinite week. At any rate it was not until the *Pedro* had been ten days at sea that I had waked to a dreary world that no longer held the father I adored, waked to know that I was alone, utterly alone. Small wonder that I was still white and jittery as the *Pedro* warped in to her berth.

I felt in the pocket of my jacket for a cigarette, and paper rustled. This was the suit in which I had been carried aboard; someone must have stuffed a last minute message into it. I pulled out the paper. It was a radiogram.

IMPOSSIBLE WAIT FOR YOU STOP SEE AVERY DUNN 200 WALL STREET IMMEDIATELY ARRIVAL NEW YORK STOP FULLY EMPOWERED SETTLE FATHERS ESTATE STOP

So far it made sense. But the signature gave me a jolt, the first, but by no means the last in this weird affair. "IRMA KAHN." The name was utterly strange to me. *Irma.* A woman's name. What on earth had a strange woman to do with my father's estate? Dad had been almost a hermit in the five years since mother left us, wouldn't so much as look at another woman. And this Avery Dunn! Our attorneys were Humperdinck, O'Ryan and Schwartz, a dryasdust firm of legal luminaries who have long monopolized the affairs of the first families of the metropolis.

I thought of looking at the dateline. My head was clear, I repeat. The message was addressed to me at Iquique, had arrived the day the *Pedro* sailed. It had been sent from the liner *City of Paris,* bound for France.

It was more than a year since my father had sent me down to rehabilitate his sadly neglected *estancia.* Maybe . . . I crushed the paper in my hand. No. Damn it! Dad wasn't that kind, he'd never . . .

A gangplank rattled to a dingy, splintered pier-floor, a whistle blasted aloft. I had to find out what this was all about, find out as quickly as I could. I jerked around, thumped down a companionway, and was down the gangplank before the last rope had been fastened. My footing heaved as if it were still the *Pedro's* deck, but that didn't slow my sprint down the long, dark tunnel of the covered pier. I was out in sun-glare and a yellow cab was veering toward me across the cobbles. I lunged for it, yelled "Wall Street. Two Hundred Wall," at the goggle-eyed driver, and scrambled inside. He started off with a jerk that threw me into the leather seat.

THE lobby man looked at me rather queerly when I asked for the number of Avery Dunn's office, but he said "Fourteen-ten," promptly enough. There was a mirror in the elevator, and I smoothed down my hair with the palm of my hand, got my tie around from under my left ear. I needed a shave pretty badly, but that couldn't be helped. At that I had to admit I was a tough-looking specimen. I stand six-four in my stocking feet, but you've got to measure me to realize it, because I'm built in proportion to my height. The Porto-Rican sun had tanned me pretty near to the leathery shade of a *mozo*, and my eyes were blood-shot and starey. I shouldn't have liked to meet myself on a dark night.

The door of Fourteen-ten didn't give me much information as to who and what Avery Dunn was. His name was down in one corner of the frosted-glass panel, painted in neat gilt letters. And under it was the one word, AFFAIRS. Big letters sprawled across the glass wouldn't have conveyed half the sense of importance those little ones did. And there was something queerly non-committal, almost mysterious about that evasive label.

When I got the door open I decided that Mr. Dunn's "affairs" must be manifold. Past the low railing that cut off a square around the entrance I could see a big room, and the rattle of typewriters was like a spigotty revolution going full blast. There must have been two dozen girls seated at long rows of little desks, all busily pecking away. Only three or four men were visible, moving around.

"Well," a snippy voice cut across my observation. "What is it?" I jerked my eyes back to the girl who sat at the telephone desk just beyond the railing. She was wearing some kind of black dress with a white collar, and there wasn't too much red on her lips. But her eyes were insolent. "What do *you* want?"

The muscles under my ears hardened a bit, but I answered, mildly enough, "Mr. Dunn. My name is Harold Armour."

Her face changed when I said it. Something came into it, no fright, but something akin to it. "Harold Armour," she repeated, I thought unnecessarily loudly. She thrust a plug into one of the holes in front of her and said, "Mr. Harold Armour to see you, Mr. Dunn. . . . Yes sir." Then to me: "You are to go right in sir. Straight back." She reached out a hand to swing open the gate in the railing beside her.

I looked at the opening and, quite unreasonably, hesitated a moment. Was some obscure sixth sense warning me of danger? Or were the first crawling worms of madness waking in my brain? At any rate, the prickling across the nape of my neck subsided almost immediately and I strode through, pounding stiff-legged toward the line of partitioned-off small offices at the back of the big room.

Even then there was nothing wrong with my observation, with the keen functioning of my thoughts. I can call up the face of each typist who flicked a quick glance at me as I passed; can spot on a diagram the position of every one of the male clerks. I can sketch for you, even now, the way the door of Dunn's office was set back in an embrasure made by two large square pillars, placed unusually close. But I did jerk that door open with uncalled-for violence and slam it shut behind me.

I SHOT a quick glance around the little room I had entered. If you spend much time in the outlands you get that habit; going into unfamiliar places your life may depend on a knowledge of every small item of your surroundings. And so I am certain, dead certain, of what I saw —*or thought I saw.*

The wall to my left, some ten feet long, was lined with book-laden shelves. So was the one to my right, except that at its further end the line of shelving was broken by a door. I noticed a diagonal scratch across the bronze keyplate of that door. Afterwards I clung frantically to the memory of that scratch, pictured it again and again as I battled with horror. Over and over, a thousand times or more, I asked myself if any dream, any hallucination, could be as detailed as that.

Opposite me a window let in light-flood on a massive desk that dwarfed the little man seated behind it. Avery Dunn was looking straight at me, his sallow face an expressionless mask. There was something faintly Mongolian about his features; a vague heightening of the cheekbones, an almost imperceptible slanting of the eyelids. And there was a peculiarly alien liquidity in his precise enunciation as he said, "I am glad you came directly from the ship, Mr. Armour."

My long legs took me across the space between us in two strides, but I didn't take the chair the movement of his pupils indicated. Oh, I know my behavior was boorish—outrageous. But remember that my parched system was clamoring for the alcohol it had been denied for nearly a month after a prolonged debauch. My actions were ill-mannered, perhaps, but not abnormal. *Not abnormal!* I put my fists knuckles down on the desk's glass

top and thrust out my jaw. "How the devil do you know," I rumbled, "that the *San Pedro* just docked? We are a day ahead of schedule. Who are you anyway? Who is Irma Kahn? What have the two of you to do with my father's estate?"

Dunn looked me over imperturbably, his narrow, glittering eyes like those of a biologist examining some new, not particularly interesting, specimen. "Irma Kahn," he said at length, "is the executrix of your father's estate. I am her business adviser." I think it was his utter indifference, his lack of resentment at my intolerable brusqueness, that inflamed me further.

"Where the hell do you come in?" I shouted at him. "I've never heard of you in my life, or the Kahn woman either. There's some monkey business here, and, by God, I'm going to find out what it is before I'm many hours older!"

I might have uttered some banality for all my bellow seemed to affect him. "I can quite understand your surprise," he responded very calmly, "and even your attitude. I expected both and prepared for them." His hands, their fingers curiously stubby, made a tent on the desk before him. "Irma Kahn is. . . ."

"Hal! Hal Armour," a muffled, insistent voice husked from my right. "Hal!" I wheeled, stared at the inner door in the side wall from behind which the sound seemed to come. "Hal! Watch out! *Watch out!*"

My jaw dropped, lax. Who could be calling to me here, using my first name? *Who was behind that door?*

"Hal! He's a . . ." the husked words were suddenly unintelligible, crescendoed into a mute shriek, and cut off. Came again. "Help! Help!" I lunged for the door, got my hand on its knob, flung it open and plunged through. I was in a long, narrow room. A man, his back to me, was struggling with another whose face I could not see. A metallic flash whizzed past my ear! A knife, thrown from behind me, plunged into the man's back. I saw blood spurt and I whirled to the menace from the rear. Dunn was out in front of his desk, his arm was raised. A second knife was in his hand, held by the weighted handle and poised for the throw that would plunge it in my own back. Steel springs uncoiled in my legs and I leaped straight for him, grabbing for the black hilt of that knife. I caught it, snatched it away. . . .

"*Mahoutma alloy! Stoot!*" The gibberish was a squealed command from my left. I twisted to it, saw . . . great heavens . . . saw a towering black giant, stark-naked, crouching just within the closed outer door. His face was an appalling spectacle of demoniac savagery and in his ebony hand a perfectly civilized automatic snouted at me!

Something crashed against the base of my skull, the world exploded in whirling coruscations of fire, and oblivion swept in. . . .

CHAPTER TWO

Screaming Faces

MY head was a swelling balloon of agony as I weltered up toward consciousness through oceans of pain-shot blackness. I heard my own name spoken in Dunn's liquid, foreign voice. ". . . Harold Armour, whose father's estate I am managing. He burst in here shouting accusations at me and when I tried to placate him he attacked me with that knife. Luckily this heavy seal was on my desk and I managed to knock him out with it before he did any damage."

"Lucky is right," a gruff voice responded. "That's a wicked blade, and he's big enough to split you in two with it."

I struggled to open my eyes. Hands were fumbling at me, a pungent odor stung my nostrils and something wet dribbled along my lips. Some of the fluid got into my throat and I swallowed convulsively. There was a minor explosion in my chest and my lids popped wide. A pink face was over mine. It had a little blonde mustache and was topped by a blue cap with a red cross embroidered above the visor. I tried to get up, found my arms were being held by iron fingers. My head jerked sidewise, I saw the glowering features of a clerk who had leered at me as I came through the outer office. "Easy," the ambulance surgeon said gently. "Take it easy, old man, and you'll be all right."

A squirrel was chasing its tail inside my skull, but my vision cleared a little and I could see, beyond the doctor, a policeman talking to Dunn. "Grab that man," I mouthed. "Arrest him! He's a murderer!"

The cop grinned, infuriatingly, and took a step that brought him above me as I lay on the floor. "That's all right," he chuckled. "You just calm down an' let the doc take care of you."

I forgot the throbbing pain in my head. "You damn fool," I howled, fighting to get away from the hands holding me down. "You . . . ass! It was Dunn killed the man inside, he tried to kill me, and you're letting him get away with it!"

The officer's eyes narrowed and his thick fingers moved along his nightstick. But the hospital man straightened and whispered something in his ear. The cop grinned and nodded. "What man?" he asked, more smoothly. "Inside where?"

"For the love of God!" I grunted. "The dead man in that room." I rolled; somehow the fellow holding me had relaxed his grip; started to point, started to say "Behind that door." And did neither!

There was no door in the wall back of

me! The shelves stretched solidly to the window! The door through which I had lunged to the unknown's cry for help had vanished! There was no sign, absolutely no sign, that an opening had ever existed in that book-lined wall!

I felt my eyes widen, heard myself gasp.

"There was a door," I shrieked. "There *was* a door there!"

"Sure," the physician said soothingly. "Sure there was a door there. But it isn't there any longer. Now you be a good fellow and let me take you to the hospital. *Our* doors stay put."

My stomach turned over as I realized that he was humoring me. Great heavens above! Dunn had made them think I was insane!

The thought sobered me. I must be careful, shrewd. I must match his guile with my own. "All right, Doctor," I muttered very calmly. "All right. I'll go with you. But you'd better take the black man with you too. He might hurt somebody with his gat."

"Hell!" the cop grunted. "He's batty as a loon."

"Keep quiet, Rafferty," the medico snapped. "I'll do all the talking." His blue eyes were shining with interest. "I want to find out just what he thinks he saw." Then, to me, "Who's this black man you're talking about, pal?"

"The fellow without any clothes that pulled a gun on me," I answered, talking slowly and carefully. "He couldn't get away without someone's seeing him."

"No, he couldn't get away." The man in the white coat smiled, and turned his head. "Anybody see a naked black man around here with a gun?"

There was a chorus of "noes," and for the first time I saw the staring-eyed girls crowding the door from the outer room. Fright mingled with morbid curiosity, on most of the white faces, but I saw pity in the eyes of one pert-featured minx. And somehow that pity made me cold, suddenly, cold all over.

"No one could have come into or out of this office without all of us seeing him," another girl said, her voice shrill with excitement. "We all know Mr. Dunn was alone in here till this man barged in, and nobody went in after him."

There was a general murmur of assent. "I heard him shouting at Mr. Dunn," the clerk who was holding me offered, "and I was just coming over when there was a crash and the boss yelled for help. I was the first one in. Those two were the only ones to be seen, and nobody could have gotten past me without my knowing it."

The floor rocked under me. They couldn't *all* be in a conspiracy against me! There was no door in the side-wall, there had been no naked negro! Great God! Were they right? Was I ... *insane?*

"Hell, Doc," the patrolman growled. "Let's get it over with. Let's put the nut in the wagon and get going."

I REMEMBERED the scratch on the door-plate. Tiny thing that .it was, it steadied me, gave me infinitesimal hope to which to cling. I couldn't have imagined that, I told myself. I tried to keep my voice even. "Doctor," I said. "Doctor. I know it looks bad for me. But will you do me a favor?"

"What is it, old man?" Bless him! He was convinced I was a madman, a homicidal maniac. But he was kindness itself, his voice gentle. May his tribe increase.

"I'd like to see what's behind this wall before you take me away."

"Certainly," he responded. "I'd like you to. Maybe if you see how impossible it is for the things you imagine to have really happened it will help us to cure you."

At a word from the surgeon my captor

released me. I was sore all over as I staggered to my feet. The burly clerk closed in on one side of me, the cop on the other, and we moved to the door. The girls scattered as we came toward them.

Dunn himself opened the door of the office on the right of his own. I looked in, and my legs were suddenly water-weak. The apparently unused room was utterly unfamiliar. Although I had only glimpsed that in which I had seen a man killed, I knew this could not possibly be the same. I had looked possibly twenty feet ahead of me into that one, this was only some seven wide. There was no break in the painted expanse of the wall on the left. And there, in a line with those in Dunn's chamber, were windows through which the sun was streaming. . . .

"Are you satisfied?" the medico asked quietly.

"Yes," I forced past the lump in my throat. "Take me away."

A black mist formed in front of my eyes and I swayed, clutching the cop's arm to keep from falling. "Come on," the policeman grunted.

"Wait," Avery Dunn said smoothly. "What are you going to do with him?"

"Take him to the psychopathic ward at Bellevue. I suppose he'll go to Manhattan State Hospital on the Island after a couple of days."

An icy shiver swept over me. Bellevue! The Island!

Dunn's reply came dully to my ears. "I should like to arrange that he go to a private sanitarium. I am in charge of his father's estate and there is plenty of money to give him the best of care."

The interne looked gratified. "That can be done," he said heartily. "But he'll have to be certified by two lunacy commissioners and committed by a judge. You'd better let me take him to Bellevue till the red tape is unwound."

The vertigo with which I was struggling

eased a bit, and I watched Dunn warily. One corner of his thick mouth twitched a bit and a film seemed to drop over his Oriental eyes. "I have some influence," he smiled. "It won't take me long to get things fixed up."

A BLOOD-FREEZING thought flared into being at the back of my tortured brain. In a public institution I should have some chance to prove, to myself and to others, that I was not insane. In a private asylum I should be utterly in the power of the evil-faced Dunn, utterly without hope. "No," I croaked. "No. I want to go with you, Doctor. Take me away with you."

The young fellow turned and patted me on the shoulder. He had to reach up to do so. "Don't be foolish, buddy," he said in the tone one used to a willful child. "If you knew what I do about the Island you'd appreciate the break you're getting."

My biceps swelled and my heart pounded. They thought me mad and would pay no attention to what I wanted! Dread closed in on me, quivering, black dread. Perhaps they were right. Perhaps I *was* a lunatic—a knife-wielding, murderous maniac. No! I thought of something. The knife with which I was supposed to have attacked Dunn! Where had that come from? I had no weapon of any kind when I left the *Pedro*. "Damn it!" I bellowed. "Don't talk to me like that. I'm being framed. I'm not crazy, I'm as sane as you are!"

The cop's fingers tightened on my wrist. "That's what they all say," he chortled with the unholy glee of the sane in the presence of the unbalanced. "All these nuts think there's a plot against them."

It was as if his hamlike fist had pounded against my jaw. I rocked back on my heels and the room swung dizzily around me. Faces, faces everywhere leered at me, and all about hundreds of fingers pointed in derisive scorn. An unhuman, horrible voice shrilled, "He's crazy! Hal Armour's crazy," broke into a cackle of triumphant laughter that echoed and re-echoed in vast spaces. Other voices shrieked and bellowed, roared and screamed, "Crazy! Crazy! Hal Armour's crazy!" and the pandemonium was threaded by the squealing gleeful laughter of insensate fiends.

I crouched, suddenly, and sprang, twisting as I leaped. My wrists tore from the grasp of my captors and I was free. Someone got a hand on my shoulder, I whirled and crashed a blow to a blond mustache on a pink face. I hurdled a desk, and dashed down a long aisle as screaming women scattered before me. Someone in an alpaca coat, piglike eyes glittering, loomed in front of me and my fist flailed out.

He was down and I had leaped his sprawled body. I stumbled and crashed against wood. Ink spilled and papers flew through the air. I saw the railing in front of me, glimpsed the insolent-eyed telephone girl with her mouth wide open and her face fish-belly gray. I thumped into the flimsy barrier, it splintered with a rending crash, and I saw the girl throw something, her earphones, at me. I dodged them, but the wires tangled around me. I plunged on in my bull-like rush, the phone switchboard dragged after me. I stopped to rip the cords away, and someone grabbed me from behind. I twisted to him, bellowing, and fists flew at me from every side. Tugging hands pulled my feet from under me and I crashed to the floor. Sweaty bodies piled atop me, swarmed over me. I was pinned down, helpless.

"Don't hurt him," the doctor's voice sounded thinly through the roaring in my ears. "Don't hurt him more than you can help."

A hand fumbled at my wrist, twisted it. I felt the sharp sting of a hypodermic needle and liquid being forced into a vein. Blackness spread swiftly through my arteries, reached my brain. . . .

CHAPTER THREE

Whips for the Mad

I OPENED my eyes. The ceiling above me was enameled a shining white and shadow-lines made a checkered pattern on it. Slowly I became conscious that I was parched, and that excruciating pain pounded in my head. I lifted a hand . . . tried to lift a hand to it but could not! Queer, I though, mighty queer. But my head hurt too much for me to raise it and see why.

Coarse cloth was under and over me, rasping my skin. That was strange too. They had taken my clothes from me, and I was lying stark naked on a bed. My tongue filled my mouth, and my face, my neck, ached dully. Something pressed heavily on my chest and other weights rested across my thighs.

I heard a door open. "You've come to, eh!" a grating voice said. "About time."

"I want my clothes," I said, and turned my head toward him.

The fellow filled the doorway. His swarthy face was like a troglodyte's, low-browed and heavy-jawed. My skin prickled as I saw that he held in one hairy hand a short, thick-lashed whip, black and snakelike. Good Lord! The walls were covered with gray, heavily quilted canvas! "Get your clothes, is it?" He growled through thick lips. "Wait till the doc sees yuh."

"The doc!" Memory hit me like a trip-hammer and horror closed around me once more. "Where am I?" I gasped. "In God's name where am I?"

The man leered. "Yuh'll find out quick enough." There was lip-licking gloating in the way he said it. "Too quick." The door slammed behind him, and I saw that it, too, was shrouded with quilted canvas. Saw also that no handle broke its surface.

Now I was thoroughly alarmed. I strained to sit up, and found it impossible. But my struggles dislodged the sheet covering me, and, forcing my head up, I saw that those were not weights on my chest and my thighs. They were broad webbed bands tightly stretched across my torso. My wrists were bound to the stout iron sides of the bed on which I was stretched and the one narrow window was covered with steel bars! Almighty God! I was strapped to a cot in the very center of a padded cell!

A scream formed itself in my throat, ripped to the surface. But I choked it back in time, throttled it to the merest whimper. I must not—something deep in my brain told me—I must not again act the lunatic they thought me. I must hold a tight grip on myself, do nothing that a sane, an utterly sane man, would not do. To do otherwise would be to play into their hands, into the hands of that slant-eyed, yellow-faced devil whose machinations had placed me here. Already I had muffed one chance at thwarting him. My blood ran cold as I realized that, remembering what the pink-faced interne had said. Two lunacy commissioners and a judge must have already decided that I was insane. Otherwise I would not be here!

"Watch yourself, Hal Armour," I muttered, half-aloud. "They can't keep you here forever if you behave. No more tantrums, no more scrapping. Don't give them another chance to say that you're crazy."

Great Jumping Jehosaphat! I was talking to myself! I stared, fear-ridden, at the shadow of the bars on the ceiling. Were they right? Was I . . . a madman?

Was this only a lucid moment, a glimpse of sanity from the twilight land of madness in which I was doomed to wander forevermore? I licked dry lips and shuddered.

"Well, well, well! So we've decided to take an interest in life." I turned to the chuckling voice. The short, roly-poly man coming through the door was the epitome of cheerfulness. "Jim Rand tells me you want your clothes." He rubbed hands together, and the fat rolls that were his cheeks lifted to a delighted smile. "We'll see. We'll see."

THE guard I had seen before followed the newcomer into the room, carrying a chair. He put it at my bedside and retreated, but I noticed that he went only as far as the door. There he leaned against the jamb, glowering at vacancy and swishing his whip against his pants leg. The fat little man sat down, fumbled for my wrist with his flabby fingers. He made clucking noises at the back of his throat, for all the world like a hen scratching up worms for its brood, and then exploded into speech again. "We might as well get acquainted," he said, and giggled. "I'm Doctor Helming, Dr. Ottokar Helming. And you are Harold Armour."

"That's one thing I'm sure of," I responded, fighting to keep hysteria out of my voice. "But I'd like to know where I am."

Helming vented his schoolgirlish giggle again. "He, he. Very good. One thing you're sure of. Very good indeed. I see that we're going to get along. And your pulse is quite normal. Remarkable. Most remarkable." His hand left my wrist, travelled to my eyelids and pulled them back. "Pupils clear too." His fingers felt peculiarly cold and clammy against my skin.

"What is this place, Doctor?" I repeated my question, quite calmly.

He pursed his tiny red mouth. "This place?" he chuckled. "A very fine place indeed. A very fine place." He waved his palm across my face, close to it. "Reflexes in order. You're in good shape, Mr. Armour. In good shape."

"Where am I?" I said again testily, then bit my lip. That was his game, of course. He was testing me, trying to get me angry. Trying to get me to flare into rage once more. Well, I'd fool him. "Not that it matters much. I don't suppose I shall have to give the address to very many taxi drivers."

Helming fairly chortled at that. "Heh, heh, heh. A comedian. A veritable comedian. No, my dear fellow, your taxi rides will be limited for a long time to come." His horrible touch stroked along my biceps, down my flanks. "What muscles," he cackled. "What beautiful muscles!"

My skin crawled under the slug-like feel of those gelid fingers. The fellow in the doorway watched with slitted eyes. He cracked his whip and the lash seemed to flick my raw nerves. I jumped inwardly. There was more than threat in the act, there was sadistic yearning, a vile eagerness to sense the crash of that black thong against flesh, to hear the howl of its human victim.

The doctor must have sensed my thought, for he simpered. "Don't be afraid of that whip, my boy. You needn't be afraid of anything here . . . if you behave."

"How about giving me a chance to behave," I ventured. "How about letting me get up?"

The doctor's lips made a little red O. "Hmm. Hmm. Do you think it's wise, son? Do you think it's wise?"

I tried to catch his eyes, those eyes that were like blue dots in a pink-white ocean of fat. "I don't want to instruct you in your profession," I said slowly, "but it would be wiser to let me get up

than to keep me lying here. If I'm strapped to this bed much longer I'll be a raving lunatic."

"Haw!" Rand spluttered. "Haw haw."

Helming looked at me, and a curious change came over his round face. Good humor fled from it; it was bleak, somehow terrifying. "You're not thinking of playing any tricks on me, are you? Are you?" Lines suddenly appeared at his mouth corners, deep lines of cruelty. "Because it won't get you anywhere. Not anywhere at all."

Can you imagine a round-faced, roly-poly fiend? That was what he looked like then. A short, fat devil whose belly would quiver with delight as he watched a damned soul fry in the bottommost pit of hell. "No, I don't like anyone who plays tricks on me, and when I don't like them," the words dripped from his little mouth, "it's . . . just . . . too . . . bad."

"Why shouldn't I behave?" I said mildly. "Will it get me anything if I don't?"

The momentary change in the fat man's appearance vanished, the amused twinkle returned to his eyes. "Fine," he chuckled, rubbing his pudgy hands together. "Splendid!"

He heaved from his chair, seeming no taller on his columnar legs than when he had been seated. "Jim," he turned to the guard. "I can see that Mr. Armour is going to be one of our star patients. Get him his clothing and give him a good room. Sixteen is vacant, I think." His insensate giggle was infuriating. "When he is ready, call me." He toddled to the door and vanished.

Rand came into the room and stood above me, his eyes cold flame. "The doc's good-natured today," he rumbled. "Lucky for you. But don't let that pep yuh up too much." He pulled the flexible length of his whip lovingly through his fingers. I saw certain crusted brown stains on it and shuddered. "Don't let it give yuh idears."

I STARED at the remnants of the meal Rand had brought to Room Sixteen and tried to fight off the black despair that rested on me like a pall. The food had been good enough, but cut small, it had been served on paper plates with a paper spoon. These now lay on the upper one of two shelves set in a recess in the white enameled wall. A comb and brush, fashioned of papier-mache, that were shoved to one side showed that this shelving was intended to be a dresser. I had eaten standing, for the only chair was bolted to the door next to a cot, also fastened in place, whose iron bars were welded at their joinings. These were the cubicle's only furnishings, and worst of all, a stout steel grating covered a small window so high up that I could not look out through it.

My eyes wandered to the door. The surface it presented to me was blank; no knob, no key-plate, showed on its smooth surface. The barrier opened outward, I had noted, and there was nothing on the inner side by which the room's occupant could manipulate the latch. Simply, ingeniously, that door was locked against escape while it gave ready access to anyone wishing to enter.

I tried to put a hand in my pocket for a cigarette, the fingers stubbed against cloth and I recalled that, although my own suit had been returned to me, cleaned and neatly pressed, every pocket-slit was sewed closed with strong thread. Somehow that little incident, more than anything else, brought home my situation.

I groaned. I was a man condemned as insane; imprisoned, helpless. Doomed to living death! A cold shudder ran through me. And then a sound twisted me to the door, a muffled scream from somewhere outside, far off. A woman's scream! My blood curdled . . . and then I remembered where I was. My fisted hands unclenched, but I quivered to the anguish in that scream. It came again louder, nearer; there was the patter of running feet; the thud of heavier, following ones. Something thumped against my door, the knob rattled, the door ripped open and someone was plunging through. I had one glimpse of a fear-distorted face, of golden-glinting, dishevelled hair, of a white shoulder against which red marks of a gripping hand blazed, and the girl swept past me, shrieking. Rand plunged into the room, his face contorted and black with fury, his whip whistling in his hands. "Got you, you she-devil," he snarled. "Got you!"

"Save me," the girl shrilled. "Oh save me!"

I grabbed at the keeper, got my hands on his arm. "Wait!" I cried. "Wait a minute." This was a woman after all, a girl. I forgot that she must be mad. "Stop it!"

His whip lashed at me, stung across my cheek. "Out of my way," Rand bawled. "Out of my way, *loony*."

THE epithet ripped my good resolutions to tatters. My fist came up. He ducked it, leaped sideways. I lunged at him— he whirled with lightning swiftness. I saw the lash—off-balance I could not dodge—it crashed across my face, searing like the sting of a scorpion.

I staggered—lunged again. And again he avoided my blow with an agility belaying his hulking body, again the black whip slashed across my face, cutting knife-like. It crashed me to the floor.

The girl shrieked! I exploded to my feet, landed a fist somewhere on him with all the frenzied strength I could put into the blow. It rocked him, but his wrist flicked and his whip whistled, curled around my waist. It flung me away from him, threw me headlong across the room. I thumped into the girl, she sprawled across the cot, and I fell over her. I felt her warm body under me, even in that moment I sensed the sweet redolence of her breath. But I lifted, bounded back at Rand, whimpering with rage. I ducked his whiplash and got another blow home. The impact jarred my elbow to the shoulder, but he shook his head, jumped back, and launched another whizzing slash.

I saw only his swarthy face in a red mist, and the black striking snake of his devilish weapon. It was everywhere, slashing at me, cutting my face, my arms, hurling me from side to side with terrific force. I tried to reach his face with my fists, connected once, once only. I might as well have battered at a marble statue. I heard someone shrieking obscenities in a shrill, crazed voice—knew it was myself. I knew dimly my face was wet with blood, my chin dripping with it. Rand's lips were retracted in a bestial snarl displaying rotted, yellow fangs, and lurid lights crawled in his black eyes. The whip cracked again across my head . . . .

Somewhere in the darkness into which I fell endlessly a girl screamed with terror, with unutterable fear. . . .

CHAPTER FOUR

Shang!

SOMEONE was sponging my head with freezing water. I beat up towards consciousness as the blankness within my skull pulsated with an agony not wholly physical. Voices penetrated to me, Dr. Helming's insane giggle, Rand's gruff rumble. "I don't let no loony make a pass at me like that." There was sadistic satisfaction in the guard's throaty growl.

"But you want to be more careful, Jim. Look at the mess you made of him. Suppose you'd killed him?"

"Suppose I had? Wouldn't be the first." That was a pleasant thought.

"No. But Avery Dunn sent him in. I didn't get a chance to tell you that before." The doctor's tones were meaningful.

"Oh yeah!" I heard, could almost see, Rand's thick lips smack. "He's one of Dunn's is he? Say, I'm getting sick of handling that guy's pets with kid gloves. There's that damn girl, and the old guy in Twenty-four. I could of smashed him in the puss this morning, crabbing about his food."

A hardness came into Helming's voice, a savage note that reminded me of the demoniac savagery I had seen in his little eyes not long before. "Lay off him, Jim, let him alone. That's our ace in the hole if Dunn and his woman get a yen to double-x us."

"All right. All right. But if it's gonna be lay off this one and that one there ain't gonna be no more fun around this joint."

Helming chuckled. "There will be fun enough to suit you. I just got a tip the State inspectors are coming through in a week to check up on all commitments."

My heart leaped. If there was to be an inspection, a check-up, I should have a chance to prove my sanity. I must watch my every move. It was my chance, my only chance and I would not throw it away. "Oh yeah," Rand growled. "We gotta work quick then."

"Damn quick. But leave it to me . . . and Shang. Say! This bird is still out. If he doesn't wake up in two shakes I'll have to give him a shot."

"Gawd, Doc, that stuff's powerful. If his heart ain't so good . . ."

That was enough for me. I groaned, let my eyelids flicker and come open. Helming's round face was over mine. It beamed. "Ah, my dear fellow," he giggled. "Feeling better I hope. Feeling better? Ready to be a good boy?"

I let terror show in my eyes. "Yes," I moaned. "Yes. Anything. Anything except that damn whip." I shuddered visibly, looked around as if in fear. But the girl wasn't there. Rand was on the other side of my cot, his stubby fingers clutching the whip handle. I whimpered as my eyes lit on it, cowered away.

"Steady, my boy." Helming put his hand on my shoulder, where the whip had ripped my jacket sleeve, and it felt like a clammy-cold dead thing. "Steady." He clucked. "You don't have to be afraid of that thing if you behave."

I bit my lips. "But he was going to hit the girl, Doctor. He was going to hit the girl with it and I couldn't stand for that. Could I?"

"Chivalrous," he simpered. "Very chivalrous. But you must remember where you are. This is a sanitarium for mental diseases, you know, and some of our . . . er . . . guests must be handled like children. They must be chastised you know, for their own good. For their own good, more in sorrow than in anger."

"Yes," I said while my eyes called him a liar as I remembered the lust to inflict pain that had distorted Rand's face. "I understand now. I forgot for the moment where I was. I am sorry."

Helming chuckled. "Do you hear that, Jim? He is sorry. Mr. Armour apologizes and he will give you no more trouble. I told you he would be a good patient. I told you so."

"Yeah," Rand said, and licked his lips. "Yeah."

"If you are up to it, my boy," the physician continued cheerfully, "I should like to take you on a tour of the establishment. You will understand better then why we are forced to apparently severe methods at times. Only apparently severe, of course."

I struggled to a sitting posture on the bed. "Come on," I said weakly. "Come on." That was what I wanted. Like a cat in a strange house I wanted to know my surroundings, every nook and corner of it. And I had another reason for assenting to a tour of inspection, unacknowledged even to myself.

I wanted to see the girl again, the girl with the streaming, golden hair and the eyes that were blue as the sea at dusk.

RAND was on one side of me as we left the room, Helming on the other. A long, dim corridor was lined by numbered doors. We moved toward a flight of stairs across the head of which a steel-barred gate stretched, ceiling-high, and we paused a moment while Rand fumbled a key into its lock.

Sound came up to me through that stair-well, a mumble of sound that was somehow unclean. There were human voices in it, strangely distorted; and there were other noises, that might have been animal mewlings or the gibberings of . . . only the Lord knows what! And with the sound came an odor, the fetid stench of unwashed bodies, of beings whose control of their bodily functions had gone with the darkening of their minds. An odor that had something in it of the grave, something of the jungle . . . an odor that clung to my nostrils all the nightmare time I was in that House of Hell, that affronts my nostrils still.

Rand's key scraped in the lock, the gate swung open. We passed through, the steel clanged shut behind us. The staircase curved so that it veiled that to which we descended, but already a cold shiver of gruesome anticipation rippled up my spine.

"Beyond the Alps lies Italy," someone boomed sepulchrally. "Forward, my men." We came around the last curve of the stairs, I heard the smack of an open-handed slap on flesh, and a lisping, sexless voice said, "Thank you, kind sir. Your caretheth are motht welcome." I could see nothing, at first, but a big room, vaguely lighted by barred windows, high up, a room filled with a seething, tumultuous throng. A dog barked, realistically, and from a far corner came the "Hoink, hoink," of a rooting sow. Underneath the tumult a monotonous moan murmured, "The bugs are biting me. One, two, three, four. The bugs are biting me. Five, six, seven, eight."

HELMING'S touch on my arm halted me at a point of vantage. "How do you like my pets," he whispered. "Aren't they sweet?" His hands went back to their eternal dry-washing. "As pretty a collection as you will find in any asylum this side of Charcot's in Paris." He giggled, complacently.

My vision cleared, individual figures began to define themselves, faces that belonged to some weird dream. Here was one without a forehead, eyes bulging as if they would drop from their sockets at the slightest touch. There someone crouched on a long stool, his head an enormous dome that overbalanced a wizened body from which it seemed to have sapped all nourishment. He looked steadily into the distance, and the sorrow lining his unhuman visage might have been for all the woes of the world since time began. A wild laugh rang out from a far corner. My burning glance twitched to the maker of the sound, and I saw an expressionless countenance whose pallid skin was so tightly drawn, whose lips were so far retracted and eye-sockets so deeply sunk that it was a veritable death's-head, a living skull that laughed on and on, with a soul-shaking horrible cachinnation that held no humor and no thought.

There were other unmoving figures in that obscene gallery, other shapes distorted almost beyond human semblance, other creatures lost in nightmare phantasm, other amorphous shapes that sat or stood, or sprawled on the filth-strewn floor weighed down by a black melancholy whose utter woe showed in their very stillness. But they were by far not the worst.

This shrieking little man with the big head who darted crazily from side to side of the great hall, his face twisted with terror, his shrill voice screaming, "Eyes, eyes. They're tearing out my eyes!" as he turned, snarling, at each wall and clawed invisible pursuers. . . .

And now I realized that these were not all men here, that there were women, women and girls, intermingled in the gibbering throng. Women among these madmen! Shadowy bulks in dark corners disentangled themselves before my reeling vision. . . .

I reached out for support to the wall. This was hell, worse than hell! It was a Doréesque vision of umbrous horror, a Dantean Hades, a scene at describing which the pen of Victor Hugo himself might have faltered. The man that permitted it—this jelly-like, giggling man at my side, must himself be a monster. My fists clenched, I started to twist to Helming, to cry out in protest . . . when the glint of blonde hair caught my eye. Good God! Was she here? The girl that had fled to me for help. I peered into the horror pit. . . .

I could not find her. But just there, where I had thought she was, I saw a doorway, and I thought the portal moved.

"Doc," Jim Rand was saying behind me. "I don't see Hen Garten. He should be here."

Helming clucked. "That's right. He's not at his post. I told him the next time he wandered off I'd fire him, get another guard."

Rand sounded uneasy. "I dunno, Doc. Maybe Shang . . ."

THE door was moving out there. It was opening, and from it there came a gibbering wail, the long-drawn howl of a soul lost in torment. The lunatics below surged away from it. I heard Rand gasp, saw him plunge past me, down the last few steps. His face was white, his whip upraised. The door at the other end of the chamber flung wide, and framed in it was a form more horrible than any I had yet seen.

The thing's torso was that of a giant, tremendous; but atop the spreading shoulders a tiny, doll's head lolled. A doll's head—but no doll's head ever showed the sheer brutality, the utter savagery of that face. Its scalp was hairless, but its great, naked chest was shaggy as any beast's. Its arms, incredibly long, were lifted high. Broken chain-links hung from their wrists, and in their great gripping hands something was suspended. . . .

"Shang!" Rand roared. "Shang!" He plunged toward it, his whip slashing a way through the cowering, shrieking lunatics. "Drop him, Shang!"

The thing howled once more; there was obscene triumph in the sound, and it threw that which it held straight at the oncoming keeper. The door slammed shut. . . .

What lay squashed on the floor had once been a man. A black whip was knotted around its skewed neck, its face was a gory pulp.

A girl crawled to it along the floor. She prodded the shapeless corpse with a long-nailed finger, and laughed.

Rand reached the body. He seized the girl and flung her away, knelt to what lay there. He only glanced at it, and turned a white face to us on the stairs. His eyes were black coals, and his mouth worked. "It's Hen, Doc. Hen! He must have gone in to feed Shang and the brute got him."

Helming giggled inanely. "I told him not to, the fool. I told him to leave Shang alone. You'd better go in and chain the fellow again."

Rand's lips were a thin white slash across his swart face. "Not me. Not on your tintype. I don't go in there."

"Some one has to. The Holmes girl is in there. If he gets at her . . ."

"I'm not going in there, that's flat. He can have the yellow-haired she-devil for all I care."

The yellow-haired . . . Good Lord! I twisted to Helming. "Who's in there? Who is it? Not the . . ."

"The girl Jim chased into your room. Yes. She's in a punishment cell, in there. If Shang gets at her . . ." His eyes were glowing strangely, a corner of his little mouth lifted. But I did not notice it then. All I thought of was that *she* was somewhere back there, at the mercy of the monster I had just seen, the monster who had done . . . that!

"Good Lord," I groaned. "You're not going to let him get her. You wouldn't do that!"

Helming spread his hands wide. "I wouldn't dare go in there. And Rand is afraid. What can I do about it?"

"What . . ." I twisted from him, plunged down into the gibbering mass of maniacs that had clotted at the foot of the stairs, as far from the door as they could get. I shoved through them, saw leering, idiot faces on every side, some still working with the contagion of fear, others already betraying the forgetfulness that is insanity's one recompense. A thin hand clutched my sleeve, dreamy eyes peered into mine, and a soft mouth said: "Wait, pretty boy. Wait for my kisses." I tore myself away and was through them.

Rand made no motion to stop me, but skewed around on his knees and watched me from between the slitted lids. The fetor here was choking, revolting. I was at the further door, reached for its knob.

From behind it I could hear a muffled sobbing. My fingers shook as I turned the knob and pushed the heavy, nail-studded door open.

EVEN out of the vague half-light of the bedlam from which I came my eyes could not penetrate the darkness ahead. I took a step forward. The door shut behind me—and I heard the rattle of a shot bolt. An oath ripped from me as I whirled and surged against the door. It was immovable. Rand had locked me in here, locked me in the darkness with the gigantic madman, the simian figure that had made pulp of a human! I was unarmed . . . Hen had had the black snake-whip and the thing they called Shang had knotted that dread weapon around his twisted neck. Panic seized me as I crouched and listened to dreadful sound that came from within, the blubbering sobbing as of a gorilla baby crying. Panic rocked me as I heard the tinkle of metal and the whisper of shuffling movement that came toward me.

I crouched, my biceps flexing, my fingers spread wide, curving, as the menace came toward me through the darkness. The blub, blub of the thing was more fearful than an animal growl would have been.

I crouched lower, and moved silently sidewise with some dim idea of evading the monster, of avoiding it in the blackness. But solidity stopped me, the solidity of a stone wall that barred my progress. I was caught, fairly caught, and Shang crept slowly to the attack!

Slowly! God how slowly that mad giant was coming! The blackness was graying a bit as my pupils widened. I could make out the shapeless bulk of him, dark against the dark. He seemed to be crouched as I was crouched, seemed to be hitching himself along spasmodically, jerking forward with each blubbing sob, jerking for-ward and gasping at the same instant, silent and motionless at the same instant. He was feet from me . . .

And then he was gone! There was nothing before me but the black-gray of emptiness. I heard nothing, nothing at all. He had vanished like . . . like something half-seen in the instant between sleep and waking, unseen when midnight terror has one fully awake!

Was this too, unreal? Like the black in Dunn's office, like the room where I had seen a man murdered, a room that never was? I bit back a scream that ripped at my dry throat, swallowed hard. There *had* been something there! Shang *had* been there, he had found a side exit from the corridor we were in, had slipped aside to avoid me. He had been afraid of me, had fled from me. It was so dark here that I could not see the side-opening through which he had gone. That was all. That must be all!

If that were so I could find the exit he had used by moving forward, by feeling along the walls. I tried and found that my arms could span the width of the corridor, that my fingertips could scrape each side. I started forward, hesitated. . . . What if he were still lurking on one side or the other? What if he should leap out at me from some ambush where he was hidden? Was he playing with me, luring me away from the door that might admit Rand or Helming to my aid? I swayed in indecision, groaned. . . .

And heard an answering moan, far ahead! The moan of a woman in anguish. A pitiful little sound, muffled and tiny in the vague reaches that seemed endless before me. I forgot myself, forgot Shang. "Where are you?" I called, remembering to pitch my tone low. "Where are you?"

My question rolled into the tunnel, reverberant. It seemed to me I could follow its progress as it wandered off into the dim passage. And after awhile—it must have been at once but to my taut senses minutes seemed to elapse—a feminine voice come back in reply. "Here. Here! Save me. Oh save me!"

THE words, the words and the very voice that I had heard before, in my room! I leaped ahead, running, reckless of Shang, reckless of everything except that the golden-haired girl was ahead somewhere, that she was in trouble, needed me.

The passage seemed interminable, my flying feet seemed to be spurning a treadmill that ripped fast and faster beneath them while I advanced not at all. But at last the corridor twisted, I saw light ahead, dull light that seemed bright after the darkness. I heard her voice again.

"Save me!"

The voice came from behind a door in the side of the passage, the light from a transom over it. I dug heels to a stop, whirled to the door. Bolts held it shut, two bolts that sank deep into dull-gleaming sockets. I flicked them loose, jerked the door open. And stopped, aghast. "The devils," I gritted. "The lousy devils!"

It was a room like the one in which I had first come to, its walls quilted with gray canvas. It was a cell, a padded cell. But there was no cot there, no furnishing of any kind. There was only a vertical framework of steel, white enameled, a vertical square framework some six feet high. And within it. . . . I balled my fists and cursed those who had done this thing with every malediction in English and Spanish and bastard Indian to which I could lay my tongue.

She hung there in chains, chains that stretched her arms horizontally from her shoulders, that held her little feet together in the center of that fiendish square. She had fainted, her head lolled forward on her bent neck, and her long hair, a ripple of falling sunlight, all but veiled the flaccid but unutterably lovely curves of

her slender form. One garment—a flimsy, pastel colored gossamer web—was all that they had left her and through it I could glimpse the golden sheen of her skin. The golden sheen of her skin, and something more! Livid red weals marked that fragile flesh, red marks of a cruel whip like those that still burned on my own cheeks.

I managed to get to her. The chains were not locked, merely hooked together so that they could be easily loosed. I unfastened the lower ones first, then the ones that held her wrists. She fell into my arms. For a moment I held her, shaken by the warm feel of her, for a moment I drank in the sheer young beauty of her face. Then her long lashes trembled against the soft swell of her cheeks, her lids opened, and I was looking into deep blue pools of fear, of terror. "Oh," she gasped, and twisted from my hold. "Oh!" She slid away from me, cowered against the wall. Her mouth quivered.

"Don't be afraid," I said gently. "I'm trying to help you." I slid out of my suit-jacket, tossed it to her. "Here, slip into that, it will make you more comfortable."

As she obeyed she searched my face. "You . . . . why you're the man who . . . . whose room . . . ."

"You ran into when you were trying to get away from Rand. Yes. I tried to help you out then but I wasn't very successful. I'm Hal Armour, at your service." I bowed.

A tiny, fugitive smile lightened her face an instant, and a little of the terror seeped from her eyes. "And I'm Nan Holmes."

Her voice was tight, husky, edged with hysteria. It brought me back to our situation, the danger we were in, the threat of the prowling maniac who for some reason had evaded me. Time enough to ask questions later. "Look here," I said. "We've got to get out of here somehow. I don't know anything about this place. . ."

"I do. There is a way out."

"Through the big room back there? I'm afraid . . . ."

"No. In the other direction. Another staircase."

"Come on then," I began. "If Shang . . . ." I stopped as her eyes flashed wide with renewed terror, stopped and whirled to the door behind me.

THE giant stood in the opening, his little head thrust forward, foam dribbling from his protruding lips, his tiny eyes fixed not on me but on Nan beyond me!

I leaped toward him, my fist arcing. But I never reached him. One long arm flicked forward, a back-handed swipe sent me reeling. I twisted, plunged back to the attack. And again the brute crashed me effortlessly away. I skidded along the floor, the wall stopped me. I was half-stunned, my senses were alert but my limbs refused to obey the frantic signals of my brain. I watched Shang's curiously bowed legs shamble slowly toward the girl, watched his hairy fingers curve to seize her, watched the avid, lascivious working of his thick-lipped mouth.

A squeezed, tiny voice whispered, "Hal! Save me, Hal!" It pulled my gaze to Nan, to the terror that struck all beauty from her face, to the hopeless appeal in her eyes.

And suddenly strength was back in my muscles! I rolled over, lifted to toes and spread fingers in a sprinter's crouch, hurled myself at Shang's twisted legs in a football tackle. My arms clamped around his knees, my shoulder struck, and he crashed down.

I had time only to yell, desperately, "Run, Nan, run!" and then the volcano exploded. I was lost in a mad maelstrom of fighting, a frenzy of threshing arms, legs, a whirlpool of bared teeth, ripping nails. The noisome thing I fought was a growling, mad animal; a fanged demon; a volcano of restless fury. But reason, civilization, was stripped from me also. I fought him fang for fang, claw for claw, in a snarling battle that knew no rules, no mercy. Scratching, gouging, biting, I was primordial male battling for my mate, he was ape-man raiding from the dank jungle. He was gorilla-man, his strength triple mine, his maniac fury unconquerable. But for minutes, for long minutes, I held him even.

And then—I don't know how—his shaggy fingers were clamped around my throat, he was atop me, his knees crushing my chest. His drooling, horrible face was close to mine; his yellow, rotted fangs bared by curled back, black lips; his tiny eyes red-blazing with maniac fury. His fingers started to close, my breath was cut off; his fingers were tightening, tightening; his face blurred, was gone in a black mist that veiled my bulging eyes; my lungs were bursting, my fists flailed at his arms that were columns of whipcord and steel; beat weakly, fell flaccidly down. . . .

CHAPTER FIVE

The Voice in the Hall

A SHRILL whistle pierced the mists. I felt the fingers crushing my throat jerk. The whistle came again . . . . above me the monster whimpered. And suddenly the hands were gone from my neck, the weight from my chest. I pulled air into my torn lungs; it cut knife-like. A nausea retched me, I fought it as the haze obscuring my vision faded. Pain pulsed in my throat, my chest, and the floor heaved under me. But I was alive, miraculously I was alive, and Shang was gone! I could see now, and he was nowhere in the room. Nan was gone too. I was alone.

I lay helpless, gasping, gathering strength for the effort to rise. A voice sounded at the door, Helming's giggle. The physician's round face swam over mine, his cold fingers were on my wrist. "You're all right, my boy," he chuckled. "All right."

"Shang," I husked, the words rasping my palate. "Shang."

"He got away. We don't know where he is. He's prowling somewhere around." Uneasiness flickered in Helming's eyes.

"Why .... why ....?"

"Why didn't he kill you?" He shrugged. "His spasm passed, I suppose. It's happened before. But come, we've got to get you to your room, take care of you. You're pretty well bunged up." He slid an arm under me, lifted. With his aid I managed to get to my feet. "How did he catch you, here?"

Something in his face warned me to be careful how I answered. Something in his face, and my suit jacket, lying crumpled in the corner. Its message was plain. "I was looking for him," I mumbled, "and found this room. Heard a sound at the door and there he was. I suppose those are the chains by which he was bound."

"Yes," Helming lied, and relief showed on his rotund countenance, was quickly hidden. "Yes. We keep him here. But he's so powerful when he gets one of his fits that nothing will hold him. When he is running amuck he is dangerous, will kill anyone he sees on sight. And all we can do is keep out of his way till the spasm passes. But he's never yet succeeded in getting out of this part of the asylum. God help us if he ever does." He wasn't giggling now, fear quivered in his tones. "But we've got to get you to your room. It's late; a good night's sleep is what you need."

I could walk unsupported by now. I followed him out into the dim corridor on which this room fronted, shot a glance to the right as my scalp prickled at the thought that Shang still lurked out there,

drooling venom. Helming's flabby hand turned me to the left. We hurried through the dimness, ten paces or so, the corridor turned again, and a staircase lifted ahead of me. "This way," he said. I started to mount. But turned back suddenly to an agonized howl that ripped out from somewhere below.

"Good God," I gasped, staring at another stairs that dipped down to darkness alongside the one I was on. "What was that?"

"Never mind that," Helming giggled, pushing me gently upward. "We have to use some pretty stern discipline here sometimes. One of our inmates was somewhat unruly, and Jim Rand is teaching him a lesson. Jim believes in the old adage, 'spare the rod and spoil the .... er .... lunatic.' It's nothing, though; the fellow is making a lot more noise than what he is getting warrants."

I was too weak to argue, too weak to resist the compulsion with which he urged me on, though gooseflesh prickled along my spine. I recalled the sadistic lust in the big keeper's eyes. No, Rand was scarcely one to spare the rod.

I could still hear those howls as we reached the head of the stairs and a steel-barred gate like that at the other end of the corridor with the numbered doors. Helming swung this open. "The lock on this is broken," he smiled. "I shall have to get it fixed in the morning. No hurry, though. Everyone here knows that these stairs lead only to Shang's quarters, and I assure you no one would try to escape that way." He giggled.

"Suppose he found he could get out through there," I asked. "What then?"

"Oh, I wouldn't worry about that. He's due to be quiet for at least twenty-four hours now, and by that time the lock will be fixed." He paused, then said meaningfully. "Of course, if he should get another spasm he'll remember that he didn't finish you off and come looking for you. But here's your room. Pleasant dreams, my boy. Pleasant dreams."

BEFORE I could voice my protest I was in my room and the door had closed behind me. I reeled across the floor, found the cot in the darkness, fell across it. For a long time I lay there, unthinking, feeling only the pain of my wounds, feeling only black despair.

But after awhile thought started again. And I had plenty to think about. Nan, for instance. Was she safe? Had she gotten away? Where was she? What was she doing in this place anyway? There had been terror in her face, fright, but not insanity. By all that was holy her eyes had been sane as mine.

As mine? I groaned. *Was* I sane? For an instant the panic question reached its livid tendrils into my brain. Even now I was not sure how much that I had seen was real, how much the product of my own fevered imagination. The dreadful quarter-hour when I had crouched in that dark tunnel, trapped, while Shang slithered closer and closer, only to vanish inexplicably . . .

Inexplicably! So much there was unexplainable in what had passed! Rand's terror, for instance, of the mad monster, and Helming's. Apparently that had not lasted for long, since the doctor had appeared in Shang's very bailiwick not long after and displayed no trepidation. The bolting of the door behind me, why had that been done? *To make sure I could not escape from the beast?*

And what was it that had saved me at the last? Not a change in Shang's mood but the piercing whistle I had heard. Who had given that whistle, Helming? Rand? If they could control Shang why had they been afraid of him? *Were* they afraid of him? I caught myself up as my speculations came

around full circle. If I kept thinking along that weary treadmill I should go mad. *Go* mad? Was I not already . . .

Damn it! I must stop thinking. Sleep. I needed sleep, God knows I needed it. My body was wracked with pain, my limbs water weak. Maybe sleep would clear my mind, bring me strength.

Sleep . . . Sleep . . .

I dreamed of Nan Holmes, her golden hair a shimmering veil through which I caught glimpses of her white body; her rounded arms, pink-tipped hands stretched imploringly to me. Her blue eyes drew mine to them, I looked deep into their cerulean depths; sank deep, deep into their peace, their promise . . .

And snapped awake! Wide awake, and quivering in the darkness with the sense of danger close at hand! I lay tensed, not stirring, and fought cold fear clutching my throat as Shang's fingers had clutched; fought cold fear and listened . . . to silence, to dead silence of the silent house. There was no sound. But I knew, knew beyond doubt, that some deadly peril threatened me. I felt its aura, froze in its icy, creeping menace.

There *was* a sound. No, not quite a sound, a sense of movement, infinitely slow, infinitely cautious movement, somewhere in the room. Against the tautness of my neck muscles I forced my head around, till I could look in the direction from which it seemed to come towards the door. A vague thread of yellow light, vertical, thin as a hairline, bisected the darkness. Imperceptibly it widened, was pencil-thick, was finger-wide. Someone —something, was opening my door! A shout tore at my throat, a scream of fear . . . but made no sound. Nightmare paralysis quenched it, nightmare paralysis made of me a marble statue in the grip of gibbering, grisly terror. Unbearable terror!

Something blobbed the dim light-line,

inch-wide now, something black, serrated. A hand clutching the door edge. A hand whose fingers were hirsute, shaggy with black hair! The hand of an ape. *The hand of Shang!!*

No! It couldn't be, it must not be. This was a dream, a nightmare of terror. That was why I felt this unutterable fear, which I could not move. It wasn't so! It wasn't . . . God! What sort of man was I to lie there, motionless, while grisly death crept into the room? I surged from the bed—*tried* to surge. Something threw me back, held me to the cot, held me helpless. *Something!* Great Jupiter! It wasn't fear that held me rigid, it wasn't terror! *I was strapped down!* By all that was fiendish, I was strapped to that bed with the same webbed bands that had been my first experience of this House of Hell!

A low growl twisted my look to the door again; a foetid, animal smell affronted my nostrils. The opening was wider now, wide enough to admit the mad giant's tiny head, wide enough, almost, for his broad, furry, twisted frame. His eyes, peering in, glowed red with the lurid light of madness, I could hear his deep breathing . . .

He was in! The door swung to behind him, so that only the faintest of light-lines showed that it had not latched. His dark form bulked against it for an instant, vanished. He merged with the darkness, only his eyes showed, his red-gleaming tiny eyes that came steadily toward me, moving faster and faster as the pad of his bare feet slithered toward me along the floor.

And now he loomed close above me, so that I could see his towering form black against the black. And now his fingers touched my cheek, his furry fingers, crept slowly down along my cheek, rasping; drifted along my jaw, under my chin; found my throat . . .

The door crashed open, light flooded in. The piercing whistle sounded, the mysterious whistle I had heard before. Shang's fingers left my throat, he whimpered, twisting to the door. My own eyes went to it; I glimpsed a figure, a woman; voluptuous curves outlined by light striking through sheer silk of a nightgown, ebony hair-coif above somber eyes. The whistle sounded once more, Shang's bulk blocked the vision from my staring eyes, he swept through the door, it slammed behind him. I heard a contralto voice, berating, its words indistinguishable; heard a squeal like that of a chastised beast, heard the pad of Shang's feet moving away, and heard no more. Heard no more . . . but lay staring into darkness, cold sweat-damp dewing my forehead. . . .

For a long time I knew only that I had been once more delivered from certain death at the hands of the giant maniac. For a long time my clogged, bewildered brain did not go beyond that bare fact. I think, in those moments, that I was as near the empty, physical shell as ever a man can be this side of the grave.

The Stygian gloom brooding about me was no blacker than that within my soul. The silent house was no more silent than any whisper of hope in my brain. I was in the meshes of a net of horror from which there was no escape, in the hands of fiends from hell itself. Or—I could not keep the dread speculation from my pain-racked brain—or none of these incredible things were real—all were the weird phantasmagoria of a mind wandering in outer darkness.

Slow footsteps moved along the hall, slow shuffling footsteps, something vaguely familiar about their sound. Good Lord, what was going to happen now? They shuffled nearer. A low moan was distinct in the hush, choked by a gasp of terror. And suddenly there were other, running footsteps, a harsh voice bawling, "Hey you!" Jim Rand's voice, enraged. "Hey!"

The other groaned. I heard Rand reach him, heard a hard thud. I knew, as if I had seen it, that the brutal keeper had slammed the prowler against the corridor wall. "Damn it! Where are you going? How did you get out?"

"I . . . I . . . my door wasn't latched. I wanted to . . . " Deep-chested tones that were yet edged with the thinness of old age. My skin prickled, and I threw myself frenziedly against the webs that held me. My God! Oh my God!

"Yuh wanted to get away. Damn yuh!" *Crack*! Crack of Rand's whip on human flesh! His victim screamed. "No! No! Don't whip me. Kill me but don't use that whip on me!" That voice again, *the voice I knew*. "Don't!" The canvas belt cut my skin as I fought against it, fought frenziedly, unavailingly.

"Jim! Jim! Stop it!" Helming's voice, sharp, commanding. "Quit it!"

"But he . . . "

The physician was nearer. "Take him to his room. And find out how he got out. Hurry." Excitement in his voice, and fear. "Good Lord, if he got away and Dunn knew of it!"

The noises moved down the corridor. A door slammed somewhere. There was silence again.

Silence, and molten ice running through my veins. No question now of my sanity, no question at all! Horror curdled my blood, and then I laughed, laughed silently and long into the rags that stuffed my mouth. Funny, oh how funny it was! I thought, actually thought, I had heard my father's voice. I had heard, real as Rand's gruff, berating tones, the voice of my father who was dead for a month! I laughed till the tears came. What a joke that was, what a funny, funny joke. *I would tell it tomorrow to the fellow with the big head who saw eyes all around him, red staring eyes.* Maybe it would make

him forget his eyes and he'd laugh with me!

Then suddenly I was sobbing, sobbing like a baby. I didn't want to be crazy. I didn't want to hear voices and see things that weren't there, I didn't want to be like those dead-eyed men in the room below who mewed and gibbered, and drooled at the mouth . . .

CHAPTER SIX

The Beckoning Hand

I MUST have slept, at length, for I next remember a chill light defining the bare room, and black bars criss-crossing a gray square of sky high up on the wall. I could not feel my body at all so numbed it was. I lay quietly for a while, and despite the throb of pain within my skull, despite the crawling horror of all that I had seen and heard, knew peace, the dull unthinking peace of utter hopelessness.

After a time, though, I became aware of racking thirst. Consciousness of it grew on me till I was suffering the tortures of the damned. I visioned lakes, cool lakes of icy water; foaming cascades leaping down bosky precipices . . .

"Good morning Mr. Armour. Good morning." I hadn't noticed my door opening, but Helming was in the room, clucking. "I hope you are . . . er . . . recovered from your last night's indisposition. You did a lot of running around, remember? And you finally got into a really dreadful fight with one of our other inmates. I had all I could do to separate you. Then after I got you back here and thought you were sound asleep you started screaming again and we had to come in and strap you down. I am very much disappointed in you. Very much."

So that was his game, eh! I was to be convinced that nothing had happened, the way I thought it did. Or . . . the worms of fear twisted again in my addled brain

. . . perhaps it was so. Good Lord! I started to say something . . . changed it to a husked demand for water. "Water!"

"Of course. Of course." Glass touched my parched lips and a cooling draught trickled along my tongue. "Gently. Gently. Mustn't gulp it all at once. That would be bad, bad."

I felt a bit better. He withdrew the tumbler, looked at me with smouldering eyes whose corners crinkled with false good humor. "Now, Mr. Armour, do you think we're going to have any more trouble with you? Any more trouble?"

"Trouble?" I said weakly. "I don't want to make any trouble for you."

He giggled. "Good boy. Sensible. Very sensible. If you remember that we shall get along." He chuckled. "Willingness is half the cure, we find. Half the cure. And the other half is remembering that you are not quite . . . normal, remembering that things are not always what they seem to you. Will you keep that in mind, my boy? Will you?"

Peculiarly, menace had filtered into his face. It had hardened, as once before; had become, for all its pink roundness, a mask behind which lurked utter evil. White lines appeared, running from flat nostrils to mouth corners, and his voice was suddenly flinty. "Armour!" he rasped. "Nothing you thought you saw last night was really so. *Nothing at all!*" He rapped out the last, and I understood.

Monstrous things crawled in the depths of his tiny eyes. I thought of Rand's black whip, of Nan Holmes chained almost nude in the steel frame, of the wretch whose howls I had heard from the nethermost depths of this hell-hole. My skin crawled. "Nothing happened last night of any importance," I muttered. "I had some bad dreams, that is all."

"That is all." The menace lifted from his countenance, but it left dread in my own heart. "And you wouldn't be foolish enough to tell anyone of those dreams? You have sense enough for that?"

"I have sense enough for that," I parroted. "God help me!"

"Splendid!" His infernal chuckle sounded again. "I have great hopes of curing you yet." His pudgy hands washed one another briskly. "And I have a surprise for you. A pleasant surprise."

What did this portend? What new outrage was germinating in his black mind? I said nothing.

"Yes, a pleasant surprise. A visitor," he simpered. "An old friend of yours has telephoned that he will be here to see you shortly."

"Who?" I managed to say. "Who is it?"

"You will see. You will see. But first we must remove those uncomfortable straps from you, get you in shape to receive your guest. We want you to look nice." He moved to the door. "Jim," he called. "Jim."

Together they took off those accursed bands, and I bit my lips to restrain a scream at the needle-stabbing pain of returning circulation. They massaged me, worked over me, getting a semblance of life back into my tortured frame. Cool water was grateful as Jim sponge-bathed me, and fresh, clean underclothing was an untold luxury. They gave back my suit too, cleaned and neatly pressed, and I began to feel like something human once again. They even brought food to me, toast, and crisp poached eggs, and steaming coffee in a paper cup.

When I had finished the roly-poly doctor collected the paper plates from which I had eaten and waddled to the door. There he turned to me. "Remember," he said softly. "Remember that I shall be able to hear every word that is said in here. The room is wired for sound." He giggled again and closed the door behind him. But almost at once there was a knock and the door opened again.

An age-stooped, wrinkled man with the flaring white side-burns of a bygone age tottered in, tears glittering in his rheumy eyes. His arms, held out to me at full length, were shaking visibly.

"Mr. Humperdinck!" I jumped forward to the ancient attorney who had watched over the Armour fortunes for a quarter-century. "Uncle Carl!" I wrung his long-fingered, bony hand. "God, I'm glad to see you!" Glad wasn't the word for it. I quivered inwardly. Was this release at last? Had he come to take me from this house of hell?

He looked at me, his shrunken lips mumbling over false teeth. Emotion was rendering him speechless, his dew-laps shook as he tried to get words out. Behind him Rand closed my room-door softly and I heard the latch click. "Uncle Carl," I said again, and the familiar appellation reminded me of happier days in the rambling old mansion on Fifth Avenue. "How did you find me?"

"The papers," he squeaked. "The newspapers." He fumbled in a pocket of the caped coat he wore, pulled out a *Herald-Tribune*. I saw the black headlines:

ARMOUR HEIR GOES INSANE
    ATTACKS EXECUTOR IN
        WALL STREET OFFICE

My ink-smudged face stared at me from the page, and my father's! Avery Dunn's too. My hackles rose at the sight of his slant eyes and thin, cruel mouth.

"Thank God! You've come to get me out of here. I should have known you would take care of me. You always have, haven't you, Uncle Carl?"

His lips quivered, and my heart sank at the look in his eyes. "Get you out?" There was pity in them, pity and *fear*. I rocked back with the appalling realization that he was afraid of me . . . that he, also deemed me insane. "Why? Aren't they treating you well?"

I thought of Helming's parting warning . . . he was listening, somewhere, to every word that passed between us. "Of course they are." My tones went flat, dead. "Yes, of course. But—" I dared that much— "But I'm not crazy, uncle Carl. I'm not!"

"No," he piped, edging toward the door. "Of course you're not crazy. I'll write a letter to the papers and have them correct that statement. You're sick." He was speaking in the cajoling, soothing manner one uses to babies and . . . *lunatics*. "You stay here for a while and you will be all right. Dr. Helming impresses me as a very fine man, a man who knows his profession. It is best for you to stay here. Your old friend advises that, Harold. Your old friend and your father's."

My mouth twisted bitterly. There was no help here, I could see that. But there were things I wanted to know. "All right," I said, meekly as I could. "All right if you say so. You know best, Uncle Carl. But sit down and talk to me. I don't know anything of how dad died. Tell me about it."

Relief showed on his face. He sank into the chair, I threw myself across the bed. "Tell me about it, Uncle Carl," I repeated, encouragingly.

"It . . . it was very sudden," he began, rubbing his thin shanks with his almost transparent hands. "I saw John the night before it happened and he was quite well. More cheerful than he had been for years. I was hopeful that the new companionship he had was bringing him out of the hermit life he had imposed on himself since your mother's death."

"Companionship!" I exclaimed, sitting up. "What . . . who . . .?"

Humperdinck blinked at me in owl-like surprise. "Didn't he write you?"

"Mails are slow to Chile," I responded. "And uncertain. To what are you referring?"

"To Mrs. Kahn of course."

"Mrs. Kahn!" This was getting interesting. "Irma Kahn?"

"Yes. Then you do know about her."

I was evasive. "A little. Who is she, Uncle Carl?"

"She *claimed* to be your father's sister, your aunt. You remember . . ."

"Yes." The old story woke in my mind. "Yes. He had a younger sister who married a foreigner of some sort . . ."

"A Eurasian."

". . . and went away, was lost sight of. It all happened before I was born."

"That is it. This woman appeared shortly after you left for Iquique and claimed to be she. I was doubtful, started an investigation. But your father insisted on acknowledging her. He took her into the house, and I must say it seemed to do him a great deal of good. But as I was saying, I saw your father the day before his death, we spoke of you—he was very proud of what you were doing with the *estancia*. He was keen minded, I remember remarking on his marvelous grasp of affairs when we started to draw up his new will."

"To draw up a will. What . . ."

The old man raised a deprecating hand. "It left everything to you. Everything he possessed, and made Mrs. Kahn his executrix. I advised against that last, but he was obdurate."

I sank back. If I were his sole heir . . .

"Had it been otherwise I should have been suspicious of something untoward, but the surrogate's court would watch the estate carefully . . . and there was no reason to dispute probate."

I said nothing, but I was tense with attention. Somewhere here, was the crux of my troubles . . . the explanation of what I was undergoing. Where was it?

"John—your father—told me that he had put his yacht in commission, was leaving the next day for a short sea trip.

'Irma,' he said, 'advises it, and I think she is right.' He did leave on that trip . . . and never came back."

"Good Lord! He . . ."

"He was lost overboard. No one saw him go. He was in the salon—so the report went—playing bridge with the captain, Mrs. Kahn and Mr. Dunn . . ."

"Dunn was on board!" I broke in. "How . . ."

"He was a friend of Mrs. Kahn's, had made all the arrangements for the cruise, hired the crew, and everything. As I was saying, your father had been playing bridge, went out on the deck for a breath of air while he was dummy, and, although the yacht was searched from stem to stern, that was the last that was ever seen of him."

I jumped to my feet. "Great Heavens above!" I shouted. "He was murdered! They killed him!" My fists clenched. "They killed him, you old fool, and you let them get away with it."

The lawyer looked frightened, rose, trembling, his old eyes seeking the exit. "Calm yourself, Harold," he quavered. "Calm yourself. Why should anyone kill him? The only one who could gain by his death would be yourself. Surely you didn't sneak on board and murder him." He said it almost as if he expected me to say that I had done just that. "You were in Chile at the time you know. In Chile."

I controlled myself by a great effort. No use scaring the old man to death. I had gotten all I could out of him. I turned away from him, walked over to the shelf-dresser, and twiddled with the papier-mache comb that lay there. "I'm sorry," I said slowly. "Forgive me, Uncle Carl. I was excited." Two comb-teeth came away in my fingers. "Of course he wasn't killed. He must have had one of his usual attacks of vertigo, must have fallen overboard. Thanks for coming," I said dully. "I . . . I appreciate it."

"I had to come. I dandled you on my knee, Harold, when you were knee-high to a grasshopper." He bit his lip; he was at the door, rapping on it.

Dr. Helming pulled the door open. "All through?" he chuckled, rubbing his palms together. "Had a nice visit, I hope. A nice visit."

Humperdinck turned in the doorway, the voluminous fold of his cape filling it. "Goodbye, my boy. Goodbye."

I took his extended hand in my right but my left was busy too. "Goodbye, Uncle Carl. Take care of yourself." Then he was gone, and I was alone again with thoughts that were a scarlet thread through the darkness of my bewildered brain.

I seated myself on the room's one chair, my elbows on my knees, my face buried in my hands. And gradually, as my thoughts wandered in those long corridors of black despair something obtruded on my senses. An almost imperceptible aroma of ethereal sweetness called to me, warmed minutely the sluggish cold stream in my veins. A tendril of scent still clung to the sleeves of my jacket, of a clean, fresh scent. It was the ghost of the white form my jacket had clothed for moments only, the aura of the golden girl whose blue eyes had twice looked to me for help, for help that I could not give her. Suddenly my breath came faster, my heart pounded hotly, my lips set in a grim, hard line. And I knew there was work for me.

The corridor outside was hushed, silent. Nothing moved out there. From somewhere came a faint murmur of sound, sound repulsive, bestial. That must be from the common-room below where bedlam reigned. I remembered how that room was peopled and caught my breath while an icy shudder took every cell in my body. If they had her there, down there in that place of evil! My teeth gritted. Even if she were in that Avernian pit I would find her, tear her from its unimaginable horror. Even from there! But somehow, calmness came back to me, somehow I felt that it was not there I should find her.

Helming had told me there was a dictaphone hidden in this room, a metal ear that eavesdropped on every sound within its range. Perhaps someone still listened at its other end. Well, I had passed through much, had had little rest. I rose, stretched and yawned. "God, but I'm sleepy," I murmured aloud. I tossed myself on the cot, its spring creaking. I waited a while, let my breathing grow slower, let a soft snore sound. I snored again, more loudly. Then I was breathing deeply, letting the sound of that breathing die away. I was utterly silent, straining my ears for any intimation that someone stirred in the hall.

The quiet out there was absolute. And the silence within my room was unbroken as I slid slowly, reining my muscles with infinite precaution, from the cot. I lowered myself to the floor, squatting there as my fingers unfastened my shoes and slid them off. Now I was stealthily crawling, moving inch by inch with taut care, so that there was not even the whisper of scraping fabric to warn any listener I had left the bed. It seemed to me that hours passed before I crossed those few feet to the door.

And now I had reached it, and my hand was lifting, silently, slowly, to purchase on the edge that fit so tightly against the jamb. Blood pounded in my ears, a muscle twitched in my cheek. My palm lay flat against wood—I hesitated—pushed. And the panel moved, moved slightly outward under that gentle shove.

My heart leaped. The two paper teeth that I had concealed between my fingers, that I had pushed into the lock-slot in that door jamb with my left hand as I shook Humperdinck's with my right while his cape concealed my act from Helming; those two paper teeth had jammed the latch so that it had not caught. The asylum-keeper's wily schemes, his paper comb that could not be used as a weapon, his knobless door that needed no lock, had boomeranged against him.

I coughed back a sudden laugh of triumph. The door swung open. I lifted to my stockinged feet and was in the corridor. It was dim, deserted. The steel gates at either end were closed, their bars glimmering in an eerie light. Was Nan up here, behind one of these long rows of dark doors on which numbers were painted? Dared I open them? What if some mindless occupant were to be startled by my appearance, were to scream and bring Helming up here, Rand with his whip? I swayed in indecision, nerving myself to the endeavor.

What was that? I twisted to a sound, midway of the hall, the sound of an opening door. There it was, the panel moving slowly outward. I gasped, started back toward my door. If I could get back there before . . . But a slim white arm was reaching out of that opening portal, a white, long-fingered hand was moving, was beckoning to me. A whisper, light, feminine, reached me. "In here! Quick! In here, Harold!"

My dash to that door was a flicker of soundless movement. I was in the room, the door shut behind me. And I was staring at . . . not Nan . . . a woman tall and stately; a woman about whose rounded, mature form a lacy black negligee clung, half concealing, half revealing; a woman whose olive features were touched with a wistful, appealing sadness; whose lustrous gray eyes, fixed on my face, were flecked with gold.

My lips moved, but made no sound. This dark beauty, this woman whose helmet of ebony hair quivered somehow with vibrant life, whose nostrils flared just enough to show the shell pink of their lining, whose curving lips were dreamy with sensuous promise, what was she doing here in this madhouse? She was no inmate; her poised, insouciant bearing told me that; the fact that her door was not locked, the unbarred window, the luxurious furnishings of her room. I took all this in at a glance, then her voice pulled my gaze back to her, her voice that was the deep throb of a 'cello, resonant, enthralling.

"Harold," she said, "Harold Armour!" and held out both arms to me. The black gossamer web fell back from them, revealed soft curves, glowing skin. "Harold!"

"You know me," I managed to say. "You . . ."

"But of course. I have a picture of you, Harold, a picture of a chubby, naked infant with a most endearing smile. That was long ago." She sighed, and a world of regret was in that suspiration. "You have changed since that picture was taken, but I still can trace that baby's lineaments in your man's face."

"You have a picture of me," I gulped. "Who . . ."

"Who am I?" A faint smile touched, just touched, the wings of her luscious mouth. "Your dear father's sister, Harold, your aunt whom you never knew. It was that picture that brought me back from France. I could not bear to think of that baby alone in the world with his sorrow, and I, his only kin, so far away. I rushed back, and when I arrived, last night, my friend Avery Dunn told me that . . . that . . ."

"That I was a lunatic who had tried to kill him. That I was in an asylum."

"Yes," she breathed, and a tear trembled in the corner of her eye. "I couldn't believe it. I rushed right out here. It was late and Dr. Helming would not permit you to be disturbed. But he was good enough to offer me this room for the night, and . . . and I have only just awakened. I heard a movement in the hall, looked out and recognized you, called you in so that I could talk to you alone. Tell me, Harold, tell me that the horrible thing isn't so."

She moved closer to me, her aura seemed to enfold me with an almost overpowering allure. I was drawn to her, drawn by something that was *not* filial, not the affection of a nephew. My arms crept up to take her within their embrace and suddenly I stiffened. This was Irma Kahn, I remembered, the Irma Kahn who . . . "I am in an asylum," I said with rigid lips. "Duly committed."

"Oh!" She seemed to feel the change in me. "But they may be mistaken. You were hysterical with grief, unbalanced at the moment. But today . . ." She made a little gesture with her hand, a pitiful little gesture.

Somehow I felt there was something wrong about her, something deadly wrong. The smouldering flame in her eye, the sensuous slow motion of her gorgeous body, the way each little movement displayed new charms, were not compatible with her role of the aunt appealing to her long-lost nephew for affection. They were rather the practiced art of the courtesan, the devious artifice of a woman fighting to awaken in the wanted male—passion! And yet, when that gesture ended with the touch of her fingers on my arm I felt an electric tingle at the point of contact, a tingle that thrilled to my brain and exploded there.

"Let me help you, Harold. Let me help you."

I fought the fever in my veins, fought the unholy sweep of desire that boiled within me. "May I ask," I ventured with tight lips, "whether it was the picture of which you spoke that brought you to my father . . . to see him die?"

"Harold!" She veiled quickly, but not quickly enough to hide from me, the sudden stab of startlement, of hate, of male-

volence that flared in her eyes. "How could you say a thing like that?" I felt suddenly like a wearied swimmer who feels firm ground under his feet at last. "I came to my brother because I was at last free to come after long years of separation. His tragic end," her voice broke, "almost killed me too." I had said so little, so very little, to induce this outburst!

But she recovered quickly. She came closer, so that she was pressed against me, her warm breath was sweet in my nostrils, her great, lustrous eyes were demanding, urgent. Her hands slid up along my arms, were around my neck. "Harold," she throbbed, "dear boy. Don't thrust me away. I have starved for love, for the love of my own, so long, so long."

I was certain now she was not, could not be my aunt. And that certainty was all the worse for me. For the kisses trembling on her lips were there for me to take, the hot pulse of her blood found an answer in the pound of my own heart. A maelstrom of desire whirled in my reeling brain, a great voice shouted in my ears. "Take it. Take what she is offering. What difference who she is, what she is? She is woman, incarnate woman, and the delights that are yours for the asking are such as you never yet have tasted."

In another moment . . . Thin sound came to me from beyond the door. A scream! A woman's scream! *Nan's scream!* It came again. I threw Irma from me, saw her reeling, saw the agonized frenzy in her eyes, and whirled, plunged out.

The faraway scream came again, from my right, from the staircase up which Helming had led me last night, the staircase that dropped down to darkness, to the mazed labyrinth where Shang prowled. Great God! I lunged toward the gate, got my hands on it, pulled. It swung open; the lock had not been repaired! I pounded down toward where Nan's cries came again and again, but fainter, further away.

CHAPTER SEVEN

Bottom of Hell

IT was a well of darkness down which I hurled myself, a well of darkness veiling the Lord alone knew what dread secrets. But far below I could hear the faint shrieks of the golden girl; her shrieks, and a snuffling, growling rebuttal that told me the mad giant had her. Shang had her, and was taking her . . . where?

I reached the first landing, where was the passage into the corridor where first I had met the madman. I stopped, listened. The cries I had heard did not come from below, from the further descent whence had come other howls, howls of anguish at which the round-faced owner of this madhouse had giggled. I whipped on, down into that mystery.

Nan's anguished screams were close ahead. Close! Was I in time to save her? The stone steps down which I hurtled twisted. I pounded around the last projecting corner of sweating gray granite . . . and crashed against something that threw me back with tremendous force, the force of my mad plunge! I sprawled, stunned for an instant, lifted to my feet, and saw that a steel-barred gate closed an arched doorway. Beyond there was a vaulted, dark chamber walled with slimy stone. The girl's shrieks, distant again, burbled into sudden, appalling silence.

I hurled myself at those bars. They were locked. I battered at them, yelling incoherently; tossed my quivering body at them. My jacket ripped from my shoulders. My arms, my forehead, dripped blood, a gush of warm liquid spurted across my cheek, but the barrier at which I battered was immovable. I clung to the bars at last, stared through them with eyes that must in that moment have been truly insane.

Dimness fronted me, dungeon dimness and blacker shadows lying across green-scummed pools that made the broken-boarded floor of the dungeon a noisome plain. Loathsome things scuttered in veiling gloom. A sudden howl of agony twisted my head to the right as my heart came into my throat. Light flooded across another arched doorway there, light somehow lurid, and beyond it . . . Oh God! . . . bathed in that bloody glare a naked form hung, its bare toe-tips just scraping the floor! The writhing form of a man hung like that from chains clamped to his wrists; his back was toward me, and across that quivering back crimson weals dripped slow-oozing, ruby droplets that ran in gory rivulets to mingle with the sweat of agony glistening on his tortured frame!

Crack! Black, snake-like, a whip lashed from the door-side and sliced across that agonized back. It wrung another howl from the man, convulsed his suspended form with a spasm of pain that jerked his taut legs from the floor. The steel cuffs to which the chains were fastened cut into his stretched wrists, and from these too rivulets of blood streamed down his muscle-bulging arms.

A shuffling sound jerked my eyes to the left, a shuffling sound and the smack of bestial lips. A misshapen thing loomed in the blackness. It came nearer, nearer . . I saw it distinctly. And rocked to supreme horror!

It was Shang! His diminutive head was out thrust from the awful spread of his tremendous shoulders, little lights were crawling in his beady eyes, spittle drooled from the corners of his thick-lipped, lascivious mouth. His hairy, simian chest heaved with crazed emotion, his bowed legs shambled through slime, and one swarthy arm hung loosely at his side, so long that its kunckles were inches from the scummy floor. The other . . . frantic protest shrieked soundlessly in my squeezed throat . . . the other arm was curled around the waist of a limp form, the form of a girl, the form of Nan!

She hung flaccid, her long golden hair trailing the mire, her upturned eyes open but staring senselessly in some strange rigor of uttermost terror. The clothes had been ripped from her torso . . . I saw the corded muscles of her matchless neck, the soft round of her breasts that a vagrant gleam of ruddy light just tipped with fire . . .

"Shang! Shang! Oh God, Shang!" I screamed to the monster in some mad hope that by my voice alone I could stop him from the horror to which he stalked. "Shang!" I thrust my rasped arms through the bars. "Don't Shang, don't!" He prowled on, and not even the twitch of a muscle showed that he had heard me. But I flared with sudden hope. He was shambling closer, closer, perhaps . . . He was right before me, my extended hands clawed for his arm. But did not reach, just did not reach! Oh God Almighty! Oh God!

The grotesque being stalked on, a red glow in his pig-like orbs, obscene expectancy in his gargoyle face, shambled on in a solitude where there was neither sight nor sound. He swerved away from me, was swallowed up by blackness this side of the red-lighted archway, by blackness veiling some dark cave, some lair to which he had dragged his prey. But just before he vanished I saw a flicker of light come into Nan's eyes, a flicker of dread awakening.

I rattled the bars, shook them as if I would tear them apart with my bare hands, shrieked my soul's torture through them. And my shrieks were answered by other screams, shrill screams of supernal agony, of terror beyond comprehension, shrill screams from the black cave where Shang had borne his victim.

"Harold! What is it, Harold?" I whirled to a voice behind me. Irma Kahn! Her eyes glowing, her face alight with strange feeling. "Why did you run from me, my dear?" Light from above struck through the tracery of her lacy garment, showed her voluptuous curves, the black coif of her hair. And I remembered! Remembered the woman who had appeared in my doorway, the woman whose whistle had called Shang from my throat. Thank God!

I leaped for her, clutched her arm. "Irma," I cried. "Irma. Whistle for him. Whistle for Shang. He's got a girl there, Nan! Call him off. Quick! Quick!"

She pulled away from me, shrugged me off. And laughed in my face! "Call him off," she gurgled. "Call him off from that girl you prefer to me! Not I, dear boy. Not I! Why worry about her when you can have me." Her eyes were suddenly slumberous. "When you can have me?"

My hand fisted, raised above her. "Call him or I'll kill you." I was frothing at the mouth. "I'll tear you limb from limb, I'll do to you what he is doing to her."

"You'd strike me, Harold," her voice husked. "You'd strike me." Her hands came up, a quick movement and the black lace fell from her, she was a white flame in the dimness, a white flame of beauty. Her head went back, her arms flung wide.

I rocked on my feet, the solid walls whirled about me. Oh God! O good God! And suddenly I was laughing, shrieking with laughter, with wild laughter that tore my throat, that ripped my lungs. We were crazy! We were all crazy! She and Shang and Nan and I! We were all stark raving mad!

HINGES squealed behind me, hinges squealed and the roar of an enraged animal thundered in my ears. I whirled. Shang was leaping through the open gate, his mad eyes glittering, his great arms sweeping out. His mouth was open and the insensate beast's roar was coming from it. I crouched, fear driving away madness, crouched to meet his attack. He plunged past me — Great Jupiter — he plunged past me and dived for the woman behind me, for Irma Kahn. I heard her scream, glancing around I saw her turn and run, a white, stark-naked figure, up the stone stairs. And after her plunged the hairy brute, the maddened giant, doubly crazed now by jealousy!

They disappeared around the stair-curve. But I whipped through the steel gate, open at last, whipped through—to met Jim Rand plunging from the red lit archway beyond. "Hey," he roared, and his whip swept up—his whip swept up dripping blood, sliced down at me. But I wasn't there. Taking a leaf from his own book I had dodged. He staggered with the force of the missed blow, my hand darted forward lightning-like, and ripped the whip from his grasp. He launched a fist-blow at me. I parried it with the whip and slashed at his face.

The reddened lash cut a weal across his cheek. He squealed, lunged at me. But I had gone completely berserk. The memory of the brutal whipping he had administered to me lent me strength, the memory of all he had done. My arm rose and fell, rose and fell, and the whip lash whistled through the air, crashed about his face, his shoulders. I remembered the howling victim on whom I had seen him use this very scourge, and slashed at him again. He crouched, sprang. His hard fists landed somewhere on me . . . I heard their thud . . . but still I beat at him with the thong that was his own weapon, beat at him through red mists of wrath, through a seething haze in which I could see only his face, dripping blood,

and the black thread of my whip snaking across it.

Sheer exhaustion stopped my arm at last. I looked down at the quivering, senseless hulk lying in the slime at my feet, the faceless horror that had been Jim Rand. A modicum of sanity came back to me, and I shuddered. Good God! Had I done this? I? Then my mouth twisted bitterly. It was a dreadful fate that had overtaken him. But it was richly deserved. Richly deserved!

I twisted to his latest victim. A glance showed me that his sufferings were over. That which hung in those chains would feel pain no longer. He had escaped in the only certain way, from the hell of insanity, from the devil that was Jim Rand. I envied him.

But there was something I still had to do. What was it? Something about a girl, a girl with golden hair. Of course. Nan. Nan Holmes. She was somewhere in here. But where?

A low moan answered me, a low moan from the darkness where I could see the arched mystery of a low doorway. I staggered to it, and through.

THE red light entered here not at all. But I could see something, a very little, in the gloom . . . could see a pale bundle that moved. I got to it, knelt to it. A wee small voice moaned a word, a name. My name! "Hal. Save me, Hal."

And I was wholly sane again. "Nan," I groaned. "Nan," getting my arms under her, lifting her. "Nan! Hal's here. I'm here, and I won't let him touch you again."

Her arm slipped around my neck, she nestled in my embrace like a little child as I struggled to my feet. "Safe, Hal. Safe," she murmured. She was so light, so light in my arms, and so sweet. I turned to make my way out of that cave. Out of that cave to where? Where in this house was safety for me . . . for Nan?

I turned, and halted. The red light out there was flickering strangely, was brighter than it had been before. A foul, acrid odor stung my nostrils . . . the pungent odor of smoke. Good Lord! As I reached the exit from the cave, came out into the dungeon proper, flames crackled. I twisted toward the ominous sound. And saw what I could not have seen when I battered against the gate, what I had overlooked in the furious melee of the fight with Rand.

A brazier had burned within the torture chamber, a caldron of fire in which I saw them scattered now—irons heated for what unholy purpose I could only guess—and guessing know renewed satisfaction at the punishment I had meted out to Rand. But now that brazier was overturned—probably while I battled with the keeper—its coals were strewn over the wood floor of that horror cell—and a sheet of fire was sweeping across the room. Even as I looked a tall tongue of flame shot up, licked at the hanging corpse!

The sight shattered a nebulous plan I had formed of hiding with Nan somewhere in this labyrinth. I must get out, get her out, at once. I leaped for the entrance where the steel gate still hung open, leaped up the staircase. I must get out . . .

At the head of the first flight I turned into the dim passageway where I had my first meeting with Shang. My skin crawled at the recollection, but I pressed on. The tunnel echoed with my incautious footsteps, and then suddenly another sound drowned their reverberations. Sounds rather; shrieks, catcalls, an agonized scream, pandemonium that was worse than anything I had yet heard! Something was going on in the common-room where the mad inmates of this asylum were gathered! I must know what it was before I dared take Nan out there.

But if I left her here, and she came to before I returned? Came to, and frightened, ran off somewhere where I could not find her. I paused in indecision. And she stirred in my arms.

"Nan," I whispered. "Nan. Are you awake."

"Yes, Hal, I'm awake." She squirmed, got her feet down, clung to me. I sensed little tremors running through her frame, tiny shoulders that spoke vividly of her gruelling experience.

A question burst from my lips, a question that had agonized me since I had found her in that cave. "Nan. Did he . . . Did Shang . . .?"

She shuddered. "No. Thank God. No. I screamed when I realized where I was, fought him off for a second. And then he heard a voice from outside, growled and rushed off. I fainted, I guess. But somehow I knew you were near, were coming to save me. How . . .?"

"Never mind that now." The faint, acrid odor of smoke warned me that I must hurry. "Listen Nan, stay here a moment. I want to take a look out there."

Her hand snatched at my wrist. "Don't leave me here, Hal. I'm afraid. Let me go with you."

"Nonsense. There's nothing to be afraid of."

"Nothing to be afraid of!" She threw a fearful look over a shoulder, a wide-eyed look into the shadows. "Shang!"

THE very name sent a pang of fear through me. I thought of her slight form in the monster's grip once more! "All right. Come along, then. But stay behind me, and be ready to run if I give the word."

It was thus that we crept through the rest of that dim passage, I in front, she behind, while louder and louder came the turmoil ahead, the shrieking tumult that was like a crazed horde of jungle beasts battling in the steamy night, while stronger and stronger came the fire-smell from behind. And thus at last we came to the nail-studded door that opened to the hell-pit where Helming's mad creatures were.

Hell-pit indeed! The door was slightly ajar, and the sounds that came from behind it transcended all that hell could offer. I singled out of the thunderous babble of sound a sepulchral voice that howled, "The Old Guard dies but never surrenders. Up and at them!" Someone else babbled, over and over, "Fly fly. It's the end of the world." I recognized the wail of the big-headed little man, "Eyes, eyes. They've got my eyes. O Holy Mother have mercy. Have mercy!" And then, cutting knife-like through pandemonium, a woman shrieked, her scream wire-edged with infinite terror! I pushed my head around the door-edge . . .

Impossible to describe that scene! The big room was a seething, boiling mass of fury, of grotesque figures milling in an indescribable, frenzied storm; swirling about some center whose neucleus I could not at the moment make out; and from there that terrorized scream came again and again, vibrant with fear, with horror. Another sound joined it, the ululation of a furious beast, the booming battle-cry of a combat-frenzied gorilla.

Suddenly the maelstrom split. Something hurtled out of it, a wizened, spidery creature bowling through the mad horde as if catapulted by some gigantic machine. I saw Shang, his long arms recoiling from the throw; his fangs exposed, ferocious; his hairy chest a mass of clotted blood. And behind him I glimpsed the white, nude form of Irma Kahn, blood-streaked, all beauty contorted from her face as her open mouth vented shriek after shriek of mortal terror.

The inferno closed around them at once, what I had seen was but the momentary flickering of a camera shutter, and the mad throng surged forward. The bang of a shot jerked my eyes to the side, to the staircase. Helming was crouching there, his face fish-belly gray, a gun smoking in his hand as it jerked with another shot at the frenzied mass that leaped, yelling and gibbering, about Shang and his mistress. Helming wasn't giggling now, his little eyes bulged out of the layers of fat, his tiny mouth quivered . . .

A CONGLOMERATE shriek greeted the asylum-keeper's second shot, and suddenly the mad horde was streaming across the floor toward him. He turned to run. His gun crashed. Arms, clawed hands reached for him, caught him. He went down, screaming, under a piled mass of horror.

All this had happened in seconds, in a time so short that my head was still moving past the door-edge, a time too short for me to have done anything had I so willed. Now my eyes swept back to where I had seen Shang and Irma Kahn. They were still there . . . the woman prostrate, the shaggy giant bending over her. I started forward, stopped, irresolute.

"Oh, go get her, Hal," the girl's whisper sounded in my ear. "You can't leave her there for . . . for those." She had read my thought. "I'll be all right. Hurry!"

I darted out from my covert and Shang rose to meet me. Ice chilled my blood. Were we to battle again, the gorilla-man and I? He crouched, steadying himself on his bowed, twisted legs and the knuckles of one long arm. His features were a leering gory mask from which his malevolent little orbs stared out, his body was mangled, torn, the great muscles exposed. As I neared I heard a whimper, half of pain, half of defiance, issue from his contorted lips. I tensed for his plunge.

But it never came! He jerked aside as I reached him, jerked aside, whimpering.

And I realized that his eyes were watching me not at all, that they were directed past me, to the frenzied mass that still boiled on the stairs. Wondering, I bent to Irma, lifted her bleeding, unconscious body, turned back to the door. And realization burst on me of what Shang feared!

For there was a sudden yell from the madmen on the stairs. The mass there disintegrated, streamed toward me. I saw red-dripping claws outstretched, red-smeared mouths in nightmare visages. I tried to break into a run for the door behind which Nan waited but panic rocked me as I knew that they must reach me before I could make that shelter. Weak, exhausted, I staggered and nearly fell, pulled myself erect and staggered on. Through a whirling, dizzy mist I saw Nan's white face staring from the doorway, her imploring arms outflung. I heard her far-away scream: "Hurry, Hal, Hurry!"

The burden on my shoulder weighed a ton; my legs moved through some viscous, clinging fluid; the obscene imprecations, the animal howls of the mad pack on my heels were louder, nearer. I could feel their hot breath on my neck, their hands twitching at my sleeves. I . . . couldn't . . . make it. "Close the door, Nan," I yelled. "Close the door and get away."

She made no motion to obey, but her finger extended, pointing. "Come on, Hal," she screamed. "Keep coming. Look!"

I twisted my head to where she was pointing, and saw the distorted faces, the foaming mouths of the maniacs hunting me. Saw them close, terribly close. But I also saw Shang's huge shaggy figure lunging to meet them, saw his bared fangs slice the throat of one screaming madman, saw his great hands reach out and snap the necks of two others, saw him

lift these last victims and use their writhing bodies as clubs to slug back the oncoming horde.

I plunged on. Nan was right in front of me. I sprawled as I reached her, sprawled through the door she held open and broke Irma Kahn's fall as I sprawled. I twisted, through the closing door I glimpsed Shang dragged down at last, heard his final howl, a howl, strangely, of triumph, and the door slammed shut, blotting out the sight. I heard the rattle of a bolt as Nan shot it home.

I ROLLED from under Irma, staggered to my feet. Nan went to her knees at the woman's side, reached for her wrist. There was a roaring in my ears, and my chest heaved, struggling for the breath that had been raped from me by the terrific exertions I had just been through, exertions that would have ended in my own horrible death had it not been for Shang. I thought of my last glimpse of the monster, of his sacrifice, looked at the woman for whom he had made that sacrifice, and contrasted the two dazedly. Shang had been evil, a prowling, dangerous monster, but his evil had come from a darkened mind. Hers was the greater sin!

Nan looked up at me. "She's dying, Hal." I bent, swiftly. There was no beauty left in that mangled face, only the hard lines of an evil life, the tortured lines of pain that wracked her even in her coma. Her eyelids flickered open, terror flared in the gray orbs that I had last seen aflame with foul passion.

Terror flamed in them, and died away. She smiled, actually smiled. Her bloody lips moved, faint words whispered from them. I bent closer. "Kiss me, Harold," she breathed. "Kiss me."

Her blood was salty on my lips. She quivered, her eyes glazed, and life fled from her with a sigh. But the smile remained, hovering about her mouth, the smile that showed she had died as she had lived. Died with the thrill of passion obliterating all else.

"Hal," Nan's voice broke into my brief thoughts. "Hal. Listen!" I was suddenly aware of a thumping echoing about me, a pounding of fists against wood. "We've got to get away from here, they'll have the door down in a minute."

"Good Lord!" I exclaimed. "I'll say we must." I grasped her wrist, started off. "We'll try upstairs." The battering of the maniac horde echoed around us in the passage, menacing. And there was something else in the passage, a red glare, the crackle of flames. I realized suddenly what the roaring in my ears was, why I had been able to see the dying woman's face so clearly. The fire from below was gaining headway, was roaring up the staircase ahead, the staircase that was our only path to safety! And behind wood splintered, and the howl of the lunatic pack was more distinct.

We broke into a run, exhaustion forgotten, plunged around the last curve in the tunnelled corridor. At its end great tongues of flame roared, red flame shot through with yellow, with virulent green. Behind a tremendous crash sounded, and thundering footsteps echoed warning of the oncoming swarm. We were caught between the blaze of hot, devouring flame and the bloody mouths, the gory, tearing claws of the shrieking mob that was hunting us down at last.

CHAPTER EIGHT

Perfect Timing

THERE was no choice, no choice at all. Rather death in the flames than what those mad men and women would do to us! Not pausing in my desperate run, I ripped off the tattered remnants of my coat, flung it around Nan's head, her golden hair. Then I had her in my arms,

the roaring chimney of fire was just ahead, and I had plunged into it.

I held my breath and my eyes were shut as the glare, the heat enfolded me. My eyes were shut, but a picture of that landing, the two staircases, was clear in my mind. I lunged for the one ascending, felt its steps under my feet, pounded upward. Heat swirled about me, heat that singed my hair, charred my skin. Heat swirled about me, diminished as I fled upward and a cooler breath told me I was through the flames, that I dared breathe again.

My eyes opened, I saw the upper corridor stretching before me, the long rows of closed and numbered doors. Pain seared me where the flames had burned, but a great joy flared within me. I had won through, won through with Nan! I had plunged through the fire at the last possible moment of escape, and nothing could stop me now. Somehow I would get out of here, get Nan out of here. I knew it then; despite the deadly peril we still were in I knew that I should win through.

I set the girl down, pulled the coat away from her head. Her face, her glorious hair, were untouched. "All right, Nan?" I gasped.

Her eyes were aglow. "All right, Hal. But you?"

"A little charred, but I'll do. Lots of fight in me yet, and we're going to need it." I grinned. "One thing we've got to thank that fire for, those fellows can't get through it at this end, and the steel gate down there will keep them back at the other. We've only one problem now, how to get out of here ourselves."

Panic came back into her face. "But Hal, we can't. The only way out is down again. The windows up here are all barred. We're shut in. Oh Hal," fear strained her voice, "we're trapped up here to burn."

That fear was echoed in my own heart. And then I remembered! "No, Nan. The windows are not all barred. There's one in that room," I pointed to the door through which a white arm had beckoned me, was it only an hour ago, "through which we can climb."

"Are you sure, Hal? Sure?"

"Of course I am. We'll be out of here in minutes. Nothing more is going to happen to us in this place."

I spoke confidently, but I was wrong. Dead wrong.

WE were in the luxuriously furnished room where still clung the warm, musky scent of the woman who lay, stripped of clothing and life itself, somewhere below. Dusk was already graying the window as I pulled up the sash and looked out. There was grass, below, a lawn edged by a tall hedge. Grass . . . across which a red light danced. I pulled my head in quickly, that red light told me that time pressed, that the rooms below must be a roaring furnace by now. "Hurry, Nan," I grated. "We'll tear these sheets in ribbons, make a rope-ladder to climb out."

She had anticipated my suggestion, had pulled the silk counterpane back, was draging the white linen from the bed. I took a sheet, started to rip it. . . and stopped as a dull pounding sounded from without!

Nan put a shaking hand on my arm. "What is it, Hal—that sound?" she quavered.

"Sounds like some poor devil caught in his room up here. I'll go and see . . . you get these sheets torn."

The corridor was already filled with a haze of pungent smoke, through which lurid luminance flickered. The thumping was coming from my left, from the end room. I ran to it—the number was twenty-four—and jerked the door open.

Jerked the door open and fell back, my jaw dropping as I stared at the apparition within.

The room reeled about me, the floor heaved. A bubbling scream rose to my lips—I choked it back and pawed at the swirling air. Good God! This little man, gray hair, shaggy eyebrows over deep-set, somber eyes—was my father! Dad! Great Heavens! It couldn't be—it couldn't be! Dad, my dad was dead!

Now again, for one horrible instant, the old terror flooded back on me, the old fear that I was insane! Insane—seeing visions, hallucinations, things that were not, that could not be! Then a familiar voice broke through to my swimming brain. "Hal! Hal my boy!"

Dad's fragile hands reached out to me. Even in that moment it wrung my heart to see how lined his countenance was with suffering, how old he was. "Hal! It can't be. It can't be Hal!"

Flame was roaring behind me, black smoke swirled around us. But I did not know it. "It is," I screamed. "It is Hal, Dad." Light flashed in his old face for an instant, then it went blank. He reeled, would have fallen had I not caught him. I lifted him, slung him to my shoulder.

"Hurry, Hal, Hurry!" Nan's voice calling from the room where was the only exit. "The fire . . . ."

"Coming," I gritted, and staggered toward the voice. "Coming." I needed the guidance of her. "Hal! In here," for the smoke-fog was dense now in the corridor, impenetrable. Choking, spluttering, I reeled into the room, heard the door slam behind me. Fresh air from the window revived me.

"I've got the rope ready, tied and tested," Nan said in my ear. My clearing vision saw that this was true, that she had shoved the bed to the window and knotted the long streamer of torn sheeting to one of its posts.

"All right, dear. Slide down, and I'll let dad down to you."

"Dad?" her voice shrilled with surprise.

"Yes. My father. And they told me he was dead! But hurry."

I WAS crouched behind the hedge that ran along what seemed a street. I was chafing dad's old hands as he lay outstretched on the grass. Nan was beside me, crouching too. Behind us was pandemonium, maniacal screams, bestial howls racketing from the dark bulk of the asylum we had escaped, a dark bulk broken by oblong holes of red flame striped by black bars of steel. Overhead the high arch of a bridge loomed, a high arch I knew. It was Hell Gate Bridge!

"We're in Astoria, Nan," I muttered. "Astoria."

"Yes," she said. "I know. Oh Hal, he isn't. . . ?"

"No. Just fainted. He'll be all right."

Feet thudded along the street. I peered through the hedge, saw brass buttons and the blue coat of a policeman. He was reaching under his coat for a gun, his face was white and staring as he pounded toward the madhouse where all hell had broken loose. I started to call to him—and choked the cry off just in time.

Good Lord! I—an escaped lunatic—a madman loose from a place where my fellows were tearing their keepers to bits —had been about to call to the law! If I had Nan and dad and I would have been prisoners again, prisoners with all the long intricacy of the law's red tape to unravel! I shuddered. Never again would I be behind steel bars—never again.

A fire siren sounded, far off.

A new terror closed in on me now, the terror of the hunted. We were pariahs, outcasts, and every man's hand against us. "Hal," Nan whispered. "He's awfully cold. I'm afraid. . . ."

A police whistle shrilled out in the street, glass smashed behind me as the officer already there broke a window to find entrance. I must get away, must find a hiding place for Dad and Nan . . . . but where? In all New York . . . . the answer flashed on me . . . . in all New York there was only one haven of safety for us, the old Armour mansion on Fifth Avenue.

The second policeman rushed across the fire-lit lawn. The fire sirens, the clangor of fire-bells, were nearer now, much nearer. I must act, act now, before these grounds were a mass of men, before we were discovered here under the hedge. But how . . . . how get to sanctuary across Queens, over a long bridge that would be an inescapable trap, across half New York?

Brakes squealed out in the street, and tires scraped. I peered again through the leafy barrier that hid us. A taxi had stopped, and its driver leaned out, gazing curiously at the blazing building set far back on its sloping lawn.

It was no conscious plan that lifted me to my feet, that sent me hurdling over the hedge, that threw me headlong across the walk and fastened my hands around the startled throat of that cabman before a sound could rip from it. Before he could cry out—but not before panic, terror, could stare from his bulging eyes to remain in my memory forever. I thumped his head against the steel post of his hack. He went limp under my hands, and I had hauled him out of his seat, had flung him over the hedge and was myself in shadow again in seconds. Seconds only it took for the desperate deed! Poor fellow—he must wake at night to see a wild-eyed, murderous-visaged maniac leap at him from the night, to see clutching hands reach for his throat . . . .

"Run for the cab, Nan," I grunted, as I tore off his cap, his coat. "Run." She obeyed, and I was close behind her with the cabbie's coat on my own frame, his cap on my head, and Dad's still limp form in my arms. I pushed my father in through the rear door, to Nan's waiting arms, and then I was behind the wheel, the motor was roaring to life, and the cab was gliding away from the flaming pyre where we had all endured so much.

IF the capture of the taxi was an explosion of action during which time did not move at all, the slow drive that followed was an infinite unreeling of tortured crawling. I dared not speed, I dared violate no rule of the road; every red light glared danger at me, every policeman was a beetle-browed menace. But I knew that in the darkness of the cab behind me were my father, my old father returned from the dead—and the girl I loved!

Here at last, was the Park on my left. Dark facades flicked past, and there was the squat, red-gabled mansion where I was born. Home! But—I gasped and my blood ran cold once more—from an upper window, wide and arch-topped, yellow light streamed! I groaned. Someone was in the house! Someone was in the upstairs sitting-room! Oh God! Was it not over yet? Were the police waiting here for us, outguessing my plans?

There were people on the sidewalk, a bus crawled past. I dared not hesitate a second—cabs were not allowed to park on this sacrosanct Avenue. The opening in the high fence invited me, where the driveway curved to the *porte-cochère*. I wheeled the cab in there, followed the old path around to the rear of the house, throttling the engine down to a merest

whisper. The stables were still back there, long unused.

How I blessed my father then for his refusal to yield to my urging that he tear those stables down and sell the useless ground. "You can do that after I die, Hal," he had said. "It was like that when I brought your mother here and like that it shall remain till I join her." Now, in our dire need, the ruined barn offered a hiding place for the cab and its precious load.

I slipped from my seat, glanced in back. Dad seemd to be asleep, so quietly he lay, his head pillowed in Nan's lap. "Stay here a minute, dear," I whispered. "I want to take a look-see before I bring you and father into the house."

Something in my tone must have alarmed her, though I had tried to keep it even. "Hal. Is anything wrong? Is. . . ."

"No," I lied. "I just want to be careful. Can't afford to take chances now. Be a good girl and wait here quietly till I call you."

I turned away, as memories of boyhood flooded back. There was a drainpipe at the corner of the structure here, a pantry roof that jutted out, and a pillar that one could climb. Soundlessly I moved, soundlessly I climbed. Just as I had done, long ago, on many a childish escapade. But no excitement throbbed in my veins tonight. Only fear. Fear for dad, and Nan. Only fear.

THE window to my old room scraped only slightly as I raised it, but it brought my heart into my mouth. I froze, listening. A distant murmur of voices came to me, but no indication that I had been heard. I slid over the sill, into darkness.

White shapes loomed in the gloom. For an instant I was startled, then realized they were the furniture with dust sheets thrown over. I knew every inch of this place, every creaking board. It would have been a sharp ear indeed that could have heard my passage as I flitted through silent, familiar rooms.

Now I was in the dark hall, was slithering toward where a line of light edged drawn portieres to show the occupied room. I was near enough to hear glasses clink, and a toast, in Avery Dunn's oily, hateful voice. "Here's to the Armour estate, my dear fellow. Long may we administer it."

Another voice answered, a voice I had often heard in this house, *Carl Humperdinck's quavering, age-thinned voice!* Good Lord! "I . . . . I don't know whether I ought to drink that toast. I . . . . when I saw the boy this morning my heart sank. That fine youngster . . . ."

"Stop!" Dunn's command cracked across the old man's trembling accents. "Stop right there. You're in this thing too deep to turn back. You started it, and you're going to finish it. The time to get cold feet was at the beginning."

Uncle Carl groaned. "Yes. Yes, I know. But when you came to me and threatened me with that old misdeed of mine I thought so safely hidden I lost my head. I was old, old and I knew the disgrace of exposure would kill me. I was weak, and you led me on slyly. You said all you wanted was some inside information about some of the families for whom I was attorney. I didn't know that it would lead to . . . . these hellish plots of yours. Two fine young people driven mad," my head snapped up to that, "my oldest friend murdered . . . ."

"Not murdered," Dunn put in, silkily. "Not murdered. The old man Armour is still alive . . . . I confess I don't like the thought of the electric chair you people reserve for . . . . killers . . . . in this country."

I heard a chair tip over as the old man jumped to his feet. "Still alive!" he quavered. "My God! Where . . . . where is he?"

Dunn laughed. "In the same place as his son, and your other little client, Nancy Holmes." My teeth gritted at that, and the red mists gathered before my eyes once more. So Nan was their victim too, she was sane, sane as I! But I did not move. I wanted to hear more. "A false bulkhead in my stateroom on Armour's own yacht, a rowboat stealing through the night from her berth in the Sound, and the thing was done. Sit down, you old fool, and drink. At least you haven't got that on your conscience."

LIQUID gulped down an old throat. Humperdinck's speech thickened. "Not on my conscience. No. An' Hal . . . . not on my conscience either. He . . . . he is really insane isn't he?" There was a pleading note in the question. "He did attack you in your office, did have hallucinations. Crazy . . . . crazy as a loon."

"No." Dunn's tone was suddenly boasting. "No, he wasn't crazy then!"

"Not crazy! But how could that be? Surely he was poised, with a knife in his hand, when your clerk broke in, ready to plunge it in your heart."

"Of course he was. But I had poised him like that." I leaned closer, the blood thumping in my temples. So it had been a fraud, that mad scene in the man's office. *A fraud!* "That little scene was my masterpiece. I must tell you about it, my dear ancient.

"You see," he went on. "I have two men whom I can trust absolutely: Hassim, an Indian Dacoit, and Abdul. When young Armour burst into my office, as I expected he would, Hassim was posted behind the side-door. At the proper moment I signalled him, and he called out, 'Hal. Hal Armour! Watch out!' You should have seen young Armour's face when he heard that. I almost laughed in his face."

"Yes, yes. But what happened then?"

"Hassim choked, then cried out for help. Armour dived for the door, flung it open. Just as I figured he would from the information you gave us as to his character. Hassim had turned around. He had his own hands at his throat, and a big mirror in the opposite wall that made the room appear twice as long as it really is wide, also reflected him so that it seemed to Armour that there were two men struggling."

"Couldn't he see the reflection of the doorway where he stood?"

"The mirror was canted a bit, so that it would not show that. And besides, the fellow had time only to glimpse the apparent fight before I threw a knife past his head and into a bladder of red ink Hassim had under the back of his coat. That twisted Armour around, and he saw the second knife poised in my hand. He leaped for me, and the instant he did so Hassim pulled a lever that turned a section of the wall in my office around, so that the door was hidden and the wall was solidly lined with bookshelves. After that Hassim had plenty of time to adjust matters in that other room so that it was utterly different from what Armour saw. It was all a matter of perfect timing, my dear sir. Perfect timing. As the young fellow grabbed the knife from me by the hilt, Abdul appeared, stark naked, and shouted some meaningless phrase at him. Armour whipped to him, and I knocked him out with the seal that was ready in my hand. It was really very simple."

"But where did Abdul come from? Surely you did not trust all your office-workers with the secret of what you were up to?"

"Small chance. My outer office door is between two large pillars. One of them

is genuine. The other is hollow, and has a secret entrance to my room. I keep the black fellow there in case of trouble. He popped out from there, did his job, and slipped back before Barclay came in. Nobody saw him."

I FELT my jaw hardening, the hot blood rushing to my head. The devil, the arrant devil! Coldly, deliberately, he had planned to make me insane, to all the world, and to myself. My fists clenched, and my leg-muscles quivered for a leap. But the old lawyer was talking again. Perhaps there would be more revelations. I held myself in leash.

"I see now how it was done." There was awe in the ancient's accents, awe, and fear. "That ingenious scheme certainly condemned him as insane from his own mouth. The girl was easy, of course. She was so cast down when her widowed mother died, so dazed, that it was simple to get a commitment for her as a melancholiac. But there are State inspections of the asylums. What if either, or both, prove themselves cured?"

Dunn laughed shortly. "By the time there is an inspection they will be really crazy. Leave that to Irma—and her charming little pet, Shang. That dear collaborator of mine is not only the consummate actress she proved herself when she won her way into the older Armour's confidence, using your information to build up her character as his long-lost sister. She is also an adept at the work she is doing now. It is marvellous to see her at it. With the brainless giant to aid her she plays on the emotions of her victims, on those strongest emotions a man can have, passion and terror, till their brains are blasted to utter darkness. As for the girl—one look at Shang's face as he creeps toward her in the dark; one feel of his hairy paws . . . ."

That was enough for me! "You devil,"

I shouted, and catapulted through the draperies. I saw Humperdinck's startled, staring face, flushed with drink, saw Dunn's slant-eyed, yellow face. I leaped for the Eurasian. "How's this for timing?" I yelled, and my fist crashed into his thin nose. "And this?" The other one pulped his gaping mouth. He hurtled away, sprawled across a sofa. I whipped around to the lawyer. "As for you . . . ."

He was backing away, his face livid. But it was not the sheer terror staring from his bleared eyes that choked the words in my mouth; it was the towering black apparition behind him, the Negro I had seen before, clothed now, but with that same snouting automatic menacing me. His lips drew away from gleaming, file-pointed teeth, I saw his finger tighten on the trigger . . . .

SOMETHING white flashed from the parting of the portieres, crashed against the black's gun elbow just as his gat belched flame. A scream shrilled in my ears as I lunged across the floor and got in a blow at the Negro's face before he could shoot again, was swallowed in a whirlwind, shouting melee of combat through which furniture crashed, thudding blows rocked me and pain shot up my arm from bruised knuckles as I pounded at a rock-like head.

"Hal," someone shouted. "His stomach, Hal. His stomach."

I shifted my attack, sank my fist in the soft belly of my antagonist. And he crumpled up like a pricked balloon, crumpled up and rolled in agony on the floor.

"Good boy, Hal." I twisted. Dad! My old dad was standing in the doorway, a tired smile on his dear face. His arm was around Nan, whose countenance was a jumble of tears and smiles.

"Dad! Was it you who . . . ."

"Threw my best Sevres vase that stood out here in the hall? No. It was this blonde young lady. I woke up, out there. She told me where we were, that you had gone into the house. She was sure that something was wrong but feared to leave me. I remembered a broken windowlock below. We got in the house, heard you yelling up here. Girl ran ahead. I got here too late to save my vase." His old eyes twinkled.

"Dear old Dad. Still up and coming. And Nan. My glorious, golden girl." I started toward them. A moan from the floor distracted me. I looked down, saw old Humperdinck, breathing his last. The bullet intended for me, deflected by the thrown vase, had found its billet in him. I moved so as to screen the sight from dad.

"Nan. There's a 'phone in the alcove behind you. You had better call the police."

"The police!" I saw fear flash, for the last time I hope, into her eyes. "But . . . ."

"No," I said gently, striding to her. "No! I have nothing to be afraid of now. There's proof here that I am sane—utterly sane. And here's further proof." I seized her, pulled her to me. And my lips found hers at last.

"I'll say you're sane," I heard dad chuckle. "Too damn sane to suit me."

SO, as it turned out, I was not insane. At least not insane enough to be committed to a madhouse. Nor, I will admit, are you. But are you sure, dead sure, that you will never be?

Think about it, tonight, when all the lights are out and you stare into a darkness where a faceless something may be lurking, its curved claws reaching noiselessly for your throat.

THE END

BLOOD MAGIC

By
G. T.
Fleming~
Roberts

All day and far into each night her ancient fingers worked busily over tiny, needle-wounded figures —while fear spread swiftly through that desolate countryside and her neighbors died one by one!

IT WAS oppressively hot. Usually Gil Fox counted upon a cool lake breeze to refresh him after the work of the day. But tonight the wind was off the land. There was a smell of tar in the air. Gil always noticed that after the sun had spent its rays upon the pine woods that crowded close upon the edge of the bay.

A whippoorwill voiced its lament, unanswered. The purling water plashed the white beach. Tonight there would be no moon.

Walking along towards the point where Devil's River joined the lake, Gil Fox made out the squat roof of old Nora Vyne's cottage where it snuggled between clustering juniper and scrub oak. He checked his ambling steps.

It was the light from the cottage window that attracted him. It was not the steady, yellow eye made by an oil lamp; rather, it was a pale, yellow glow that varied into red, that danced and faded like fox-fire above a swamp. It was the light of an open fire.

It was still July.

Gil Fox plodded through loose sand. The woodsman's native fear of forest fires hurried his steps. Nora Vyne was old, very old; but not even the chill proximity of death itself could have induced the old woman to light a fire on a night like this.

As he hurried over the board walk that approached the old woman's cottage, Gil Fox could hear the crackling of flames. He rapped on the door and entered without waiting for an answer. The rough stone fireplace was a maw of crackling flame. There was the stench of scorched fabric from a scrap of black cloth that smoldered on the hearth.

That scrap of cloth? Old Nora Vyne's black cap, of course. But where was Nora?

Firelight picked out a huddle of blue gingham on the floor to the right side of the fireplace. Gil Fox bit his lower lip. It wasn't just a bundle of cloth; it was the weazened little form of Nora Vyne, herself. Her thin, gray hair formed a disheveled mass above her white, upturned face—a face that he remembered as one of remarkable sweetness. But now all that was changed. Staring eyes gleamed up at him—dry, lifeless, china eyes. The jaws were open, silently screaming. The full, blue gingham frock was stiffly starched with drying blood from a dozen wounds!

Dead? Of course she was dead. Fox had known that the minute he had set eyes upon the old lady's shriveled form. He tugged his eyes from the face that was death-frozen horror. The fire! He sprang across the room, seized a poker, and dug at the charring sticks of wood. The fire had been built of thin, pine boards like box siding. One end of a single stick had not completely kindled. With nervous haste, Fox raked out the stick onto the hearth, beat through the flaming

brand with his poker until he had broken off the unburned portion of the board. He picked it up, hot and smoking. The board had come from some sort of a packing case. He could make out the black stenciled letters on one side:

ORE
GAN

The fast burning brands in the fireplace were yielding less and less light. Shadows crept from the corners, stealthily moving closer, waiting to make their final, smothering, kill. Gil Fox shuddered. Moving shadows animated that wrinkled, dead face upon the floor. He'd have to put a stop to that!

He walked on steadied legs to the table, scuffed a match on his trousers, and flamed the wick of the oil lamp. Replacing the glass chimney, he adjusted the wick with habitual care. That did for the shadows!

He crossed to the old-fashioned phone, twisted the crank a long and three shorts. "Mis' Dowell," he said when the connection was made, "is Doc around?"

Mrs. Dowell informed him that the doctor was at the general store, probably having a game of cards. Gil Fox hung up, cranked again until Peter Crandon, postmaster and storekeeper, asked who was speaking.

"Want to talk to Doc Dowell," said Fox. He listened to Crandon's snagging voice as he summoned the doctor.

"Dep'ty Fox talkin', Doc," said Gil. "There's been another killing—old Nora Vyne. Same an' similar sort of business. Bleeding from ten-a-dozen wounds. And there was a fire in the fireplace!"

Gil could hear Dr. Dowell's long-drawn breath whistle between his teeth. He would be over as fast as his rattling car would take him.

Gil Fox hung up. He turned reluctantly from the phone and its contact with the living to face the room where death had intruded. He picked up the lamp from the table and carried it over to the body. For several seconds he stared down at the wrinkled face. Then his eyes wandered down the blood-stained gingham skirt to the worn, black leather shoes. At the very hem of the skirt, he saw that a narrow strip of cloth had been torn away.

IT SET him wondering. A week back, Nan Weeks, who was Nora Vyne's sister, had been killed the same way. Examination of the base-burner stove showed that wood had recently been burned there. Looking through Mrs. Weeks' stock of house dresses, they had found that an eight-inch strip of cloth had been torn from one of them. It worried Fox. He didn't believe in coincidence playing much of a part in murder.

Outside, a motor raced; it took power to plow through white lake sand. Eagerly, Fox flung back the door. Eagerly, he listened for Dr. Dowell's cheerful voice. The car died with a sigh, and there was the doctor's lean shadow moving across the sand.

"Well, Gil?" Dowell called. He was near enough now so that light from the door tinged his rugged features, his gray mustache, and the unlighted two-fer cigar that was firmly socketed between his teeth.

"Another murder," Gil husked. "And good God! Why does *it* always pick a woman to butcher?"

Dr. Dowell kicked his shoe toes on the steps, strode across the sill—and there he stood.

It rasped Gil's nerves to see the doctor standing there, his gray eyes riveted on the body. The deputy sheriff swore hoarsely. "Come out of it, Doc!"

"The same *thing*," Dowell whispered around his cigar. "It'll be hard on her sister, Mrs. Nunerly. Ever stop to think what it would be like to lose two sisters

inside of a week, Gil? It takes you down pretty low." He stepped across the room and knelt beside the body. "Pretty low," he repeated. There was a desperate note in his voice as if he had to keep talking to keep his nerve from cracking.

"And what's it all about?" asked Fox. "I've never met murder head-on, but I always had a notion there had to be a motive. Try fittin' your motives in. Jealousy? No octogenarian blades are fightin' over the Vyne sisters. Gain? What have they got that anybody would want? About all they own is that chunk of beach some guy panned off on them in a land swindle. All right. Try the revenge angle. The Vyne family never had enemies. Peaceable folk, I'd say."

Dowell wasn't listening to Gil Fox. Professional interest had pulled him out of a bad case of nerves. "Six wounds, as I count them, in her torso," he said. "Four-five more in her arms and legs. The method of infliction—well, nothing I've ever seen before. Something like a gigantic needle!" Dowell stood up, mouthing his cigar.

"What lighted the fire in the fireplace?" Gil asked.

The doctor silently shook his head. "It don't click with anything sane!"

"I've got an answer," said Fox. "*Whatever* killed old Nora Vyne comes in boxes!"

"Huh?"

"Boxes," repeated Gil. "Clean, pine boxes." He pointed at the dying fire. Some of the pieces of wood still retained a semblance of their original form though now crisp and charred. "What comes in boxes, Doc, that can kill?"

"Lots of things—but nothing that kills without human agency." After a moment of reflection he added, "I don't think so, anyway."

Gil sighed, started to turn towards the door, and stopped. "Did you notice the piece of goods cut from the hem of her skirt?"

"No!"

Gil indicated the rent in the cloth. "Suppose," he said, "some damned idiot wants a piece of gingham bad enough to commit murder to get it. . ." He stopped. Dowell's gray eyes fired with a new light. "Well?" Gil demanded.

"Maybe," said the doctor, "somebody cut off that piece of goods *before* Nora died. But that—" he allowed his scraggy gray brows to hide his eyes— "but that's impossible," he concluded.

"Why? Can't you cut up a woman's dress while she's alive?"

"No-no," Dowell hastened. "You don't understand. It's absurd, of course. I'm a man of science. You, Gil, you're up-and-coming, and civilized. You and I, Gil, just don't believe in that sort of stuff— magic and the like!"

"Lord no!" Gil spat. Dr. Dowell was the last man on earth he'd expect to get brain softening! "That damned box, Doc. Who brought it? Boxes don't walk!"

"You looked around outside? There hasn't been much wind today. Might pick up a footprint or something."

"Never thought about it," Gill admitted. He picked up the lamp and, holding it above his head, shouldered through the door. Dowell followed.

"Your shoes and mine, Doc, have pretty well mussed things up," Gil said. "Hold on! Here's wheel tracks. See, your tire tracks cross 'em. Looks like they were made by a wagon. I can't remember of seeing any two-wheeled wagons around here."

Excitedly, Dowell gripped the deputy's arm. "Express;" he shouted. "If there was a box, that box came by express. Don't you know that two-wheeled handcart that Dave Dicky uses to deliver crates with?"

Gil nodded absently. Simple-minded Dave Dicky could not have found room in Gil's mind at that moment. His every sense was focused on one thing—a small impression in the sand. It was the mark of a bare foot—a very tiny bare foot. "Look!" he said hoarsely. "There's something to cogitate on!"

Dowell stared at the footprint, then looked querulously at his companion. "Any bare-footed kid might have made that. You can't pin murder on a baby!"

"No," Gil snorted, "nor you can't pin it on magic either."

The doctor scowled. "I'd think twice about that if I were you. I don't say there's anything supernatural about this, but I wouldn't forget what the school children say about old Mother Maggie who lives across the river."

Gil scoffed. "They call her an old witch, don't they? Well, put any old crone in a shack like hers in the woods the other side of a creek called Devil's River, and you'll get the same yarn from any school kid. You're gettin' childish, Doc.

"But we'll drop the argument and get the body to your car. You'll have to get her to Skinner's undertakin' parlor."

SOME time later, Gil Fox entered the Hardwood Point General Store, a market for groceries and gossip. There he found three men: Peter Crandon, the moon-faced proprietor; Dave Dicky, a little toothpick of a man with somewhat vacant looking eyes; and Toadstool Palmer, a cripple who had occupied the back room of Crandon's store building as far back as Gil could remember. He was a piteous character, was Toadstool. Remarkably sensitive about his legs, or rather his lack of them. In spite of the summer heat, Toadstool was always to be seen sitting in his wheel-chair with a gray wool blanket tucked around his knees and dropping to the foot rest of the chair. Crandon, in whom Toadstool had implicit trust, was the only person who knew what had happened to Toadstool's legs. And Crandon would say nothing more than, "Train cut 'em off at the knee, po'r guy."

Seeing that Fox volunteered no greeting, Crandon's voice rasped, "What's the news, Gil?"

Fox shook his head.

Dave Dicky, the station agent's helper, volunteered this bit of information: "Mis' Nunerly's girl Lucy is comin' home tonight, Gil. Guess you'll be glad enough of that—eh?" Dicky uttered a cracked laugh.

Gil's cheeks flamed, and the rising color brought a titter from the three men.

"Yeah," said Gil. "I knew that some time ago. But I've got to talk to you a minute, Dicky."

Did Dicky's eyes shift uneasily as he climbed down off the counter and amble over to Gil? No way of knowing what went on in Dicky's brain—if he had one.

The station agent's helper followed Gil to the door. "What's it?" he jerked, when they had gained the steps.

Fox took a firm hold on Dicky's denim shirt. "Did you deliver a crate or a box to old Nora Vyne's house today?"

Dicky's eyes revealed nothing. "Sure," he shouted. He turned and yelled back into the store. "Didn't I lug that box over to Miss Vyne's place today, boys?"

Crandon confirmed Dicky's statement with a grunt. Toadstool shrilled, "Sure you did!"

Gil felt uneasy. The admission completely disarmed him. "What'd that box have in it?" It was a foolish question, he knew.

"I ain't the kind to open 'spress packages, Gil Fox!" shouted Dicky. "You're tryin' to make me lose my job, you are."

"To hell with your job!" snapped Fox. "That box was mixed up in murder!"

Gil knew he had spoken too loud. The next moment, Crandon and Dicky were crowding around him. Toadstool had wheeled his chair up to the door and was waiting breathlessly for the news.

"You—you mean somebody's been killed?" Crandon asked in an awed whisper.

No use denying it now, Gil thought. Aloud, he said, "Nora Vyne was not only murdered; she was butchered!"

"Like her sister, Mrs. Weeks?" Crandon pumped.

"Same an' similar," Gil admitted. Then he turned to Dicky. "You wouldn't know where that box came from?"

Dicky shook his head. "It was just a prepaid box I found in my shed along with the other stuff to be delivered. If I checked up on the where from as well as the where to I'd be likely to get mixed, I would."

"Sure as hell!" Gil grumbled. He wheeled, tramped down the steps, and walked across the hard road—Hardwood Point's one street and as yet unglorified by a name. He sat down on the steps in front of his house, lighted his pipe and thought. He heard the whistle of the night train from town, heard the train stop and chug away again. He wondered if Lucy Nunerly had been among the passengers. He had intended to go meet her. Now, there was something else on his mind.

He got up, rounded the house, and angled across a thinly wooded piece of land that stretched on the east side of Devil's River. He knew where he was going. Why? He wasn't sure. He had seen something in Dr. Dowell's gray eyes— something that told him he ought to investigate a certain shack down by the river. Magic? Well, damned if he'd believe that sort of thing! But old Mother Maggie *was* a queer piece. He couldn't any more than get his eyes clawed out calling on her!

THE crossing of Devil's River required a keen sense of equilibrium. Townsmen who called a shallow creek a river also called a span of logs eight inches wide a bridge!

On the other side, he left the beaten path and pushed through a wall of mammoth wood-fern.

A hundred yards or more through the woods and he came to a little clearing. He could see the yellow light that seeped through Mother Maggie's one dirty window. The hut was a low, solidly constructed place of rough-hewn logs chinked with white plaster. The dooryard reeked with filth. In the dark, Gil stumbled over some soft, bulky form that suddenly begot short legs and ran away uttering high-pitched squeals. Just one of the old woman's pigs! School children swore that Mother Maggie ate raw pig flesh. Probably just a wild tale. . .

He approached the door quietly, avoiding anything that resembled a pig. He didn't believe in spying on people, but he'd just take a squint through the old woman's window. If he didn't see anything, he'd go away again. After all, he felt like an ass taking any stock in Dr. Dowell's idea. . . .

Fox crouched a moment below the window. Straightening up, he looked into the room. The place was a filthy combination of living, eating, and sleeping quarters all in one room. A cot at one end was covered with dirt-caked bedding. In the center of the room was a rustic table centered with a shapeless, fleshy mass that made Gil's blood turn to ice water. It was the carcass of some animal, torn as if by the jaws of savage beasts. The old crone's supper, no doubt! Beside the revolting mass were lumps of tallow-colored something tied with bright bits of colored cloth.

Mother Maggie, herself, sat beside the black and empty fireplace. She was repulsively fat, greasy, and dirty. Her head was bald except for a strand of dun-colored hair that fuzzed down over her ears. Her two front teeth were so prominent that they hung down over her lower lip when her mouth was closed. She was smoking a cob pipe. Her fat fingers were busy with a piece of tallow-colored material. Her great bare feet continually patted the floor as if keeping time to savage music that throbbed within her brain.

It was a matter of minutes before Gil could tear himself from the window. The incredible scene sickened him, but at the same time held him with a strange fascination.

He lowered his head and shoulders lest his movements attract the attention of the creature within the shack. He hurried around to the door, stepped upon a log that served as a front step, and pressed his shoulder against the door. It was fastened in some flimsy fashion. He backed off a few paces, hunched his broad shoulder, and charged against it. It broke open, boards splintering and hinges squawking. The gaseous stench of rotting offal assailed his nostrils, nauseating him.

Mother Maggie sat in her chair. Her pipe had dropped into her lap; her small piggish eyes showed no sign of alarm. Instead, her mouth dropped open, revealing her yellow snags. Her laugh was a thick, burbling sound that shook the chair in which she sat.

Gil Fox strode across the room to the table, his eyes fastened upon the woman's ugly face. "What are you doing?" he asked harshly.

Again the thick, liquid laugh. "I'm agoin' t' kill Miss Lucy," she blubbered.

Gil's eyes dropped to the table. The rotting mass of flesh was the half eaten carcass of a hog. But the tallow-colored lumps—Gil's hand darted towards one that was bound around the middle with blue gingham. His fingers, touching the thing, jerked suddenly back as if they had encountered a hot stove. He looked at his hand. Two fingers were marked with glistening drops of blood—his blood. The lump of yellow wax was barbed with needles!

With a coarse cry, Mother Maggie sprang from her chair. With incredible speed for so large a woman, she bounded to the table. Her small eyes were flaming at Gil. Her huge paws scrambled over the table, sweeping the yellow lumps to the floor. Gil dove for two of the lumps, seized one in each hand, and backed towards the door. The woman padded after him, spitting foul language, and clawing at his clothes with her filthy fingers.

Gil beat her off as best he could; but as he gained the door, her flying fingers broke through his guard. Her jagged finger-nails raked deep furrows in his cheeks and came away tipped with crimson. She stopped as if she had encountered an invisible wall. Gil Fox continued to back into the night, his eyes fastened upon the repulsive figure in the doorway. She extended her hands before her, staring at her blood-stained hand. A slavering, idiotic smile possessed her features. Slowly, she stuffed her crimsoned fingers into her mouth. Her tongue lapped hungrily at the blood—Gil Fox's blood!

"Good God!" Gil pivoted and ran headlong into the woods. He did not stop running until he heard the rippling tinkle of Devil's River.

HIS shaking legs dropped him to the pebbly bank. He unclasped his fingers from the yellowish lumps he carried in both hands. He groped for his match box, struck a light, and picked up one of the objects. It was a crude model of a woman's body fashioned in yellow wax. About the waist was knotted a narrow strip of cloth—blue gingham. Upon the

irregular base of the statuette, letters were scratched—"Nora V." The entire figure was quilled like a porcupine with steel darning needles. The needles had pierced his fingers, too, as he had run with the figure.

The second lump of wax was very much like the first except that a piece of pink material encircled the waxen waist. Upon its base were the letters—"Marthy N."

A gasp of incredulity escaped Gil's lips. Witchcraft! One figure represented Nora Vyne—and Nora Vyne had died of a dozen wounds. Back in Mother Maggie's shack he had left another figure. No doubt it represented Mrs. Weeks, Nora's elder sister. Mrs. Weeks had died the same way! And here was a statue of Mrs. Nunerly, the youngest of the Vyne sisters. Could she, too, be dead?

Gil flung the filthy wax images into the creek, balanced his way across the narrow bridge, and pelted through the woods towards Martha Nunerly's house. But if he did find her dead, what could he do? You couldn't arrest an old crone for pricking wax figures with darning needles. The days of witch-burnings were over. In the truth itself, Mother Maggie had a perfect alibi. Such things just couldn't be! Alibi? Gil wondered as he ran. Could he smash that alibi. . . ?

A shrill scream that throbbed with terror ripped the hot, still air and dwindled to a wavering cadence. To Gil Fox, that scream was like the sting of a gadfly. It was unmistakably the scream of a woman—and it came from Martha Nunerly's cottage!

He crashed through undergrowth, branches tearing at his face. The earth beneath him was slippery with pine needles. Twice, in his headlong dash, he had fallen only to rise again with desperate resolve to *stop that killer* whether man, witch, or demon.

He broke through the woods into a

clearing that was Mrs. Nunerly's back lot. The back of the house was dark, but the yellow glow of oil lamps came from the front room.

Fox stopped. Nothing could be gained by breaking into the house with the noise of an invading army. He proceeded across the lot on tiptoe, creaking up the steps, and tried the back door. It was unlocked. He inched it open, stepped into blackness and closed the door behind him.

He listened carefully. Shrieks of terror that would out in spite of every effort to muffle them came from the kitchen door. Fox dropped to his knee and fixed his eye to the keyhole. Upon the floor, he could see the head and torso of a woman. Her thick, white hair was blood-matted. Dark stains of long-dried blood blotched the ragged cloth of her dress. It was Martha Nunerly. Butchering death had come to her as it had come to her sisters.

Standing against the wall back of the body, was the figure of a young girl. At first, Gil failed to recognize her, so completely was she trussed up with wide cotton strips that had apparently been torn from a sheet. But above the gag that strained her jaws open, Fox saw horror-wide eyes. Blue eyes they were—the eyes of Lucy Nunerly, the old lady's daughter.

The girl's eyes shifted from her mother's stiffened body to some *thing* that the edge of the keyhole shuttered from Gil's gaze.

A rustling sound. A huge figure blotted across the keyhole. A shrill voice that Fox failed to recognize called: "Palmer, all set?"

The front door swung back. There was a rumble of wheels on the front porch, and Toadstool Palmer, seated in his wheel-chair, rolled into the room. A curious change had come over the cripple's usually mild face. It was a look that mingled cunning, hate, and blood-lust until the twisted features had become a hideous, gargoyle-like mask.

Skillfully, Toadstool guided his chair to the side of the girl. From beneath the blanket that hid his disfigurement, he drew a strange weapon. It was a butchers' sharpening steel ground to needle sharpness. An excited titter passed the cripple's twisted lips. With a sudden movement, he threw aside the encumbering blanket and squirmed from his chair to the floor.

On the other side of the door, Gil Fox was paralyzed with surprise. Toadstool Palmer had *legs*. But what legs they were! While the upper part of Palmer's body had developed to something just below normal proportions, from the waist down he was a dwarf! More than that—the tiny, twisted legs, the little feet were those of a child!

TOADSTOOL capered about the terrified girl, his bare, baby feet pattering on the floor. He feinted with his needle-weapon, tittering with insane glee.

"Stop that, Palmer!" the shrill voice demanded. "Finish the job quickly. She's the last one."

The repulsively formed creature halted in front of the girl. He braced himself on his little, wavering legs. His lance was poised.

Lucy Nunerly's eyelids closed upon the death that faced her—death in the form of a crazed, malformed fiend.

Gil Fox's legs stiffened. His sweating fingers yanked at the doorknob. His shoulder drove against the panel, and he flung into the room.

Toadstool spun on his twisted legs. Fear drove the fiendish glare from his eyes.

But so intent was Gil upon the crazed little killer that he failed to notice the huge man in oilskins. Something prodded him in the back. "Put up your hands!" the voice commanded. "Or I'll blast ye to hell!"

Slowly, Fox turned. His hands crept upwards. The face of the man in oilskins was veiled with black cloth. Eyes thoroughly sane calmly surveyed him. A single-barreled shotgun nestled in the crook of an arm.

"This one first," said the masked man. He stepped in front of the girl, his gun nosing at Gil.

"I ain't goin' to," Toadstool whimpered. "I'm scared of him."

"Kill him," commanded the masked man, "like you did the women. He'll stand still. If he's wise, he'll take your steel through the heart rather than buckshot in his gizzard."

Toadstool advanced, hopping on his tiny legs. Gil stood perfectly still. He felt the point of the weapon pierce his clothing and prick his skin. Suddenly, a broad smile spread across his features. Toadstool seemed hypnotized by that smile—a smile on the face of a man inches from death!

"All right!" shouted Gil. "Give 'em the gun, Sheriff!"

Toadstool whirled around. The masked man shouted, "It's a bluff!"

Gil's right foot shot out, landed in the small of Palmer's back and pitched him straight into the masked man. The shotgun roared. Toadstool's head suddenly became a pulpy mass of crimson. As the deformed creature fell forward, Gil saw his steel weapon snag through the masked man's sleeve and rip into the flesh.

Springing over Toadstool, Gil launched a smashing blow with his right. It landed in the middle of the man's chest and sent him reeling back against the wall. He fell flat, striking his head against the baseboard. He lay still as death.

Gil Fox went over to Lucy and got busy on her bonds. Her more than grateful eyes embraced him as he worked. When the gag was removed, she murmured, "They killed my mother. I found

her like that when I came in. Then, *they* came!"

"Take it easy, Lucy," Gil said soothingly. "I think your mother's been dead for some time—two-three days. They got both of her sisters. You would have been the last of the Vyne family."

Tears welled into her eyes. She braved them back. "No, Gil, not the last. Dave Dicky's mother was a Vyne."

Dicky, the killer! "Why, what could he gain—"

"The land, Gil—the big stretch of beach. I learned about it in the city. A big summer resort promoter was talking about it. It's worth thousands now!"

"But Dicky's a numb-skull!" Gil insisted.

"And Gil," the girl went on, "when I got off the train tonight, that old Mother Maggie met me and asked for a piece of my dress. I refused, and as I left the platform she tore a piece from my skirt!"

GIL nodded. "She's crazy as a bedbug. You see, the real killers thought up a swell alibi. Mother Maggie thinks she's a witch. The killers paid her to charm the Vyne sisters into the grave. She used the old method of making wax images clothed in scraps of cloth taken from the clothes of her intended victims. She stuck the figures full of darning needles that they might die of many wounds. This method was used at the request of the real killers, simply because when the bodies were found with so many wounds they thought somebody would suggest witchcraft. Somebody did!

"Mother Maggie is just vain enough about her spells to admit the killings. You can't burn witches these days. What can the law do?"

"To think that Dicky could figure all that out!" Lucy exclaimed.

"He didn't!" Fox insisted. "The way the real killer worked—except tonight when he was after you—was to build pine boxes just big enough to hold Toadstool Palmer and his butchering weapon. The murderer stole some express labels to stick on the boxes. When one box had been addressed to a particular victim, Toadstool was slipped inside. Then the killer put the box in the shed from which Dicky delivered his packages. Dicky's too dense to do much checking up. Toadstool, having spent most of his life in a chair, wouldn't mind being crated up in a box for an hour or so.

"Once the box had been delivered, Toadstool would open the lid from the inside, jump out, and kill his victim. After the job was over, Toadstool burned the box, and made his getaway.

"What the real master-mind behind all this thought he would do was to kill all the Vynes except Dicky. The killer had learned the value of that strip of beach, and he knew he could buy it from Dicky for a plug of tobacco. The murderer stood in a good way to clean up a stack of money!"

"But who is the—the murderer?" Lucy insisted.

Gil pulled the piece of half-burned wood, that he had taken from Nora Vyne's fireplace, from his pocket. He pointed to the letters:

ORE
GAN

"Those are the last letters of a two line address, I figure. Might read something like this:

CRANDON'S GENERAL STORE
HARDWOOD POINT MICHIGAN

"Then the boxes in which Toadstool was hidden. . . ?"

Gil nodded. "Were made from wood crates that had been shipped to the store."

He crossed to the silent figure of the masked man on the floor. Handcuffs jingled from Gil's hand. He pulled off the black cloth that covered the face.

"Peter Crandon, in the flesh!" he said.

Dead Man's Bride

By
Wyatt Blassingame

I CAME out of Eve Wingard's home humming Mendelssohn's Wedding March and so happy I couldn't tell whether or not my feet were touching the ground. I was on my way home to tell Uncle Edward that Eve had promised to marry me. My uncle had been father and mother to me since I was a child. I knew that he loved me and that he liked Eve Wingard. He would be very happy when I told him.

I had one foot on the running board of my roadster when I saw the man across the street. The sight of him jerked me to a halt and cut the song from my lips. He was a tall, thin man wearing an old-fashioned cutaway coat and pinch-leg trousers, but it was his face with its high forehead and dark eyes and thin, cruel mouth that held my attention. He was

Novelette of Eerie Dread

The boy and the girl were passion-ately in love. The Undead who menaced their happiness should long before have abandoned all fleshly fancies. Yet Eve Wingard, vibrant with life, was needed in that shadowed realm where the dead walk always.

watching me and smiling but it was not like any smile I had ever before seen on the face of a human being. There was something ghastly, something blood-chilling about the thin curve of his lips and for a moment I had the idea that he was smiling, not at me, but at the things which would happen to me in the future—horrible, unnameable things which he knew about and which I could not possibly avoid.

Shrugging, I slid under the steering wheel, kicked the motor into action. When I had gone a block I turned and glanced back. He was standing motionless, still watching me.

Somehow I didn't feel like singing any more. . . .

I have never seen a man look so strangely as my uncle Edward did when I told him that Eve Wingard and I were to be married. There was horror and pity and a terrible agony etched in the deep lines of his face from which the blood had drained suddenly, leaving even his full, kindly lips a pasty gray. I had expected him to clap me on the back and say, "Good boy!" in that deep, rumbling voice of his. Now the sight of his face with its gray lips and that strange, mingling of terror and pity in his dark eyes struck me like cold spray.

My uncle Edward raised a slow hand and pushed it through his graying hair. His hand was shaking and there were little beads of sweat on the knuckles. His voice was scarcely above a whisper when he said, "John . . . you . . . I . . ." He paused and I could see his tall, erect body stiffening, bracing itself for what was to follow. But his voice came softly, anxiously, "You . . . you love this girl, son?"

The lines jerked hard around my mouth. Even Uncle Ed couldn't question me about Eve. "I love her and I'm going to marry her," I snapped.

For a long moment we looked squarely at each other and I could see the pain growing in his eyes. Then my uncle Edward put a hand on my shoulder. He said, "All right, son. I don't doubt you love her. That's what makes telling you so hard. But I've got to tell you and you've got to listen."

MY uncle turned away as though he could not face me and his voice was hoarse. "You can't marry Eve Wingard; you can't marry at all."

For a moment, hearing the tone of his words, I had little chills along my back. Then abruptly I was angry. "Why not?" I demanded.

My uncle turned his eyes toward mine once more and what I saw in his face smothered my anger in a blanket of eerie premonition. "You don't know much about your family history, John, and it won't be easy to tell you. But there's no escape now. Sit down." He gestured toward an overstuffed chair near the French windows and turned and went out of the room. When he came back a moment later he had an old-fashioned miniature which he handed me. He said: "One of your ancestors, Casey A'Hearn."

I remember that the French windows were open and that August sunlight poured through them. It made a bright rectangle on the hardwood floor and touched on one arm of the red leather chair on which I was sitting. I raised the picture, holding it in the sunlight, and looked at it. And my body jumped as though electricity had snapped at my muscles. It was the face of the man who had stared at me as I came out of Eve Wingard's.

"Why . . . why . . ." I stammered. "I saw this man just a little while ago as I left Eve's."

My uncle staggered backward and the muscles jerked along his jaw. For one moment he stood quivering, then he sank into a chair before the big, empty fireplace and dropped his head in his hands. "God help us," he said.

Again I felt that weird chill along my spine as though some dark shadow had passed over me. "What . . . what's wrong with seeing the fellow?" I asked and while waiting for his answer my hands clinched on my knees in fear.

Uncle did not raise his head. "Casey A'Hearn died in 1850," he said.

I jumped half erect and stood there for

a second trembling. Then I dropped back into my chair and began to laugh. "What's this you are handing me? Or do you mean that I saw one of Casey's progeny? All the DeJarnett's look alike, and I reckon, as the A'Hearns are kin to us, they'll look the same way."

FOR a moment my uncle did not speak but sat staring into the empty fireplace. I watched him, leaning forward with my hands on my knees. Then he began to talk but not once did he turn his pale, thin face toward me. His voice held a deadly seriousness. "The trouble started with your great grand-uncle, Lacey DeJarnett, and with his first cousin, Casey A'Hearn. They both lived at the old family estate just north of Birmingham. Both the house and the land had been inherited by your uncle Lacey. Casey A'Hearn thought the property should have come to him and he never forgave your uncle. I don't know whether it was in an attempt to get back at your uncle Lacey or whether it was the man's naturally weird inclinations that drove him to the study of black magic and devil worship. All of this happened, you understand, years before I was born. But it has come down to me through the family.

"If Casey hated your uncle because he inherited the property, that hatred grew to madness when your uncle married Miriam Whitfield. Casey gave himself up entirely then to the study of devil worship. He moved back into a hut in the mountains at the far side of the plantation where he died in 1850. But before dying he sent word to your uncle Lacey that no man who inherited this estate would ever turn it over to one of his own children.

"No man ever has. A week after Casey died, Miriam Whitfield went mad. Three weeks later your uncle Lacey's horse ran

away with him and the bodies of both the man and his horse were found at the foot of a ravine beside the road. The estate went to Lacey's nephew, William. The week before William was to be married his fiancée disappeared. There were rumors about where she was seen and about things that happened back in the mountains on moonless nights. They were incredible stories and no one except the negroes and the poor whites on the place believed them . . . that is, before the thing that happened to William. After that everybody moved away from the old house. The negroes had already left the place. No one has lived there since then but two other men have inherited it. One of them married before the thing happened to him, the other died two days before his wedding. The things which happened to them were terrible enough but the fate they brought upon the women they loved was even worse."

My uncle raised his face toward me and I could see his gray lips twitching. "And so you see, John," he said very softly, "why you can't marry Eve Wingard."

I CAME to my feet then, hot anger prickling the skin of my neck. "By God," I said, "this is a fairy tale. You can't expect me to believe that a man who died in 1850 can . . . can . . ."

My uncle did not answer but sat staring at the floor. Finally he looked up and said, "You inherited the place, John, from your uncle Macon, who went mad the week before he married. His fiancée, Macon said, was dead, but no one ever found the body to bury her."

I thought then of Eve Wingard, with her close cropped gold hair curling about her head, and of the softness of her mouth. I stepped toward my uncle and he stood up to face me. "Listen," I said, "I don't believe this damn thing you've told me. It's absurd. But for Eve's sake I'm going to prove that it's wrong. I'm engaged to Eve Wingard, but I'll leave her here where she will be safe. I'm going to that old place and live there. Prove that your bogey rumor is foolish."

My uncle started. He put his hand on my shoulder and his fingers clenched hard. He started to speak, stopped. When he did speak his voice was scarcely above a whisper. "Don't go, John. The others have all tried this and . . ."

"To hell with it," I said. "Is there any one living there now?"

"I don't know. No one has been to that place in thirty years. Legend says that two old servants stay there." He paused and there was no laughter in his eyes when he added, "They are supposed to be the same two servants who were there in 1850. They had been the helpers of Casey A'Hearn."

I snorted. "How do I get to this place?"

"Go north of Birmingham about twenty miles on the Gasden Highway, then take a road that turns off to your right. It wanders out through the mountains. You won't find many persons, but anyone can tell you how to reach the old DeJarnett estate."

I looked at my watch. It was twenty minutes of four. "I can be in Birmingham by five o'clock," I said. "I can find this place before dark."

I felt my uncle's fingers digging into my shoulder. "Will you call Eve and tell her that I've left town on business?" I asked. "Tell her I'll be back in a week."

My uncle did not answer and he looked at me as a father might look at the corpse of his son. "Don't worry," I said, "I'll be back and I'll bring this Casey A'Hearn with me." I turned and went out of the house to where my roadster was parked against the curb.

CHAPTER TWO

Vanished Horseman

THE road which turned off to the right of the Gasden Highway was little more than a winding trail threading its way around heavily timbered mountainsides. I had gone perhaps ten miles before I found a small, dirty cabin squatting like a mangy dog beside the road. There was an old man in overalls sitting on the front porch and two half-naked children playing in the yard. I stopped the car and leaning over the door called to the old man to ask him where the De-Jarnett plantation was.

He lunged to his feet, mouth hanging open. For a moment I thought the old man was going to run into the house and not answer, but he only stood there and stared at me, and the way he looked made my back feel cold against the leather seat of the car and the muscles of my throat grew hard and dry. Finally the old man said, "Are you one of the DeJarnetts?"

"Yes."

"God!" he said, and sat back down in his chair heavily.

I became angry then. "Are you going to tell me where the place is?"

"It's right up this way about four mile. Then you turn off to the left and go a couple more. You'll know it when you see it."

I said: "Thanks." And started off.

The trees made the road like a tunnel of shadow and dusk hung in an impenetrable cloud behind me. I kept thinking of the way the old man had looked at me and remembering the story which my uncle had told. Somehow the gathering twilight filled me with a weird feeling of horror hanging like the dust cloud just behind me, ready to roll over me like a great wave whenever I stopped. I tried to shrug off the feeling, tried to tell myself that the whole thing was foolish; that the story was just some superstitious concoction. But it didn't work. There was sweat on my hands where they gripped the wheel and the back of my neck felt cold.

Where the road turned off to the left it began to wind upward. On the right the mountainside was sometimes a sheer bluff towering above me and the road was little more than a ridge with the left side dropping off to show the tops of trees fifty feet below. I kept close to the right wall and drove slowly. It was the time of day when dusk is thick and almost impenetrable and yet too early for the lights of the car to do any good. I kept thinking that I had seen this place before, that I had traveled this road and that some horror had overtaken me. If I had believed in transmigration I would have said that some time in ages past I had been killed here. It gave me an eerie, unpleasant feeling. I knew that I had never come this way before and yet the sheer drop on the left seemed to pull me like a magnet. I had to fight myself to keep the car close to the right hand wall.

And then without warning it happened.

I SWUNG a sharp curve in the road coming to a space where sunlight glittered. Twenty feet ahead the shadows shut down heavily and just inside these shadows I saw the thing. I saw the horse rear on its hind legs, saw the rider, his face gray and terrified, jerk at the reins. My car was almost on them. I snatched the wheel toward the left. The horse plunged at the cliff and vanished.

The car skidded wildly, sending little pebbles in a fierce rain against the fenders. The chasm at the edge of the road leaped toward me. I jerked the wheel hard to the right and slapped on the brakes. The tires whined and the car rocked. I felt the left wheel drop suddenly over the cliff and the car swaying to plunge downward.

Somehow I stabbed my foot on the accelerator and tugged at the steering wheel. I heard the wail of the rear tires in the gravel, felt the car shudder as the front wheel climbed back onto the road. Then I almost smashed against the cliff on the right before I steadied the machine. I cut the motor and stepped on the brake.

My hands were sweat-coated; my heart was a hard thing pounding at my ribs as I got out of the roadster. My knees felt weak and I thought once I was going to fall. There had been something ghastly familiar about the horse and rider, about the man's gray, terrified face, the wide forehead and the dark eyes.

And then I knew abruptly that it was the face of a DeJarnett.

I had to walk back to the spot where the horse and rider had disappeared before I could bring myself to look over the edge of the cliff. There were no trees at this point and I dreaded what would be so horribly clear lying at the foot of the sun-coated cliff.

Then I stepped to the edge of the road and looked over. For a moment I could not believe the thing I saw. I felt suddenly sick at my stomach and the muscles in my shoulders were cold and quivery. Some wild, unnameable desire tugged at me, jerked me like an invisible hand toward the edge of the bluff. I felt myself wavering and had to leap backward to keep from plunging over.

And then, still unbelieving, I moved back to the side of the road and looked over once more. Sunlight fell in a mellow effulgence along the ragged side of the cliff, turning the clay to a bloody red. Fifty feet below a small brook wound between rocky ledges. Beyond the brook elder bushes and blackberry vines made a low wall.

But there was no bloody corpse of horse and rider at the cliff's foot. The man and the horse had vanished.

I stood there staring, looking up and down the road, thinking perhaps I was not in the right position. I knew that no man or animal could have gone over this cliff and lived. Yet of the pair which I had seen plunge downward there was no sign.

I stepped backward, my hands clenching and unclenching at my sides. I turned slowly to look at the spot where I had first seen the horse. Ten feet up a small sweetgum clung to the edge of the bluff and waved slightly in the twilight wind. I looked down at the road and except for the mark of my automobile tires there was no sign that it had ever been traveled. Then I looked up at the sweetgum swaying in the shadows and tried to laugh but somehow the sound was clammy and guttural.

I tried to tell myself that what I had seen was merely an optical illusion. My nerves keyed up, I had come out of the sunshine to see this sweetgum swaying in the shade, and had mistaken it for a horse and rider. I had known such things to happen; yet I couldn't convince myself. The face of the horseman, the high forehead and the dark eyes, had been too horribly clear. I went back to the other side of the road and looked over once more. The rock-edged brook, the wall of elder and of blackberry vines, showed clearly in the sunlight. Nothing else.

There had been no horse and rider. I knew that. It had been nothing but an optical illusion.

And then I remembered that my great-uncle Lacey had plunged over this very cliff some eighty years before. My knees were weak as I went back toward the roadster. For a moment I sat thinking of the story my uncle had told me, of the fear and terror and pity which had showed in his face. Then I almost turned back when I thought of Eve Wingard. I hooked a hard finger over the car switch, clicked it on viciously and kicked the starter. "By God!" I said aloud, "Ghost or no ghost, I'll take a look at this place!"

Gravel cracked against the fenders like burning brushwood as the car started forward.

CHAPTER THREE

A Cup For Blood

ALMOST abruptly I came on the old house. The road had been winding steadily upward when, coming around a sharp curve at the very peak of the mountain, I saw the place bathed in late sunlight. Somehow I never doubted for a moment that this was the old DeJarnett home, and the sight of it sent tingling along my spine that weird premonition of horror which I had felt before.

It was a big, square house sitting some hundred yards back from the road across a barren lawn. It was built after the fashion of the old Colonial homes of the pre-war South but there was none of the lightness and grace which usually went with this architecture. The place seemed heavy, dismal, like a giant hunchback crouched and waiting, waiting for some hideous thing through interminable time. The paint was gone from the building, leaving the walls an ugly gray. There were wide, latticed windows, but the blinds were pulled closed and I could not tell whether there was any light inside the house or not. With cold hands I swung the car up the drive and stopped before the wide, rotting steps.

I slid across the seat and out the right hand door of the car, eyeing the house with a wily speculation. And even as my foot touched the running board, the door of the house swung open and a man came out. The long, level rays of the sun shone cleanly in his face. I looked at him and sat motionless on the edge of the car seat with one foot still resting on the running board. I could feel the corners of my mouth twitching and I knew that my eyes were wide and horror-stricken, for I had never seen a man like this.

He was old, incredibly old, and yet he was stiffly erect. Age seemed to have shrunken his head so that the skin of his face lay in great wrinkled folds from which hollow eyes peered darkly. He was totally bald, yet his dead did not glisten as the head of most bald men. Even here the skin was wrinkled and dirty. And I knew without question, even as I had known that this was the house I sought, that this man was the servant of whom my uncle Edward had spoken.

The man came down the steps moving with the stiff awkwardness of age. He pulled the car door open for me and said, as though he had known me all his life, "Welcome home, sir."

I did not answer him, for I could think of nothing to say. I did not ask if this were the DeJarnett home or if he were the servant in charge, for I knew these things instinctively. I remember the creak of the running board as I stepped on it and the crunch of my shoes on the gravel.

The old man said, "Your bags, sir?"

I turned and looked at him and for the first time it occurred to me that I had brought no clothes except the ones I wore. I replied, "I don't have a bag."

He said, "Yes, sir," as though he had not really expected one, and turned to lead the way into the house.

THERE were candles burning in the great hallway, glistening on the wide, paneled floor, on the dark railing of the circular stairway which coiled like a snake upward into darkness.

Beyond the stairway I saw something move for a second and then it had merged into the darkness at the back of the hall. Somehow I knew it was the old woman who with her husband took care of the house.

The ancient servant had turned into a room on the left and I followed him. It was a high, paneled, old-fashioned living room with family portraits on the walls, a great open fireplace and a giant chandelier in which a dozen candles flickered yellowly.

"If you will wait in here, sir," the old man said, "I shall have your bath ready in a few moments. Martha has prepared dinner and it will be waiting for you."

"Thank you," I said. The old man seemed to glide through the doorway and vanish.

And then I realized that his feet had made no sound as he moved. There was no sound in the great house at all except the whisper of my breathing and the dull thud of my heart against my ribs. Silence rushed like a black river through the house and I stood there motionless, waiting for something which I did not understand.

The old man had gone and I had the eerie feeling that he had never been there at all: that he was like the horse and rider which I had seen . . . or thought I had seen. I laughed nervously, making a tiny trickle of sound which seeped into the black silence of the house and faded. Then I turned and began to examine the room in which I was standing.

The candlelight left the wide walls of the room in semi-shadow, but I could make out the dull outline of old-fashioned portraits. I stepped close to the one which hung above the mantel and peered upward to examine it. There was a man in the stiff riding costume of the middle nineteenth century. I could scarcely see his face in the semi-darkness but what I could see cut me like a sudden whip of terror. There was a thin-lipped, cruel mouth that even in the shadows were viciously red; a thin long nose with flared nostrils and above them black, wild, maniacal eyes in which madness glittered like fire. It was my ancestor, Casey A'Hearn, who had laid a curse on every man to inherit this house and on the women whom those men loved. And it was the man I had seen watching me as I left Eve Wingard.

I sprang backward from the portrait as I might have from some wild animal, terror gripping the muscles of my throat. Then I laughed again and I cursed myself for a superstitious fool, and I turned back toward the center of the room.

Under the massive chandelier with its guttering candles was a large, square mahogany table and on the table there lay a single book. I wondered why I had not noticed the book before for it lay opened almost in the center of the table. I leaned over to look at it. A dull, rust colored stain smeared the bottom of both pages, and then I noticed the weird Gothic lettering: "Book of the Devil." Picking up the book to look at it more carefully, I discovered an eerie feeling about the leaves, as though they were made of some soft, fleshy tissue. I started to laugh nervously, but at the same moment found that my right thumb resting near the bottom of the page had become stained with the same stuff that smeared the book. I dropped the book as I would have dropped a hot iron . . . for the stuff which stained the pages . . . was blood!

I WAS standing there staring at the blood on my thumb and feeling horror running like a cold mist through my body, when I heard the old man speak. "If you will go to your room and bathe, sir, dinner will be served as soon as you are ready."

I looked up wildly for I had not heard any sound as he came along the hall or into the room. But there he stood inside the circle of the candlelight, his face and head a massed tangle of wrinkles. I began to rub my bloody thumb slowly against my coat.

"All right," I said, "show me the way."

He turned soundlessly and went through the door. For a moment I could not follow him for my feet seemed frozen. For as the old man had moved without a sound out of the circle of candlelight and into the dimness of the hallway, I saw that no shadow preceded him. Candlelight lay on the polished hardwood floor as unruffled as though nothing but a wind had passed.

From the hall I heard him say, "This way, sir."

In that moment I felt a wild impulse to rush from the room, to fling open the rotting front door and dash down the steps. I wanted to see the solidity of the roadster I had left in front, to see things to which I was accustomed in the common, every-day world. And then before I could move, I thought once more of Eve Wingard, her eyes, vividly blue under the gold of her hair, watching me. I knew then that I could never leave this place until I had proved the thing I came to prove. I could not go back to her until I knew that I brought no curse with me. The idea of leaving her, or breaking our engagement, never occurred to me even then.

I heard my voice answering the old man, "All right, I'm coming." And then I felt the cold muscles of my leg move and heard the thud of my shoes on the hardwood floor.

From a bracket in the hall the old man took a candle and led the way up the spiral staircase. I watched him raise his feet one after another and though I were less than a yard behind him I heard no sound. He moved as silently as the light which flooded ahead of him.

It was a large, square room to which he conducted me, with a massive, old-fashioned, curtained bed, a great chest of drawers and a low washstand, on which was an old-fashioned pitcher and bowl. There were four big windows in the room but the blinds were drawn and for the first time I became conscious that the air in the house was stale. It had the heavy, dead odor of air in houses long closed, houses where no human being has lived for year on year.

The old man placed the candle in the bracket above the washstand.

"Dinner will be ready when you come downstairs," he said.

WHEN I came back down the stairs carrying the candle, the old man was waiting in the hallway. "This way, sir," he said, and led me into the dining room. It was a large room with a long, linen-covered table in the center. On the table was a candleabra and two chairs were drawn up. The old man stepped to one of them and pulled it back. The table cloth was a heavy linen and the silver-ware at my place was massive and mono-grammed. Before the chair opposite me stood a cluster of empty wine-glasses but there was no silver placed there. At one side of the glasses was a thin china cup and the candlelight playing on the fragile porcelain made the thing look as though it were alive.

Before I could ask the old man said, "This place is for the Master. He will be here soon." The words touched a cold finger to my brain and I shuddered. I felt my eyes swelling in their sockets. Whom could he mean—the Master? I was master in this house. The old man must be crazy, I told myself, and shrugged. Living in this house long was enough to drive any man mad. And then

I thought of the thin, cruel face in the portrait, of the man who had smiled so strangely, watching me leave Eve Wingard.

The servant walked around the table and stood for a moment looking down at the wine glasses. Then he reached out a lean, wrinkled hand and touched the fragile cup. I could have sworn that he was caressing it. His voice was a husky whisper. "This is the cup for the blood."

I came half way out of my chair staring at him. "What the devil!" I gasped. The old man looked at me and though there was no change in his sunken eyes, I thought the wrinkled lips curled upward in a smile.

He turned without a sound and went out of the room. A moment later he was back bearing a bowl of soup. I did not hear him leave nor return but a half-minute later he was pouring Sauterne into a wine glass.

I had barely started the second course when I heard the chair opposite me scrape on the floor. My head jerked up and my breath made a loud whistling noise. As if they had materialized out of the air two men stood opposite me. The old servant pulling back the chair and another man in the dark, formal dress of 1850.

"Who . . . who?" But the words clogged in my throat and made no sound. For already I knew the man opposite me. He was the man whose portrait was hanging over the old fireplace in the living room; the man who had died eighty-four years ago cursing my family.

He was a handsome man with a cruel, terrible sort of beauty. He gestured courteously toward me as he sat down. "I apologize for being late," he said. His voice was low and cultured, but there was a sound in it which made the blood clabber in my veins. He sank into the chair and there was no sound as he touched it, but the chair scraped as the servant pushed it forward. "You came earlier than I expected," he said.

I had forgotten the food before me. My hands were clenched on the edge of the table and I was leaning forward, gazing at him. "You . . . you expected me?" I asked, and somehow the question sounded foolish.

"Certainly." He laughed quietly. And there was the servant again, standing over his shoulder and pouring wine.

I HAD lost any form of appetite and barely touched the food which was brought to me, course after course. No food was placed before the man opposite me but his wine-glass was refilled many times, and as he drank, his left hand toyed with the cup which the servant had said was for blood.

My own conversation was limited to stuttered monosyllables. A weird sense of inescapable doom had settled on me. I felt as though I were locked inside a tomb from which escape was so totally impossible that I could not even bring myself to try. In the deep silence of the house there was no sound except the voice of my host. And I sat there waiting, waiting for what was to follow without any idea of what the thing would be; yet I knew that it would be horrible and that there would be no escape.

Almost suddenly it struck me as odd that this man should play host in the home which belonged to me. I had been telling myself that the man was real, that he was a human being and that the old servant was a human being and that they were usurping a place to which they had no right. I straightened in my chair to ask the man who he was.

Then out of darkness the servant materialized behind him once more with the wine bottle in his hand and before I could speak the man said, "You will tell Martha to have the wedding chamber ready.

There will be a marriage tonight." He said the words as though he were ordering a candle lighted in the other room and the servant accepted them as casually.

"Yes, Mr. A'Hearn," and then he moved silently backward and vanished.

Casey A'Hearn turned to me again and took up the story which he had been telling.

I had finished eating my meal when the thing happened so suddenly that it left me aghast, unable to move. Casey A'Hearn was talking about his afternoon's ride and then in the middle of a sentence, his face changed. The quiet, courtliness went out of it as light leaves a room when a candle is snuffed. His thin lips curled back from wolfish teeth, his eyes blazed, there was a wild, snarling sound in his throat as he surged to his feet. His thin white hands caught the table cloth and jerked. The candelabra crashed over. The yellow lights gutted high and went out. There was a clash of glasses striking the floor and breaking but even in the deep gloom I could see that he held the thin porcelain cup in his hand.

I did not move from my chair but sat there frozen by the suddenness of this thing and by the terribleness of the face opposite me. Then fear lashed me to my feet and my chair went over with a crash as I staggered erect.

For a moment Casey A'Hearn's face worked terribly and his long teeth seemed to glow in the darkened room. Then I heard him snarl, "Don't cross your knife and fork like that . . . . in this house!"

Even then I tried to struggle against the certainty of the thing. I knew that unconsciously I had made a cross of my knife and fork after finishing the meal. My uncle Edward had taught me this old fashioned manner and I had come to do it unconsciously. I tried even then to say it was not the cross that had transformed Casey A'Hearn. I kept telling myself, "The man is human; this is all a play or a dream; he is a human being and he is only acting." But I knew that there was no acting about the thing I had seen.

Then again out of the silence the servant materialized and I heard the scratch of a match and saw the yellow flame spurt up. Silently the old man lighted the candles and replaced the candelabra on the table, and as silently I stood watching him, motionless.

And then the utter quietness of the house shattered like a glass ball. From outside came the raucous blasting of an automobile horn and with the sound anger blasted my body into motion, driving the fear and horror from it. I spun and leaped toward the lighted hall.

For I knew the horn that I had heard outside. It belonged to the small Chrysler roadster which Eve Wingard drove.

CHAPTER FOUR

Decaying Faces

THERE was no sound behind me as I dashed down the hallway and out the door. The sun was gone now and dusk had thickened into a gray darkness through which the headlights of an automobile jabbed white fingers. "Eve!" I cried, "Eve!" and went stumbling down the decaying steps.

She was getting out of the car, smiling. I could see her gold hair in the gathering darkness and the pale blur of her face. "I came right out when I got your note," she said cheerily.

I was gripping the door, keeping her inside the car. The expression on my face must have shown that something was wrong and the smile left her lips to be replaced by an anxious trembling. She put her hands quickly on my shoulders.

"Why did you come here?" I demanded. "How did you find this place?"

She looked at me puzzled. "I came when I got your note," she said again. "You told me how to get here."

I looked at her in wild amazement. "But I didn't write you any note. I didn't know how to get here myself until a little while ago."

"Why, John . . ." There was a strained sound in her voice and I saw the new question which came into her face. "Here's the note you sent." She reached behind her and took her purse from the seat and opened it. For a moment she fumbled inside then I saw her brows knit and she lowered her eyes to the purse. She looked up at me again dazed. "Why . . . . Why, it was here," she said. "I know I had it in here. It couldn't have slipped out."

And then before I could answer, her body jerked stiff and she screamed.

Whirling I saw the servant. He had come down the steps with that shadowy silence of his and in the deep dusk his face was a wrinkled mask of evil, and even as we watched he stepped quietly to the automobile and raised the hood. He reached out a wrinkled hand and there was a sound of wires tearing from their sockets.

I darted forward, caught him by the shoulder and spun him around. "What the devil!" I said. My right fist was clinched and I would have struck him but something held my arm. I turned and it was Casey A'Hearn, smiling blandly.

The old man said, as though nothing had happened, "Did the lady bring any bags?"

I told him no, and turned back to face Eve Wingard. She was looking past me at Casey A'Hearn and her eyes were wide and frightened. A'Hearn bowed toward her gracefully.

"I am Casey A'Hearn," he said, "Mr.

DeJarnett's kinsman. Come in. We have been waiting for you."

I swung on him. "I'll be damned if she does," I said. "She's going back to Tuscaloosa now."

A'Hearn made a gesture with his right hand. "But her car won't run."

"She can go in mine."

A'Hearn appeared half sorry, half pleased. "I think yours had an accident also." He nodded to where my car was parked and I turned to follow his gaze. The gravel under the rear of the car was dark and wet and I could see the jagged hole that had been torn in the gas tank.

"Let's go inside," A'Hearn said again, and his voice was utterly bland. "I had prepared for both of you anyway."

WHAT it was that held me then I do not know. I can't explain the feeling that came over me, the feeling of helplessness, the feeling of a pre-destined and irrevocable doom. Whatever it was, Eve Wingard felt it too because without another word she stepped out of her car. A'Hearn took her elbow and led her up the decaying steps. I followed and I knew that behind me came the old servant. The rotting steps creaked under my feet and there was no sound when the old man came up them, yet I knew that he was close behind me.

A'Hearn led us into the living room. He paused beside the table underneath the chandelier. Eve Wingard stopped beside him. I stepped close to her and took her hand in mine. Her fingers were cold and small curled in my palm but the feeling of them gave me courage. I did not know what was to come but I swore then that whatever it was nothing should happen to Eve Wingard. Even then I did not doubt my ability to protect her.

A'Hearn gestured toward the open book on the table and his voice was conversational. "That is blood on the leaves of that book," he said, "blood some eighty-four years old. It is the blood of the girl Mr. DeJarnett's great-grand uncle married. The blood of the girl I loved." He paused and I heard Eve gasp, felt her body shrink close to mine.

Casey A'Hearn reached out a thin white hand and thumbed the leaves of the book. "And this," he said pleasantly, "is the book on which I swore revenge against Lacey DeJarnett, against each one of his descendants who should inherit this house and against the girls they should love." He turned to look at me. The thin mouth was smiling quietly, but in his eyes there was a wild and furious glitter. "I made that vow," he said, "eighty-four years ago. I have not failed to keep it."

Eve Wingard swung to face me. Both her hands were caught in mine and her red mouth was half open. In her eyes there was a terrible knowledge even before she spoke. "And you . . . . you . . . ."

"Yes," I said. "I inherited the place. I found out today."

Casey A'Hearn was smiling when the two of us turned to look at him. With utter silence he left the room and went into the hall. He came back carrying a candle and the light made the dark hair above his high forehead burn with an intense blackness.

"Perhaps," he said, "you would like to see how well I have kept that vow. Look!" And he moved across the room to where a portrait hung against the wall. He raised the candle to show on the thin nose and high forehead of a De-Jarnett. "Your great-grand uncle Lacey." He moved on holding the candle up before three other portraits, naming the men as he went. Then he said, "Come," and went out of the room.

Why we followed him I do not know. Perhaps if at that moment we had fled from the house there might have been some chance of escape, though I do not think so. If we had tried to escape, the things which happened anyway might not have been so horrible. I do not know. I only know that we followed him as if drawn by a magnet and that Eve's hand was very cold as it clung to mine, and that I could feel the soft touch of her shoulder against me.

Down the long hallway toward the rear A'Hearn went soundlessly holding the candle above his head. At the end of the hall there were no lights so that his candle seemed to burn brighter and brighter as we went and the blackness of his hair shining in the light of the candle seemed to grow in intensity. And I noticed too that the hand holding the candle had taken on the delicate whiteness of the porcelain cup—the cup which the servant had said was for blood.

"Oh God!" The words tore from Eve's throat in a choked whisper. "Look!" She was pointing toward the floor at Casey A'Hearn's feet. We could see his feet moving utterly silent in the candle light which made a golden circle on the floor. A'Hearn held the candle shoulder high and the light flickered downward across his body.

But there was no shadow cast across the floor!

There was a door opening to the right of the hallway at the rear and A'Hearn paused before it. He looked at me with a mocking light in his dark eyes. "The family has always been an honest one," he said, "and so I kept my vow well." He reached out his left hand and opened the door.

THE wind from the door made the flame jerk and quiver; then the light lapped out into darkness and I saw that beyond the door stone steps led downward. A'Hearn stepped to one side and bowed for us to proceed.

For one brief moment then terror was greater than the inexplicable feeling which had controlled my movements, which had drawn me as a man hypnotized is drawn to follow the command of the hypnotist. I thought of catching Eve up in my arms and dashing away from the darkness which yawned like the open mouth of a grave. Then once more the feeling of inevitability overcame me. Holding tight to Eve's hand I stepped past Casey A'Hearn and through the doorway. A'Hearn followed pulling the door closed behind him.

Eight stone steps led downward to a stone floor. The candle light flickered dimly moving from step to step as A'Hearn came down and the shadows of Eve and me were black and grotesque ahead of us. Then we were on the bottom and A'Hearn said, "Come this way." He stepped past us and held the candle shoulder high.

Eve screamed; a hoarse choked cry that caught in her throat and made little sound. I staggered backward and I heard my teeth scraping together. My heart quit beating but seemed to swell until it pressed against my ribs, aching. We had stepped backward into darkness and I could hear Eve's heavy breathing though I did not see her, and I could feel her finger nails digging into the back of my hand.

A'Hearn was standing motionless, holding the candle at his shoulder, and the light of the candle flamed in a yellow glow across the things beside which he stood.

Time had eaten the faces of the four corpses which lay on a flat stone table, though there was no odor of decaying flesh. And though each face had rotted partially away the expression of horror and of a terrific, unbelievable agony remained visible. I knew somehow that these four men had gone insane before they died, and I knew also whom they had been in life.

They were the men whose portraits Casey A'Hearn had pointed out to us in the living room above—The men who had inherited this estate before me.

And at that moment a thought struck me which was more horrible than the decayed faces of the four men. I felt a shudder run through my body shaking it as a leaf is shaken by the wind. I opened my mouth to question A'Hearn but no sound came. I could feel Eve's fingers digging into my hand and even in the darkness without seeing her face I knew that she too had the same thought.

And then I heard her voice. "What . . . . what became of the four women?"

CHAPTER FIVE

Married to Death

CASEY A'HEARN turned to look at us, moving the light so that it flicked out into darkness and touched on Eve. I could see that the blood had drained from her face, leaving the rouge on her lips a vivid scarlet. A'Hearn smiled, almost gently, but there was something unbelievably ghastly about the smile.

His words had the half hungry tone which sometimes creeps into the voice of a man love-making, and his dark eyes fastened upon Eve. "Their bodies did not decay; they were married . . . to death by the hook which you saw upstairs. Married, as you shall be."

The words themselves made little sense. It was the tone of the man which gave me his meaning, and when I heard him hot anger drove the fear from my body, and drove away any reason which might have been left in my brain.

I knew that the sound that I heard came from my own throat but it was more like the sound of a dog snarling.

I dived headling into A'Hearn. My head struck him just above the waist and I felt my right fist crash against his face. A'Hearn went backward as a curtain might have swayed before the wind, but he did not lose his feet.

I crashed face down on the stone floor, rolled over and was on my knees when the candle suddenly snuffed out. Darkness struck like a black tornado in the room. Eve screamed and I dived forward, arms flung wide. I thought I touched the hem of her dress and then there was nothing but blackness and the sound of my own breathing.

"Eve!" I shouted. "Eve!" My voice rumbled and echoed through the darkness, rocking back and forth like lapping water, dying slowly. There was no answer. I took two wild steps forward and stopped. I had no idea which way to go. The darkness had cut off all sense of direction.

I remember standing there terrified lest my outstretched hands should touch those decaying faces. I remember thinking that if I should touch that flesh something horrible and unnameable would happen to me. And for a long moment I stood motionless.

Then the thought of Eve stirred me into furious action. I lunged forward shouting her name. My right ankle struck something and I fell heavily on the stone floor. My forehead hit hard and the darkness spun with tiny lights.

It must have been a full minute before I could move again and in that time there was no sound except the gradually dying echoes of my voice.

Gradually the room steadied. I fought myself into a sort of calmness. Digging matches in my pocket I struck one on the stone floor. As yellow light blazed up I rose slowly to my feet and then stopped. The light flickered out into darkness, flamed across the horrid faces of the four corpses stretched in a row less than a yard in front of me.

I noticed that my hand holding the match was shaking but I fought to make it steady. Circling the altar on which the bodies were stretched I found the stone steps and went up them to the door. The match suddenly burned in my fingers and I dropped it and darkness swept like a wave over me. Groping I found the doorknob and twisted it. The door was locked and did not even tremble under my grip. There was utterly no sound as I flung my weight against the door and yet from beyond there came a voice. "The Master wishes you to remain in the basement until the bride is ready. Then you and your kinsmen will be brought out to attend the wedding." The servant's words died as smoke might fade away, and though there was no sound beyond the door I knew that he had gone.

FOR a full minute I stood there, sweating hands gripping the doorknob, shoulders hunched and trembling. What had he meant. . . . "when the bride is ready"? And what had Casey A'Hearn meant when he said she was to be married to death? I tried even then to tell myself that this whole thing was some ghastly joke, that Casey A'Hearn and his servant were human beings whom I could touch with my hands, beat down with my fists if necessary, but I kept thinking of the half rotten corpses lying on the altar like stone in the darkness behind me. I thought of A'Hearn's eyes as he looked at Eve and the sound of his voice as he said that her body would not decay in death. And I remembered my Uncle Edward saying that the sweethearts of my kinsmen had died but that the bodies had never been found.

For a short while then I went mad. I pounded against the door with my fist, crashed my shoulders time and again against the open panel but the door did not even tremble under my weight and gradually I sank to my knees exhausted. It was as I rested there on my knees, hands flat against the door in front of me, that I heard the sound. It seemed to come from a long way off and yet it was not loud. It was the low moaning cry of a person who has lost all hope. And I knew somehow that it was Eve.

The sound of her voice ran through me like an electrical current and restored some slight reason to my brain. I knew that it was impossible to escape through this door but perhaps there was some other exit. Striking a match I stepped back down the stone steps into the basement.

The light from the match seemed small and crowded in the darkness. The basement was large, square and empty except for the altar on which the corpses lay and the small box over which I had stumbled. But high up on the far wall was a window only slightly larger than a porthole. Standing beneath it I could hear the wind brushing past outside.

How I wriggled my body through that window I have never exactly known. I went through head first, my shoulders bent almost into a circle. I found that my fingers were scraped bare of skin and the nails broken as I hung there like an empty sack half in and half out of the window. The night had a heavy thick darkness through which I could scarcely see the black silhouetted line of trees a half mile away. A strong wind had come up that felt cool on my face as I hung there. Then I wriggled through and fell to the earth two or three feet below.

I don't remember running but I must have done so. I must have fled like a blind madman for suddenly I realized that I had stumbled and fallen and was lying on the rocky earth panting heavily. I could feel blood oozing from my fingers on the rocks beneath my hands. I did not know how far I had come until I turned and saw the house looming darkly a hundred yards away and when I saw it I remembered the cry that I had heard and I remembered Eve Wingard.

IT wasn't easy to go back toward that house. The place itself had an inexpressable evil like some giant beast waiting in the darkness for me to come close. I said aloud, "The men are human. The men are human." But the words sounded empty and I did not believe them. I remember crunching my shoes over the rocks and the sound seemed to give me comfort. I did not know what hope I could bring to Eve Wingard. I did not know what I intended to do once I reached the house but I knew that I could not leave her there. I kept listening to the sound of my shoes and tried to make my mind concentrate on each separate crunch as I walked. I knew that if I looked ahead into the things which might be happening in that forbidding house that I would go mad. I began to drag my shoes so that they would make a louder sound. I reached the house and circled it to the front where the two automobiles stood.

I remember the cold feel of the fender as I leaned over it looking at the motor of Eve's car and wondering if I could repair the damage the servant had done. Every wire had been torn loose, and I shook my head. I was no mechanic and would not know how to begin replacing them. And then grimly, my hands cold and shaky, I turned toward my own car. From under the seat I took a heavy tire-iron, and, smiling half grimly, half insanely, I went up the decaying steps and across the wide porch.

The front door swung open when I pushed on it and I stepped into the wide hallway where candles flickered dimly. I stood there balanced on the balls of my feet, shoulders pushed forward, head cocked slightly to one side. For a long moment there was no sound except the moan of the wind outside the door and the tiny guttering of candles. The hallway was gusty with the sound and then from above me there came a low groaning. It took me perhaps a minute to recognize that it was a voice mumbling monotonously. Cautiously I went toward the spiral staircase and circled upward into darkness.

I remember the feel of the tire-iron as I gripped it so hard it dug into my fingers. I kept shifting my grip but always holding it tightly, squeezing it as hard as I could.

Keeping my left hand on the bannister as I went up the stairway, I remember feeling how clean and smooth the wood was and saying to myself that these were human beings in this house who kept it so spotless. And then I reached the second floor and the mumbling was even louder. It was pitch dark and I stood there holding to the head of the bannister for a long while before I saw the light. It was a thin sliver of yellow and I knew that it seeped under a doorway. My heart was big and hard in my throat and my lungs ached against my ribs as I went toward that light. What was beyond it I did not know . . . . I dared not guess. I shifted my grip once more on the tire-iron, catching it near the end. Then I pushed my left hand out of the darkness and groped for the doorknob.

Abruptly the door swung open.

Yellow light flooded the room and reached out in a soft rectangle across the hallway. There was a strange sound that tore from my throat as I looked past he old servant into the room beyond. The old man stood holding the door open for me to enter looking as if he had expected me and opened the door at my knock. But it was not this that sent horror curdling through my blood and made my eyes swell in their sockets with unbelief. It was the things beyond him.

EVE WINGARD stood in the center of the room. She was wearing a bridal costume with a long flowing train. There was a dark rust colored stain that smeared the front of her dress and made ugly streaks across the whiteness of her veil and I knew that that stain was blood. The girl stood on a small, slightly raised altar and to each side of her tied to her arms to keep them erect was a corpse with its face half rotted away. Propped against the wall behind her were two more bodies and I recognized them as the men who had been in the basement; the men who had inherited this house before me.

There was a small brazier of hot coals at Eve's feet and before this stood Casey A'Hearn. Resting on the top of the altar before A'Hearn, was the blood-stained Book of the Devil. He spoke and I knew that he was addressing me though he did not turn his black, mad eyes from Eve's face.

"We have been waiting for you to come and witness the ceremony. Your kinsmen are already here."

I made a growling sound in my throat and stepped across the sill. The candle-light glittered on the tire-iron over my head. I saw the old servant's eyes move upward although there was no light in them and he tried to dodge. Then I brought the iron down, putting all my weight behind it.

It made a loud, crunching sound as I struck the old man's wrinkled head. I heard the skull crack under the blow and sheer force drove the old man downward. I knew that I had killed him and I leaped forward toward A'Hearn without another glance at the servant. I swung the tire-

iron high again, gripping it with both hands.

A'Hearn turned slowly, calmly toward me. There was a black and hideous mockery in his eyes that drove the last bit of reason from me. Snarling, I started the iron swishing downward at his head.

Something cold caught my wrists and held them; stopped them suddenly as if they had struck a stone wall. The weight of the iron almost tore the thing from my fingers. I don't know what it was that made me spin around although I had heard no sound behind me and the thing that had stopped my hands had done so like an invisible cord stretched above A'Hearn's head. But turning I saw that it was the old servant who held my wrist. There was no blood on his head though I could see the crease where the iron had struck, the dent in his forehead above the crushed skull.

A'Hearn said quietly, "How did you expect to kill a man who has been dead over eighty years?"

Perhaps it was at that moment that I went completely mad. I tried to fling myself on the servant, tried to batter his ace with my fist, but the old man held me as though I were a child. Dimly I became conscious that his hands gripping my wrists were cold, with the clammy chill of a corpse.

"We had best tie him," I heard A'Hearn say, "or he will interrupt the ceremony."

I felt the old man pushing my hands behind me and I felt some sort of cord binding them though there was utterly no sound except the beat of my feet against the floor as I struggled and the wheezing of my breath. A'Hearn and the servant moved as silently as the candlelight flickering against the wall. Then with my hands and feet tied I was pushed against the wall and turned so that I faced the altar and the persons who stood there. For the first time now I realized that Eve had spoken no word since I entered the room, and looking at her I realized that she was either unconscious or in a trance. Her head lolled slightly backward so that her face turned upward. Her eyes were wide and staring yet there was no light in them, and the reflection of the flickering candle showed there only dully. Her mouth was half open and horribly red against the whiteness of her face.

OF the things that happened after that I have never been certain. Looking back toward them I have the feeling of a blind man caught in a wild storm, whirled wildly through strange and unknown places. I remember A'Hearn's voice rising and falling, rising and falling like the wind that beat against the latticed windows. I remember the flame in his black eyes and the porcelain-like whiteness of his hands. And I remember that he read from the book he held above the thin china cup which the servant had told me was for blood.

There was a blaze of saffron light as the brazier of coals burned high. I remember A'Hearn raising the brazier and holding it toward Eve, her wild sharp scream, the smell of burning flesh, and then the mad silence that beat through the room.

There was the bright glitter of a knife in the candle light, of a blade that flickered like a white flame as A'Hearn moved it toward Eve Wingard's throat. There was a short, choked cry and I remember how red the blood looked against the whiteness of her flesh. I remember the dark stain on the front of her dress grew brighter, larger.

Then there was A'Hearn's white hands and the white china cup. With the blood in it the cup itself turned a glowing red like a great ruby glittering in A'Hearn's porcelain fingers. And then the man raised the cup and drank.

I don't remember when the ropes about my wrists came loose. I don't even remember struggling against them. Though I must have done so during that furious and mad lapse of time which I cannot recall. I don't remember tearing the ropes from about my ankles but I know that suddenly I was on my feet, stumbling through the doorway and racing down the dark hallway sobbing. And I knew that the servant was racing close behind me though there was no sound and though I did not once turn to look. Twice I struck against the wall, staggered and kept running then there was a streak of gray across the hallway and I knew that I had reached the latticed window. I flung the sash upward and was clawing at the lattice when cold hands touched my shoulders. The hands jerked me over backward in the darkness. There was a wild tearing of wood and I felt part of the latticed window come away in my hands.

The cold hands reached my throat now, and I knew that I was helpless in their grip. But I struggled like a mad man. I swung up the wood that I held and lashed out with it and I remember the sound of the words that came involuntarily from my lips. . . . "Oh God! Good God! Help me!"

IT was a scream of a fiend in torment that whipped along the hallway and set my eardrums throbbing like a plucked string. Then the hands were gone from my throat and I felt what was more like a stirring of wind than any other movement. I lashed out again with the portion of the lattice which I held but struck nothing.

I could see the gold rectangle of light reaching out into the hallway from the open door and abruptly I saw the old servant plunge through it headlong. I heard him shriek what might have been words, though I did not understand them.

I came to my feet and pounded along the hallway. There was a prayer bubbling from my lips though I was not conscious of the words I uttered. Then I went lunging through the doorway into the room where Eve Wingard and Casey A'Hearn had been a half minute before. I saw A'Hearn close against the far wall holding the girl in her blood-stained dress. And I saw that she was clinging to him and that her eyes were still dull and lifeless.

I surged toward them, muttering my prayer and swinging the lattice. I saw then that I had torn the center piece from the window and that the bottom brace had clung to it making a cross. And as I swung it there came a light into Eve's eyes, a mad and furious light. She ducked, raced past me into the darkness of the hallway . . . . and her shoes made no sound.

A'Hearn snarled as I swung at him with the cross. He dodged and it struck him on the shoulder flinging him to one side. Then I jumped, still praying, with the cross raised over my head, and found that the room was empty.

I searched throughout the house for Eve Wingard. I went praying, cursing, shouting. There was no sound except the sound of my own voice and the moan of the wind about the eaves. I stumbled back into the room upstairs to find only the four decaying corpses and then I went out of the house and down the long road which I had traveled that afternoon.

I have never seen Eve Wingard since. There are rumors that she has been seen in the mountains near the old DeJarnett home, but those rumors have never been proven to be fact. It is certain that her automobile, in perfect condition with no wires torn loose on the motor, was found parked before the house. That is all!

There were some questions, but men do not believe me now and I live alone with my uncle Edward. A child came to the house last month and when I answered the door-bell he turned and ran screaming to the street. Since then I have remained in my room.

THE END

A Night In Camberwell

By
John Flanders

A grimly realistic little tale of one dark night's adventure that you will not soon forget. . . .

AT THE head of the stairs I heard a door cautiously opened and a murmur of frightened voices. I reached for my revolver.

I had been drinking an enormous quantity of whisky that evening: I can't stand this chilling London drizzle, and when it comes on I have to get my sunlight artificially. So I had spent the evening in the Enchanting Prospect Bar, tête-à-tête with an immense Dutch salamander whose mica eyes were as red as hell itself, scraping my feet over a nice floor-sand as white as sugar, and absorbing a liquor that would have damned Saint Anthony if he had ever taken the trouble to cross the island of mud on which the Enchanting Prospect is located.

In the streets an ugly autumn wind was stirring the puddles and the rotting leaves, and I wasn't able to get up courage enough to stick my nose outside till Cavendish, the proprietor of the Bar, politely but firmly persuaded me out of the door of his terrestrial paradise. I had a difficult time of it getting home.

My little house in Camberwell is cold and damp, and I live there all alone. There are mushrooms in the corners like fantastic livid tumors, and the journeys of the slugs draw patient silver bands along the walls every night. But an Englishman's house is his castle, and I am ready to defend my tarnished silver and my three or four valuable paintings against all acquisitive comers. And now. . . .

Silence again. It was not even broken

by the friendly tick-tock of the Flemish clock in the entry. I concluded that the robbers had already carried it off, and I turned furiously angry.

My case is melancholy enough at best. When I come home late at night, I have no wife to scold me a little and then confirm her forgiveness with a kiss, no dog to meet me with a boisterous welcome, not even the twin night-lamps of a comfortable cat's eyes. On that cruel, chilly night the bright whisky dreams had suddenly deserted me at a street corner like fickle friends, and it would have been a crumb of comfort to be greeted at least by the clock, chanting cozily in the thick darkness of the corridor:

"You're back . . . I'm glad . . . I'm glad. . .
You're back . . . I'm glad . . . I'm glad. . ."

I have tried sometimes to make the clock say something else, but I have never succeeded. My imagination doesn't work well in the small hours of a cold night, and I could never fit any other words to her rhythm.

And now they had robbed me of this one friendly companion. . .

The first stair creaked under my prudent step. Then I heard a whisper again, and an object fell and smashed noisily into bits.

I have several vases of Bohemian and Venetian tulips in my room. I take a great deal of comfort in the sight of their silent flames.

The lamentable end of my vase pierced me to the heart; but my attention was distracted at once by the dry click of a pistol-trigger at the head of the stairs.

I stared stubbornly up into the darkness. I could not understand why no light came through the little bull's-eye window which ordinarily spreads over the landing a few feeble rays from a distant row of street lamps.

Then something scraped along the wall above me. I ducked hastily, just in time to get out of the way of a red bar of light.

The ball struck my hat.

"You rascals," I cried, "I've caught you!"

Another burst of flame.

I lifted my revolver and fired in the direction from which the shot had come. A body fell, heavily, without a groan.

I FELT around in vain for the electric light switch. I remembered with exasperation that I had disposed of my last match in a vain effort to light the moist mixture in my pipe.

I reached the top of the stairs. My foot slipped in something smooth and soft and horrible. I bent slowly down, in anguish and disgust.

Ah!

A pair of hands clutched at my throat.

Two enormous hands, cold and hard as steel.

In that perfect silence, broken by no cry, no hateful expletive, they gripped my neck with the system and the certainty of a machine. My vertebrae cracked, my breast filled with molten lead, strange lights danced before my eyes. I knew that my last moment was at hand. Then, all at once, of its own volition, my revolver went off.

The air rushed into my lungs again. The hands let me go. I heard a low groan in front of me on the dark landing.

A low groan . . . very low . . . then the silence again.

The silence . . . the night . . . dead bodies I could not see, an incomprehensible tragedy in which I had played a blind part. Then Fear leaped on my back and threw me howling out into the street again.

As I staggered through the door, the fog came. In two minutes the cruel shroud settled down over the street, shutting off the side streets, covering the buildings, muffling my voice as I cried for help against the assassins, thrusting an icy gag of terror into my aching throat. I ran after distant human silhouettes which melted into the fog when I came near them, I knocked at doors which remained cold and deaf and indifferent. . .

I could find nobody. Nobody heard me, and the terrible silence of my bloody house was on my heels as I fled through the cunning complicity of the fog.

AFTER two hours of this hopeless flight, in the dawn of a grimy morning which wept soot from a thousand chimneys, I found myself again on the threshold of my ghastly home.

I opened the door, trembling in all my flesh with the presentiment of the spectacle which the darkness had concealed from me. And I heard the tick-tock of my friendly clock.

There it stood, gravely swinging its pendulum.

"You're back . . . I'm glad . . . I'm glad. . ."

And neither on the staircase nor on the landing above was there any sign of death or violence. And my vases, every one in place, greeted me smiling, in all their discreet tones of rosy dawn, of honey, and of ocean blue.

Nothing had been disturbed in all my little house. There was not even the print of a bloody shoe.

And yet. . .

There is the hole of a pistol-ball in my hat.

There are two burned cartridges in my revolver.

My neck is sore from the pressure of fingers . . . thin fingers, monstrously long. . .

I have consulted my oracle, my whisky bottle, and now I know what happened.

I wandered into the wrong street, into the wrong door . . . a key opens many locks . . . and streets often look alike.

Good God! Somewhere in London, I have no idea where, in some street I had never entered in my life, in some house I had never heard of, I killed two men I had never seen . . . and I shall never know whom or what or where. . .

Waiter, another whisky!

Next Month—

A New, Fascinating Different Sort of Terror Novelette!

SATAN'S ROADHOUSE

By CARL JACOBI

On All Newsstands August 24th

HANDS

By
Henry Treat Sperry

A plain tale, simply told, by a man who lived two lives—and suffered much in both!

IT HAPPENED on the night of October twelfth, in my ancestral home near Huntleigh, Massachusetts. The events of that night mark the turning point in my life, and so far as this record is concerned, nothing that preceded it is pertinent. It is as if I, Robert Mercer, have lived two lives—the first, that of an ordinary, fairly fortunate young man, born into a conservative, well-to-do family—and a second, one which I sincerely hope is nearing its end, as different from

Beyond the Grave

Novelette of Nameless Fear

the first as night and evil are different from day and virtue.

But before I begin my tale I must assure the reader that what follows is a simple, reportorial statement of fact. I must beg indulgence for those portions of it which seem completely incredible. I can only say that they happened to me.

The house had been home to my family for generations. I myself had returned from Paris to take up my residence there but a short time before. I had come back to marry my childhood sweetheart, Sylvia Blanding, and our wedding day was but a week distant. The Blanding and Mercer farms adjoined—the families had been neighbors since Revolutionary days—and now at last they were to be united.

That night I retired at ten o'clock. I was always alone in my house at night, for my cook and housekeeper slept at her own home, a mile or so down the state road, and my chauffeur had his quarters above the garage. On this occasion, after

retiring I read for perhaps a half-hour; then, becoming drowsy, I put aside my book and switched off the bed lamp.

Then I slept. I slept soundly, untroubled by dreams or subconscious forebodings. Yet when I awakened, hours later, I was instantly aware, through some mental process too swift and mysterious to report, that a fundamental, all-embracing change had occurred in my life!

My eyes opened to behold a luminous gray shape, poised immovably above the footboard of my bed! No sound came from it, and at first I could discern no form to it. Yet as I looked I saw that it had a form. Dim though it was, there were limbs, a gray body—and a face without features. The thing had human shape!

How shall I express it? This ghostly form did not seem of itself to have caused that mysterious change which had occurred in my mind. It was as if I awoke with full knowledge of what had happened to me and that the luminous shape was but a symbol of it. And I was struck with a feeling of horror which I cannot hope to convey in words—a horror far out of proportion with the weirdness of the thing above the footboard of my bed.

Yet even in the extremity of my horror, I noted the cold October moonlight pouring in from the tall north windows of my bedroom, making silvery washes across the polished floor, and marked the oddity that the eerie shape seemed akin, in the nature of its luminosity, to that moonlight. Was the thing moving now? Or was it merely shimmering—vibrating within itself? I tried to thrust out of my mind the consciousness of the change which had come over my mind and personality like a thunder-clap, and decide on a course of action. I felt an impulse to address the ghostly shape and ask it what it desired of me; but I thrust this idea out of my mind as being starkly mad.

AT THE same moment I remembered the presence, on the south wall of my room, of a couple of crossed javelins—heirlooms which had been handed down for no one knows how many generations. And oddly enough I felt then that, with one of these ancient weapons in my hand, I would be better able to cope with the weird form. For I knew without thinking that I must cope with it—to save myself!

However, it was a good five minutes before I finally mustered enough courage to slide slowly over to the right side of the bed and lower a foot tentatively to the floor. Here I paused; I was somewhat reassured to note that the shape had not changed its relative position. Cautiously I lowered the other foot to the floor and, trembling violently in every limb, slowly stood erect.

I felt my knees go suddenly weak as I saw now that the vibrating movement of the thing was increasing in rapidity. This seemed to my mind to presage a threatening advance; and somehow I felt completely incapable of escaping the onslaught of the thing, should it attack me.

There was only one mode of relief open to me—action—however ill-considered or ineffective. I could stand the strain on my nerves no longer and resolved to risk everything on a dash for the javelins. I sprang with all the agility I possessed for the south wall.

But quick as I was the gray thing was not less swift. Although it maintained the same relative distance from me that it had while I was in my bed, it arrived at the place where the javelins hung at the same moment I did! I wrenched one of them from the wall and turned to confront the eerie shape. It now hung comparatively motionless, pulsatingly poised a few feet above the floor—ready, it seemed, to leap upon me!

Complete panic claimed me. My breath

came in a painful gasp that seemed to leave my throat raw. I jabbed madly at the wavering shape.

I had no real hope that my thrust would have any effect. I would not have been surprised if the weapon had passed through the thing with as little result as if it were composed of a glob of moonlight.

Yet the shape exploded with a deafening detonation! It was as though a piece of field artillery had been discharged in the room. For some moments I stood, stunned and deaf, unable to realize what had happened and somewhat of the impression that I had been blown to bits.

Eventually my mind functioned again; my ears regained their ability to hear. I was alone in the room, I am sure; even the shape was gone; yet the first sound to reach my ears, after they had recovered from their temporary deafness, was a human laugh—low but clear, coming I could not tell from what direction! Human—and yet surely it had been uttered by no living being. In it were contempt and derision diabolical in their intensity. It was the laugh of a fiend from hell!

I STOOD rooted to the spot, sick with terror, as the last notes of the hideous sound died away. I waited, trembling. But when it was not repeated, I did a strange thing. I lay back on the bed, seemingly calm!

It occurred to me, merely as an idea, that I might call Mason, the chauffeur, or even go out and spend the rest of the night with him in his quarters; yet I made no move to do so. I seemed of a sudden to be lacking in all initiative, to have no real desire to leave the house. A harrowing thing had happened—a thing unearthly yet none the less real. And its final impact upon me had been so great that I no longer felt even terror!

Yet I did not sleep again. I lay on my bed, exhausted and mentally numb, until dawn. Such thoughts as I had during that time were vague and imponderable—I do not even remember them.

With the coming of dawn I seemed to think more clearly again. Whatever had caused my listless numbness, it was slowly leaving me. Now I remembered vividly the events of the night, and my reason told me to scoff at them as at the disordered imaginings of a nightmare.

Yet I could not scoff. I knew those things had happened. And oddly enough, now that the lethargy was leaving me, fear was coming back. I felt that I was in danger; I knew that I needed aid.

I tried to plan a course of action. By now it seemed the height of folly to call Mason. Somehow I knew he could be of no help to me. . .

More than anything else in the world, I wanted Sylvia. I wanted to talk to her, to look into the calm blueness of her eyes and find peace again. I wanted the soft coolness of her white hands on my brow, dispelling my troubles. Were I but to call Sylvia she would come to me and comfort me.

Would to God I had done so! Then, though it might not have changed what was to happen, at least she would have known—and understood—when the fatal hour came. . .

But masculine pride intervened. Here was I, I said, having allowed myself to be made into a terror-wracked weakling —and I wanted to call on the woman I loved for aid. She above all others must not see me as I was now. In the end, I forced all thought of Sylvia from my mind.

Naturally enough, the one I finally decided to seek out was my closest friend, the one who was to serve as best man at my wedding—Dr. Howard Crandall of Boston. I could 'phone him and ask him for medical advice—ask him to drive out and examine me. And in the back of my, mind was more than that. For Howard, besides being a physician of reputation, was Research Officer for the Massachusetts Psychical Research Society. He had talked to me often of the strange happenings he had, at the first through scientific curiosity, witnessed and investigated in this office—happenings and manifestations for which he could find no possible explanation by human means. In our talks, I had played the materialist and the scoffer, had chided him for what I called his belief in spirits. Now, I did not feel like scoffing—felt even that his knowledge might help me. At least it might prove to me that I still retained my sanity, a thing I had begun to doubt. I would call Howard as soon as I had breakfasted.

I arose to find myself still somewhat dull and groggy, dressed and made my way downstairs. To my surprise I found that Martha, my housekeeper, had not yet arrived, though it was now nine o'clock. All that day she did not appear; the reason I never learned. . .

THE day was dark, the sky heavily overcast with low-hanging clouds which carried the assurance of rain before many hours had passed. Abruptly, now, I was assailed with a fear of the coming storm and of being alone for another moment in this great house the atmosphere of which, so calm and peaceful before, had abruptly become surcharged with an inexplicable threat. Terror was upon me. And if it sounds like the abandoned terror of a coward, it must be remembered that I was struggling with an assailant which seemed to attack my mind at the same time that it manifested itself outwardly. Again I knew that a profound change had occurred in my mental processes. My own mind was not master of my body—yet it had a master!

I could stand this no longer. I would call Howard at once. I stumbled to the wall telephone and put in the call for Boston.

Once I had done so, relief flooded over me like a refreshing wave. I felt somehow strengthened. I sat down beside the telephone and waited confidently.

But the relief was only short-lived. Even as I sat waiting, it began slowly to be replaced by fear—a creeping fear, that seemed to presage a return of the stunned horror I had felt in the presence of the eerie shape. I turned in my chair, half-thinking to see some hideous nightmare thing making its way toward me from behind.

There was nothing there, and I knew even as I looked that there would be nothing to see. Nothing to see, and yet the fear crept upon me, increasingly stronger. It seemed it must soon overwhelm me— *it seemed that it meant to overwhelm me, before I could talk to my friend!*

And then, like hope flashing in the darkness of dread, the telephone rang! I staggered to my feet. It seemed I would never reach it, never be able to raise the receiver from the hook. Yet by an effort of will I did so.

"Hello Bob," I heard Howard's cheerful voice calling to me across the miles.

Yet I could not answer, for at that instant something seemed abruptly to be constricting my throat—something that might almost have been human fingers! For that first moment I could only gasp into the mouthpiece in an agonizing attempt to speak. Terror, blind, unreasoning terror overwhelmed me. When at last I did manage to speak it was only to whisper hoarsely:

"Howard . . . Howard . . . for God's sake come—quickly! . . ."

I could manage no more. I tore at my throat in a futile attempt to loosen the invisible fingers that were choking me into insensibility. Then, as if it were the work of a fiend angered at my partial success, the receiver ripped loose from my clutching fingers. The telephone was jerked sideways from its fastenings, as though dealth a smashing blow with a sledge-hammer! It hung dangling from the wall by its wires.

As I looked at it with startled eyes, the fingers, momentarily loosened, tightened again about my throat. There was a roaring in my ears; lights danced before my eyes. I felt myself falling . . . falling into space.

And as I fell, there dinned in my ears the mocking sound of fiendish laughter. . .

CHAPTER TWO

Voice from Beyond

IT WAS nearly an hour later that I came back to consciousness to the sound of pounding at the door and the wildly ringing bell. I was sprawled upon the floor. My tongue was swollen and my throat parched and dry. I was weak and sick; yet for the first time in twelve hours my brain seemed perfectly clear and I felt master of myself. I struggled to my feet and feebly made my way to the door.

It was Howard Crandall. He had driven at top speed from Boston to reach me. His face reflected his concern and alarm as he saw mine. He entered quickly and closed the door behind him, supporting me, as he did so, with a strong hand under my arm. He aided me to a chair.

"Bob!" he exclaimed as he did so. "What the devil happened to you? Who . . . what was it?"

He eased me into the chair and stood over me, holding my pulse and regarding me with searching, worried eyes.

"I . . . I wish I really knew," I said weakly. "Damn it, Howard, am I ill . . . am I going mad? I'll tell you what's been happening here . . ."

Briefly, I told him. I was hardly begun

before he had drawn up a chair, facing me, his gray eyes snapping with interest. He could hardly contain himself until I had finished.

"Good Lord, Bob!" he burst out then. "Why man . . ." He broke off, laid a hand on my shoulder, then said quietly. "No, Bob, you're not going mad by a long shot. And it isn't advice from me as a medical man that you need, but . . ."

He stopped again; it was obvious that only through great effort was he managing to retain some degree of professional calm. "I'm going to look around a bit," he said. "If I don't find. . ." And then he was off, almost at a run, through the house.

I was still too weak to want to follow him, and I sat and waited for his return. He was gone a long time, and he ransacked the house from cellar to garret—searching with truly scientific thoroughness, as I realized later, for some slightest shred of evidence that would admit of the possibility of some natural explanation of the things that had occurred. But when he came back again his excitement was even more evident.

"Bob," he said, and there was a trace of awe in his voice, "there's something tremendous loose here . . . something astounding. It looks as if you have turned into a remarkably potent physical medium. . . . Still," he added, and it seemed to me that even he showed a trace of fear then, "it can't be that either. . . . It's more like the Charlotte Armand poltergeist case that Price recently reported in Arcachon, France, only more powerful—much more powerful. . . ."

A little of my confidence had returned with his presence. "Good Lord, Howard," I said with a half smile, "what the devil are you trying to make out?"

HE DID not smile. He sat silent for a long moment, staring thoughtfully down, before he answered me. Then he said: "Bob, I don't know. I don't myself admit the existence of spirits. If we workers in psychical research didn't keep to our attitude of scientific inquiry, God knows where we'd end—in the madhouse, perhaps. What we try to do is to investigate the actuality of such astounding things as have just happened here, to see if there is any possible way in which they could have happened naturally—explainably. Sometimes there is—more often there is not. So there's one thing we can't deny—that unbelievable, fearful things do happen, where there is no possible natural explanation of their so happening. *There is no possible explanation unless we admit to the existence of an unknown force not open to scientific analysis.*"

"Good God," I said, and my voice sounded strangely flat and subdued. "Then you think—"

"I don't know," he interrupted tensely. "I'm a medical man; I could say you've been the victim of nervous hallucinations. But hallucinations don't rip telephones from the wall. I could even say that you're telling tall stories and up to silly trickery. Knowing you as I do, I know how absurd that theory is. But as a scientist interested in psychical research, I'm going to admit both possibilities and investigate myself."

He paused momentarily, and there was a troubled light in his eyes. "Meanwhile, Bob," he said then, "as a friend only, I'm going to advise you to leave this house—at once. . . ."

I looked at him searchingly, a little astonished even after all that he had told me. "But Howard! You don't really think it's as bad as that! . . ." I think I was secretly hoping for reassurance.

He leaned over, placed a hand on my knee. "Yes, Bob," he answered. "I do . . . think it's as bad as that. What it

is I don't know—but one thing I'm certain of—it means you no good. I mean to stay on and find the meaning of this mysterious force. I think I'll get Mrs. Crumb down from Boston and see what she can do. A lovely little old lady. . . . She's not a professional medium—never accepts money. But she's a true sensitive and always gets results. Between us we should be able to track this thing down. Until we do—well, there's on need to mince matters, Bob—until we do, you're in danger of some sort—very real danger—as long as you stay in this house. I want you to leave for a few days. Take a run down to Boston—or better still, go over to Sylvia's. I don't think you'll have any trouble once outside this house. . . ."

Howard's suggestion brought upon me again with renewed force my desire to be with Sylvia in this time of trouble—a desire that had not really left me since I had first thought of calling her. Yet, for a reason I could not then have put in words, I was afraid to call her. With some vague premonition of what was to come, I feared to have her near me. . . .

But I wanted to take Howard's advice. I could go to Boston as he suggested. After all that had happened, it seemed wise and sane. And yet, I found myself hesitating.

"It's all very well for me to go packing off," I said, "but what about you and Mrs. Crumb? Don't you think you'd be taking quite a chance? This force, as you call it, doesn't strike me as a thing to be trifled with. Not judging by the power it's already shown. . . . I'd much prefer you to forget the whole business and leave with me. I've troubled you enough."

"Indeed, no," he assured me. "We have thoroughly adequate ways of protecting ourselves against these so-called malign forces. But you run along and forget the whole thing for a few days. In the meantime, I want to see this thing through. I'm sure Mrs. Crumb will want to as well, once she knows what's happening."

I doubted then, and still do, that Howard had any real idea of the terrific power of the murderous force he so lightly challenged that day. I argued with him for some time; but his professional interest was strongly aroused and he would not listen to me. I soon came to realize that he would gladly risk any danger to witness a demonstration of the talents of the thing that had assailed me.

"In that case," I said flatly and yet finally, "I'm staying on, too. I'm seeing it through."

God knows I did not want to stay. I spoke those words in a voice that seemed not my own. Howard looked at me searchingly, and I think he felt the strangeness of my tones.

He argued to no avail. I would now that he had used physical force to propel me on the way. And yet, I am sure it would have helped not at all. Even then I knew without the thoughts forming into words that even had I gone away, I would have come back. I knew that I was not myself any longer; that an invader had entered my mind, my very soul; an invader so strong that he could direct my actions and the words I spoke. At times in my strength I might fight him off— yet sooner or later, when I was off guard or weakened, he would come back. *Already my will had ceased to be my own.*

And so I stayed. Stayed on to learn that the horrors which had been my lot were but paltry things compared to those to come. . . .

IT WAS just getting dusk when a knock came at my bedroom door. It was Howard. Having failed to persuade me to leave the house, he had at last adminis-

tered a sedative and packed me off to bed. I had slept soundly, and awoke much refreshed.

While I slept he had sent Mason—who still knew nothing of what was transpiring in the house but fifty yards removed from his quarters—to Boston with a note to Mrs. Crumb. She had returned with him. And now, Howard assured me, she was in the process of preparing an excellent dinner for the three of us.

I bathed and dressed, then went downstairs to meet Mrs. Crumb. Pleasant odors were wafting from the kitchen, and there I found her—a sweet-faced little old lady with white hair and kindly blue eyes. Her hand-clasp was surprisingly strong and firm, and for the time it seemed to drive away the feeling of dread and unnamable horror which had so long possessed me. There was confidence in that hand-clasp—confidence of her ability to deal with the enigmatic thing which was dominating me.

But a short time before, Howard informed me, she had fallen into an involuntary trance. She had received a warning from one whom she called her guide, that a powerful intelligence was attempting to establish connection.

"So now your mind can rest at peace, Mr. Mercer," she assured me. "We will bring this restless spirit to terms."

She, at least, apparently had no doubts as to the nature of the *force*, in contrast to Howard's conservatism in labeling it. Somehow, this appealed to me. She accepted the existence of malignant spirits with a calmness which robbed them of much of their menace.

Poor woman! How tragically ignorant she was of the boundless horrors beyond the gates at which she knocked!

After dinner we repaired to the library. We seated ourselves before the log fire Howard had built in the fireplace, Howard and I on the divan and Mrs. Crumb in a chair on our left.

She sat down and closed her eyes at once. Howard and I sat in silence, smoking our after-dinner cigars and watching her. In a few moments her breathing became heavy and regular and she slumped far down in her chair, seemingly in deep slumber. But at last she stirred restlessly, as if troubled by dreams, and muttered something unintelligible. Her fingers fluttered on the arms of the chair. I looked at Howard; he nodded.

"It's coming through," he said.

Abruptly, Mrs. Crumb straightened in her chair, as if awakening, although her eyelids remained closed. For a moment her lips moved inaudibly. Then, seemingly, she spoke. But the voice she spoke in was so different from her own that, involuntarily, I looked about the room to see what stranger was present—although the sounds obviously were coming from her lips.

The voice was clear and loud, and definitely that of a man!

"I am John Alcott, Mrs. Crumb's control," it said. "I am having great difficulty in coming through to you because of the presence of a very powerful intelligence—a cruel intelligence. I must warn you—"

Abruptly, the voice had stopped, as if a telephone plug had been pulled from its jack! Mrs. Crumb again slumped in her chair, seemingly deep in slumber, and for a time silence reigned in the room, broken only by the crackling of the fire on the hearth. But to me that silence was filled with dreadful portent of nameless evil.

Then, without warning, a second voice crashed into the silence—a voice much more powerfully masculine than the first. This time Mrs. Crumb did not change her position, nor did her lips appear to be moving, although strangely, the voice seemed to proceed from her mouth.

"The time has come for vengeance!" cried the voice. Uncannily, it seemed to fill the room with reverberations and echoes. "I have waited long. At last I have developed my power to the point where no living person may thwart me. Be warned! At last I have found the instrument of my vengeance. He is mine! Let him alone!"

The voice paused, yet the echoes rolled eerily about the room. I felt coming over me once more the nameless terror which had shadowed me for so many hours. Now it seemed certain that it would engulf me. Angered by my helplessness, my body was yet drained of every ounce of strength and will to fight. I turned to Howard for strength—but momentarily even his face reflected the stark horror which shone in my eyes. Then he shrugged and nodded reassuringly.

The voice returned. "You are skeptical of my power," it said in ominous tones that would have seemed theatrical but for the force of conviction they carried. "I shall strive to convince you. But whether or no, remember—" and here the voice rose to a roar that dinned in my ears like the trumpets of Doom—"I have a serious and fatal mission to perform. *Interference means death!*"

The voice ended in a thunderclap which seemed to shake the house to its foundations!

WITH a low cry, Howard sprang to his feet and stood peering about the room, as if expecting to find someone lurking in the shadows. He strode to the wall and flicked the switch, turning on the lights in the chandelier. Obviously, we three were the only occupants of the room. . . .

Howard came back and resumed his seat. "Extraordinary, extraordinary," he muttered thoughtfully. "Never saw anything like it."

I waited in silence for a further word from him; but he seemed wrapped in thought, unconscious of my anguish. I could bear it no longer.

"Howard!" I burst out. "For God's sake, what does it mean? Am I—?"

A crash drowned my words. At the far side of the room, an entire row of books had seemingly been dashed from the top rack to the floor!

I wanted to scream madly, to dash from this house of horror. Yet I stood helpless, chained by an unthinkable dread.

Howard, with an appearance of calm, walked over to inspect the books and the wall. Barely had he satisfied himself that no explainable agency had been responsible for the crash, when chaos descended.

One after another—singly, at first, and at last, all those remaining in a final crescendo of destruction, every movable thing in the room on shelves, hanging from the walls or resting on the tables, was swept crashing to the floor. Books, vases, bric-a-brac, pictures, lamps—all crashed about us as if we were experiencing an earthquake. Or, as if the end of the world had come. . . .

Then again there was silence. I was trembling in every limb. Looking into my eyes, Howard must have seen the sheer terror written there. Perhaps hoping to quiet my fears, he shrugged his shoulders with seeming indifference, and spoke.

"You have done a great deal of childish damage, force or spirit or whatever you are," he said, "but that is all. It is not difficult to exercise strange powers over inanimate objects; but what will this avail you? You need not think you can control my friend, or any living being, and cause them to work whatever fiendish ends you pursue."

A laugh came—the laugh that was that of a fiend! It rose higher, higher, louder than ever I had heard it before, till it filled the room. Then the voice spoke again.

"Why," it said, "do you think Robert Mercer did not leave this house today as you advised him? Why did he not go elsewhere, where my power for the time at least would not have been so strong over him? Do you think he did not want to go? He did . . .but I willed otherwise! *His will is helpless in my hands—helpless until my vengeance is fulfilled!*"

Involuntarily, Howard shuddered; but he quickly gained control of himself. "Not," he answered, "while Mrs. Crumb and myself are here to battle with him against you."

"Fool!" said the voice. "You do not know against what powers you have pitted your poor strength. Leave this house, while life is in your body and reason in your brain. Death—and worse than death —will be your portion if you strive to divert my descendant from the charge I shall put upon him."

And when Howard made no reply, the voice added: "If still you do not fear my power, then tomorrow you will. If both you interferers do not leave this house— tonight—then a greater horror than you can even dream of is in store for you. Tonight! . . ."

And with a sound that was like the sweeping of a hungry hurricane, the voice was gone!

We were brought back to reality by a startled cry from Mrs. Crumb. She had awakened from her trance to see the shambles about her. Apprehension was on her kindly old face.

"What does this mean?" she asked dazedly.

Howard explained to her all that had happened. When he finished, Mrs. Crumb closed her eyes for a moment, and I could see a shudder shake her small frame.

"It is dreadful," she said. "It is a truly malevolent spirit. It may be we can do nothing. I had a terrible vision —oh, it was far worse than anything I have ever experienced. Hands—horrible, bony hands—I could see nothing else. They came to me out of the dark, then receded. Each time they came closer. At last I felt their cold, cruel touch upon my throat. . . ."

"You must go at once, Mrs. Crumb!" I burst out. "Both of you must go. You can do nothing for me. You must go to save yourselves!"

She looked up at me. A great fear lighted her clear, blue eyes, yet she shook her head.

"Oh, no," she said. "We could not leave you—in his grip. Never. We have a great task before us. We may not be successful, but we must strive to reason with this discarnate being. He must be turned from his terrible purpose. . . ."

She paused, looked off into space with that pathetically frightened expression lurking in the depths of her eyes.

"Ah, those hands," she whispered. "I am fraid. They were so long and curved and white—so strong and cruel. . . ." She gave a little, choking gasp, and finished almost inaudibly, "They—they—the ends of the fingers seemed to have been dipped in blood. . . ."

CHAPTER THREE

Hands That Kill

IT WAS late, that night, when at last we retired to our separate rooms, for such troubled sleep as we could gain. For hours, it seemed, I had argued with Howard and the kindly Mrs. Crumb, begged them to leave this dwelling of mine that had become a house of horror. All to no avail. . . .

"I have devoted my life to this work," Mrs. Crumb said firmly. "I am not going to leave it because danger threatens."

And Howard growled: "I'm going to stick with you, Bob, and see this thing through. I'd be a fine physician to let myself be frightened by a lot of melodramatic threats from apparently sourceless voices. It's the most amazing thing I could ever hope to meet with in a lifetime of psychic research, and I want to track it down. This house, where the strange force first manifested itself, is the place to do it. Furthermore, it's obvious that whatever the thing is, it's mesmerized you to the point where you *can't* leave the house—and I'm certainly not going to leave you here to fight it out alone. That's final, Bob. Now, let's get on to bed. . . ."

Frankly, the thought of spending another night in that house terrified me; I was certain that sleep would be next to impossible. But Howard and Mrs. Crumb were able to soothe my fears a little. Both were confident—foolishly confident, God knows!—that there would be no further manifestations that night. Both felt that on the morrow they might be table to exorcise the evil influence which seemed to have enveloped me like a shroud, leaving me a terror-stricken weakling. How they proposed to accomplish this I do not know. Mrs. Crumb, I remember, mentioned the possibility of "enlisting the aid of good spirits;" Howard did not explain. Yet their confidence, their very self-assurance in the face of the threat, calmed me a little. As much from a spirit of bravado as otherwise, I found myself at last going to my room and retiring.

And strangely enough, I slept at once. . . .

In retrospect, I can fully understand the evil source of that suddenly-induced slumber. Ah, how trustfully, how blindly we mortals relinquish consciousness in the seductive arms of Morpheus. We regard it as a friend—a priceless boon that "knits up the raveled sleeve of care," giving sanctuary from the troubles of the day!

But I have cause to know sleep as a traitor—as a siren who can lure away the guardsmen of the inner temple in volition and leave it unprotected against the invasion of the shadowy enemies of mankind—who live in the dark and whose only weapons are the unconscious bodies of living men.

For a long time my sleep was troubled by vague dreams. They were fearful dreams—nightmares of twisting shapes which no words couched by humankind can express. Nightmares in which I seemed to be one with chaos and confusion, and one with the whirling cosmos. All the while, terror had me tightly in its grip—and yet I did not awaken.

Then, with the abruptness of a lightning flash, the whirling vagueness took form and color, became a picture.

I seemed to see the room in which Mrs. Crumb was sleeping—and yet I could not have said that I was there, in the room. On the bed I could see the little old lady, peacefully sleeping. The vision came closer.

As that happened, Mrs. Crumb seemed to awaken with a start. She opened her eyes. I could see into their depths. In them stark terror was written! Terror —and something else I could not name.

I followed their sticken gaze—and knew then what else it was I could not name.

For out of nothingness two hands had come, two hands that crept slowly upon her. They were hideous hands, long and curved, white and somehow cruel hands. And the ends of the fingers were red—as if they had been dipped in blood!

Closer they came to her. She opened her mouth as if to scream—but the scream was but a choking gasp. For already the hands were about her throat, throttling the breath of life from her body.

I wanted to cry out, to tear at those encircling hands. But I was helpless, seemingly incorporeal; I could do nothing. I stood, silent and unmoving, while life was torn from the helpless little woman's body; watched as that body relaxed in the lassitude of death. Then the hands left her throat.

And as they moved away, back into nothingness, I screamed aloud. For I knew in the dream that the hands were my own!

I CAME awake, then. I found myself in my bed. My pajamas were dripping with sweat, but fear was a cold and clutching thing in my breast.

As I came awake, the door burst open and Howard rushed in. His sleek hair was tousled and there was worry in his eyes.

"Bob!" he burst out. Then relief spread over his features as he saw me still in bed. "What was it? I was awake and heard you cry out. Nightmares, I suppose. . . ."

"Mrs. Crumb!" I cried in answer. "Has she—what has happened to her?"

He looked puzzled. "Mrs. Crumb? Why, I'm sure she's all right. Her door was closed when I passed it. She's sleeping. What *have* you been dreaming?"

So real was the terror of the moments just past that I leapt out of bed. I would have rushed past Howard and out the door, had he not restrained me.

"Calm yourself, old fellow," he said. "You've been having nightmares and you're not awake yet."

"But Howard!" I cried. "I dreamed that a horrible thing happened to her . . . to Mrs. Crumb. We must go to her— now!"

He tried to hold my arm, muttered something about not disturbing the poor woman's sleep. But I shook off his detaining hand. I rushed madly down the hall, stopped at the door of Mrs. Crumb's room. I pounded madly, and when no answer came, I tried to open it.

It did not move. I realized, then, that it was locked—soundly bolted from the inside with a modern lock. And yet, that knowledge gave me no comfort. I threw all my weight against the door.

Howard had followed. He must have sensed some reason now, in the terror he had seen in my eyes, realized that no answer had come from the occupant of the room. For he placed his sturdy shoulder beside mine.

After tense moments, the door crashed inward. We rushed to the bed.

The horror of that moment will live in my memory as long as my body lives. My reason totters when I think of it, and because of it, and one other moment that followed, all that I ask of death is forgetfullness. Yet knowing what I do now of the life beyond, I know that death can never bring me that one boon. It is the final curse put upon humanity by the forces that evolved our existence.

Ghastly gray in the faint moonlight that sifted in through the window, Mrs. Crumb's face stared up at us. It was horribly contorted with agony and terror. The little old lady was dead. She had been throttled, and her neck still bore the marks of the fingers that had chocked her!

Something snapped in my brain at the sight. I collapsed to the floor as blackness overwhelmed me. . . .

WHEN I recovered consciousness a few moments later, I was back in my bed. Howard sat in a chair at my side, watching me anxiously. As soon as he saw that I was awake he began talking to me, quietly and steadily.

"You must get a grip on yourself, Bob," were his first words. "This is a terrible thing that has happened; but our only salvation lies in keeping our heads clear and our courage up. . . ."

He talked on. . . . Then he did not know? It was plain he did not know. . . . I rose up in bed and stared at him. He broke off abruptly and looked at me in vague alarm.

"You fool!" I screamed. "Don't you realize that *I* killed her?"

For a moment Howard was thunderstruck; but he quickly recovered from his surprise. "Nonsense," he said. "The door was locked on the inside. Didn't we nearly break our shoulders opening it? . . ."

I sank back in the bed with a bitter laugh.

"And you," I said, "are Research Officer for the Massachusetts Society for Psychical Research!"

How I cursed myself then, for having trusted his and Mrs. Crumb's theories regarding the mysteries they dabbled in. Why had I not followed the dictates of an inner conviction which, but a few hours before, had warned me that my only safety lay in having myself locked up—in a prison, if necessary—until I could be sure that I was no longer haunted by the discarnate demon that hovered about me? Had I done so, Mrs. Crumb might have been saved. Now. . . .

"You're quite right, Bob," Howard was saying. "I deserve the rebuke. Yet I still do not believe that you killed her, that you are a murderer."

Strangely, it seemed then, in that moment the face of the woman I loved, of Sylvia Blanding, flashed before my eyes. It seemed to give me strength. I climbed out of bed. "In any case," I said with more firmness than I had been able to muster for hours, "you've done enough coddling of me. There's been murder in this house, and I lie in bed, treated as if I were an invalid."

Howard nodded. "Again you're right. I had planned to notify the authorities of Mrs. Crumb's death as soon as it seemed safe to leave you. I'll drive in with Mason, since the phone isn't working. . . ."

"And I," I said with decision, "am going with you. I shall turn myself over to the police, and confess to the murder of Mrs. Crumb. That will force them to lock me up."

"But Bob!" Howard protested. "You can't do that! You didn't kill her . . . and even if you did, you weren't responsible at the time. . . ."

"Perhaps not," I answered. "And neither is a mad dog responsible for his killings. Howard, at present I'm as dangerous as a mad dog. Remember that Mrs. Crumb was killed only because she stood in the way; but this fiendish force that is driving me has a darker goal in sight. He will kill—or force me to kill —again. Someone—some person entirely innocent of wrongdoing, perhaps, will not be safe until I am behind bars. It is the only way."

For a time Howard continued to protest; but in the end he was forced reluctantly to agree. It still lacked an hour of dawn, but we felt that no time should be lost. He went to his room to dress, while I did the same. I was putting on my coat as I heard his footsteps on the stairs. He was on his way down to call Mason.

I stepped out in the hall to join him— and stopped dead in my tracks.

Moving toward me down the dimly-lighted hallway, with sinister sureness, was the ghostly, luminous shape I had seen the preceding night!

I turned to flee; I opened my mouth to cry out; and then it was upon me.

It struck me not as a hard object, but as a thing without body. It struck with the force of light, and it seemed that the light of a million worlds was about me,

was ringing in my ears and filling my body and taking possession of me. . . .

CHAPTER FOUR

The Grave's Revenge

I CANNOT say that unconsciousness claimed me then, though I would to God that it had. It was unconsciousness of a sort, and yet I was conscious. I can only describe it by saying that another being seemed to have entered my body, my soul. And yet, in a still far corner of my brain, there lurked a remnant of the self, of the soul that was I. And lurking there, it knew dimly the things that my body did, knew the horror of them, and yet was powerless to control it!

At first I remember only that an indescribable wave of cunning seemed to sweep over me, urge me into action. It was that cunning, I know—though it is but dimly remembered now—that caused me to slip softly down the back stairs of my house, unknown to Howard, while he was on his way to call Mason. It was that cunning which caused me soundlessly to open the door, to slip into the night with the quiet of a creeping snake. And then I was free.

Free—for what? I did not know then —and yet I knew. I knew that I was on my way to consummate a greater horror than yet had been my lot. I knew that the force which had me in its grip was now driving me to the fulfillment of the destiny to which it had appointed me.

That little part of me that still lurked in my brain knew these things, and a great fear was upon it. The fear of the thing I was about to do, though I knew not what it was, was a greater fear than I had ever known before. And yet, feeling this, the part that was I was powerless to act!

I do not know the path I took that

night. I did not know then. I remember the feel of thick grass under my feet as I made my way through fields and meadows no longer familiar. Sometimes I walked, sometimes I ran stumblingly; but always I went forward, with the certainty of doom.

The grayness that precedes the dawn seemed to have transformed the leafless trees in the fields into gaunt specters, and they reached out their naked branches toward me as I passed, like skeleton fingers: I remember that. I remember dimly a garden wall that I stealthily slipped over, and a locked door that I somehow opened. And stairs that I climbed with the whispering silence of a shadow.

These things I remember but dimly, as they registered faintly on the small corner of my brain that was myself, and they did not seem what I later knew them to be. But from this point on all things that happened came more clearly to me; and as they did so the stark terror in me mounted. Yet I went on. . . .

I was in a room now, into which the morning grayness was creeping like the pale face of death. In the far corner was a bed, and on it a sleeping form; I crossed to it and bent over the sleeping one. And my hands were closing about a smooth white throat, slowly, inexorably closing.

I looked into the face; and in a blinding flash I remembered. And as if the flood-gates of hell had been loosed upon me, horror swept over me in a torrent.

For the face of the sleeper was the face of Sylvia Blanding! And my hands were about her throat!

GOD in heaven! What words are there to describe the horror of that moment? I tried to cry out, to warn her, and my words were soundless. I tried to draw my hands away from that slim white throat, yet they were held there as if in a vise. Slowly they closed more tightly, and I was powerless to stop them!

Then—horror greater than all horrors —Sylvia awakened! Her blue eyes opened and she looked up at me with a nameless fear in them. Looked up and saw that it was I!

Oh, God! I thought. Why can I not die—die spiritually and physically—at this moment? Why—why are the lurking horrors that dwell beyond the pale of death permitted to visit the innocent living? Why can I not call out to her—if only to tell her before she passes through the Shadow that it was not I who killed her?

I tried—God knows I tried. And I spoke. Yet I swear it was not I who said these words that I heard myself saying, in a voice that was not my own:

"You die, Sylvia Blanding—and with you dies the Blanding line! May you all burn in hell!"

These words came from my mouth, yet they were not mine! And as they were ended, and I looked down into the fear-stricken eyes of my beloved, a laugh sounded in the room. It was the laugh I had heard before—the laugh of a fiend from hell.

Somehow that sound filled me with such horror that the small place in my brain seemed to grow a little larger. And slowly, a little strength that was my own flowed into me. My mouth opened again, and words that were my own came forth.

"God help me!" I cried.

And almost with the words, I felt my strength grow greater, and my hands drew slowly away from Sylvia's throat.

Yet even as they moved away, I saw other hands appear to take their place. These others seemed to come from my own body, to extend from my own hands. They were white and cruel, and the ends of the fingers were red as if tipped with blood!"

While I tried with all the strength of my will and body to fight those hands, to struggle with them and pull them away, their grip grew tighter. I saw Sylvia struggle feebly, saw her terror-filled eyes distend as her white brow darkened.

Dimly I realized then the thing that I must do to save Sylvia. Those clutching fingers were not mine—yet they came from me and without me they would be powerless. I must destroy myself!

Not all my strength coud tear those hands away, but the power of movement had returned to me. My eyes focused on a weighted brass candlestick that sat on a stand beside the bed, and I knew what to do.

As in a dream I picked it up. I raised it high above my head. Silently I prayed for strength to do this thing.

And with all the power of my body, I sent the heavy brass stick crashing against my own skull!

There was only blackness then. . . .

CONSCIOUSNESS came back to me but slowly. I saw first that I was in bed, and then that I was in a room strange to me. I felt a cool hand upon my brow, and looked up into Sylvia's eyes!

For a moment I felt that I must have died, and that Sylvia, too, had died. But as I saw the troubled smile on her lips as she looked down at me, I knew we still lived. I knew before Sylvia spoke that I had succeeded only in making myself unconscious with the blow, but that it had been enough—that the hands had left Sylvia's throat even as I sank to the floor.

"Sylvia!" I said. "Thank God. . . !"

She smiled now more happily. "You must be very quiet, darling," she whispered. "You fractured your skull—to save me. But Howard says you're coming through. . . ." She leaned down and kissed me, and I knew the first happiness I had known since the awful nightmare began.

Howard entered the room then, and his eyes lighted up when he saw that I was conscious. "I knew you'd make it, old man," he said with manifest relief.

He had trailed me to Sylvia's, I learned then, too late to stop me. But it was he who had spirited me away into the hills, and with Sylvia's help had tended me.

There was a dull throbbing in my brain, but aside from that I seemed well. I raised myself on my elbows and looked about me. Across the room from me was a mantel, and above it a mirror. Looking in it, I beheld a strange being that was myself.

I was not yet thirty then. But beneath the bandage that encircled my brow, deep lines were written across my face. And my once black hair was white!

Seeing this, full realization of all that had happened flooded back to me. I thought of Mrs. Crumb—and I sat bolt upright in bed.

"Howard!" I burst out. "What is there for me to do? Shall I give myself to the police?"

Sylvia's face paled at my words. Howard thought a long time before he answered. "No," he said at last, "not that. Above all, not that. I have had one session with the police. They think you mad; they half thought me mad as well. If you gave yourself to them, they would lock you in a madhouse.

"And that," he said, "would be hell indeed, for you are sane. The world may think otherwise, but I know you are not mad.

"There is but one thing to do, Bob—and that is to flee. Escape to another country. I will help you."

"And I," said Sylvia, "shall go with you, Bob darling."

"No," I protested. "You must not go,

Sylvia. You must be far away. You don't know—"

"Howard has told me—everything," she said quietly.

"But this force . . . this fiend . . . he might make me kill you yet. . . ."

"I shall go with you," she repeated.

THANKS to Howard, we made our way to this remote spot. Here we were married, Sylvia and I, and here we live simply, almost in solitude. I have tried to forget the horror of those two nights and a day, and with Sylvia I have found happiness, and almost I have found peace.

Together we have delved into the darker pages of my family history. . . . More than a hundred years ago, there lived a fiend who bore the name of Mercer. He lived with the devil in him, and he died with a curse on his lips for the Blandings, and for their children who came after them. . . .

You might say that it was but the blood of this fiend, running through my veins, that caused me to do the things I did. But Howard, who has seen destruction wrought, and heard the voice shaking the very walls, would not believe you. Sylvia, who has felt and seen those cruel white hands about her throat, would not believe you. And I, who have gone through two nights and a day of hell on earth, I would not believe you.

I think I have beaten the fiend. Though he still desires Sylvia's life, I am sure that he can never force my hands about her white throat again. With but frail human strength, I have beaten him.

Have I? Sometimes of an evening, when Sylvia is singing about her tasks inside our cabin, and I sit alone outside the door, with the smell of the pines in my nostrils and my eyes on the distant hills, I wonder. . . . Will he come back to claim me in the end?

And so, though Sylvia and I are happy, I can never quite say that I have found peace. . . .

THE END

IN OUR NEXT ISSUE!

A Savory Assortment of Tasty Terror Dishes
—Served Piping Hot From the Printer's Cauldron!

Blood-Tingling Terror Tales by—

James A. Goldthwaite, Fleming Roberts, Frances Bragg Middleton and other Masters of Mystery Fiction!

...OUT AUGUST 24th...

TERROR

By
Hugh B. Cave

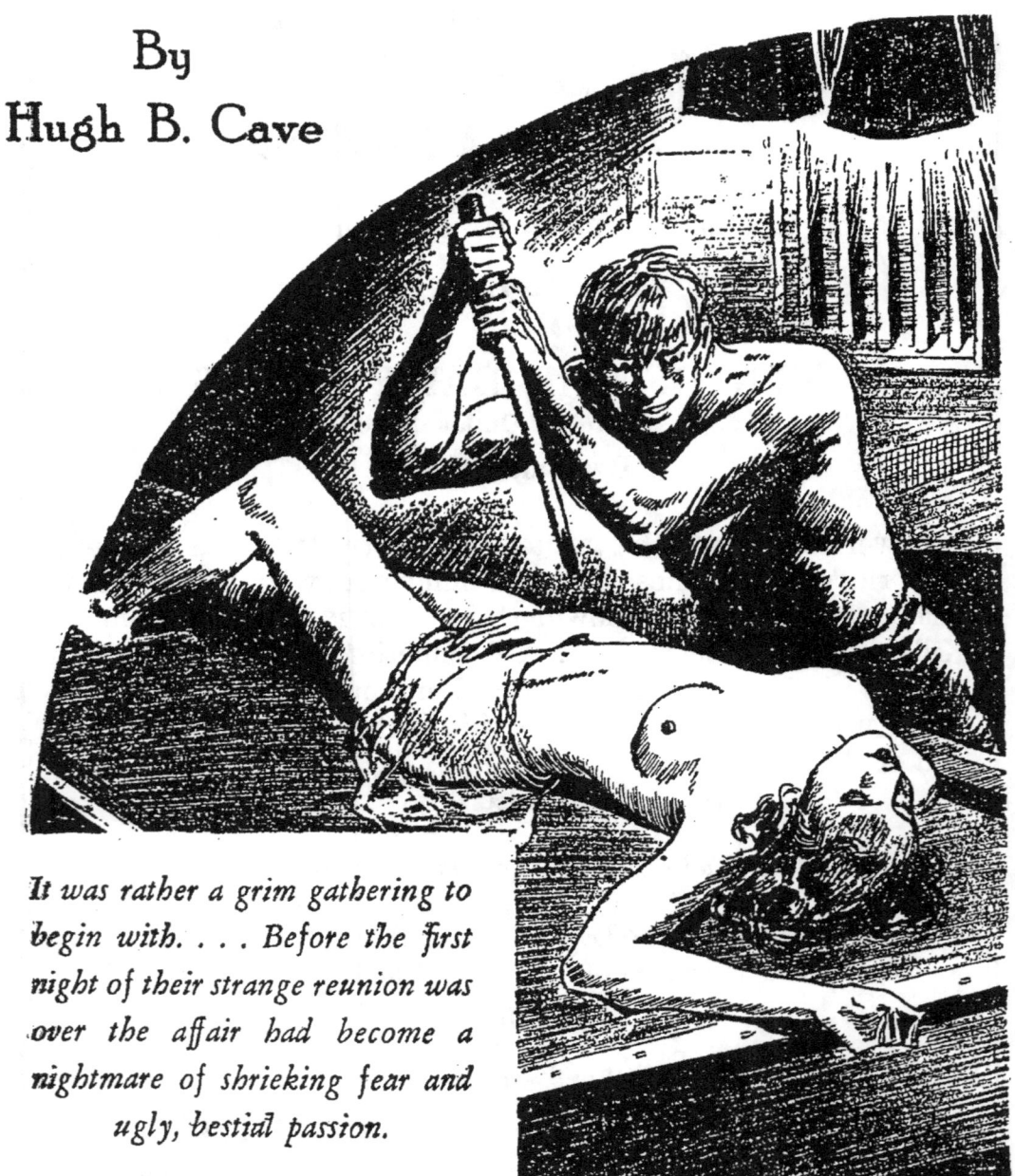

It was rather a grim gathering to begin with. . . . Before the first night of their strange reunion was over the affair had become a nightmare of shrieking fear and ugly, bestial passion.

"LIFE'S a strange thing," Ruth Little said. "When I looked into all those faces at the dinner table this evening, it seemed impossible to believe that those same men had been—"

She shook her head. "I shouldn't even remember it. It isn't fair to them. They're all successful business men now, some of them even wealthy. They have outlived their pasts."

ISLAND

Mystery-Terror Novelette

mind, brought with it sinister forebodings. He turned his head, looked back at the owl-eye windows of the huge house that loomed out of gray vapor behind and above him, fifty yards distant.

Ruth was right, of course. The men in that house were no longer criminals; they were respected members of society, and prison walls were but vague memories out of the shadowed past. Still—and Deen involuntarily tightened his grip on the slim waist of the girl beside him—it was a strange house in a stranger setting. Somehow not quite the place for a young, lovely girl, especially the very charming

Vance Deen nodded silently, leaned his rangy body against a pier-post and stared moodily out into the gray winding-sheet of fog that covered the dark Atlantic. The fog had eaten its way into Deen's girl who had promised soon to become Vance Deen's wife.

Privacy Island. Here, at the invitation of Alden Goyette, who owned the island and the solitary house upon it, had come this group of men whose names were on prison records: men who, because of the firm but humane leadership of Warden Byron Little, had succeeded in finding themselves again, in winning their way back to a normal life.

A week-end gathering of ex-criminals, in a luxurious home on a privately owned island off the Maine coast, with Warden —now Ex-Warden—Little, his wife and their daughter as guests of honor.

"I don't like it," Deen said aloud.

"You're silly, darling." Ruth Little rose on tiptoe and pressed her warm lips to his cheek. "Look. The fog's getting thicker. That means the motor launch can't come back from Owl's Head tonight. We'll be castaways."

"I don't like that, either."

Deen stared again at the big bloated house in the fog; its owlish windows were yellow, baleful, staring back at him like animal eyes full of hunger. The whisper of black water against the pier-piles, beneath him, seemed somehow to be an insistent voice of warning.

He shrugged himself erect, forced a laugh. He was being an idiot. There was nothing at all sinister about the place; everything was perfectly in order. He bent and kissed the girl beside him. "It's late," he said quietly, "and getting cold. The place for you is in bed."

He lifted her in his arms, carried her from the pier and up the flagstone path that led to the house. Holding her close, so that the warmth of her body crept through his light clothing, he felt again, for no sane reason, that evil uneasiness, that premonition of impending danger. But the girl's head was on his chest, her dark eyes looking up at him. He smiled,

held her closer and whispered: "If anyone should ask you, I'm in love with you, even if I should be building roads in Bangor. Don't let my gloomy thoughts—"

The words stuck in his throat, were gulped up by another sound from the big house just ahead. A door in an ell of the building clattered open, crashed back against the wall. Out of the yellow rectangle lurched a fog-distorted shape, a staggering, stumbling shape that screamed in throat-rending agony as it ran blindly across the lawn.

The shape was a woman—a large woman, near-naked, a mop of whitish hair cascading over her face, swirling about her rounded shoulders. Her hands were at her throat, her full breasts heaving. Like a huge blundering animal she reeled and stumbled through the mist-whitened darkness.

Then there was something else, Deen saw as he hastily lowered the girl in his arms and took a step forward.

Over the threshold had come another blurred shape, short and squat, stumpy arms extended. On thick legs it rushed forward, pursuing the fleeing woman. Bestial sounds, oily, guttural, spewed from its face—a face that was blurred by the swift lunging movements of the man's body. But those animal sounds were all but smothered under the shrill intensity of the fleeing woman's screams, wild shrieks that ate their way into Vance Deen's soul and sent him hurtling forward to defend her.

The oncoming monster saw him, stopped with a convulsive jerk and stood momentarily rigid. The woman had stopped, too, and Deen realized that her vibrant screams were caused as much by agony as terror. She was clawing with both hands at her half-clad body, turning in ever-widening circles, stumbling, staggering like an animal with its back broken.

Deen spun toward her, aimed himself

in a direction that would cut off the monster's advance. But there was no need for that. The squat shape had rocked backward, whirled in the fog and now was racing with huge strides back toward the open doorway. For an instant the bent body was silhouetted against a yellow oblong of light; then it had rushed over the sill, dragged the door shut behind it.

The stricken woman fell before Deen got to her. Fell and lay screaming, writhing, in wet grass. White-faced, shuddering at the sight that met his gaze, Deen flopped to his knees beside her, winced as her shrill shrieks stabbed into him.

The shrieks stopped. The woman's half-exposed body arched itself in a final convulsion, thumped back and lay still. Deen stared down, felt his flesh go cold.

Behind him, Ruth Little came slowly forward, looked down and put both hands to her mouth in horror.

THE woman was dead. From head to hips her large body was naked: only torn remnants of a black dress clung to her arms, her legs. Blood bubbled from her throat, oozed from a scarlet knife-gash and spilled through the hollow between large breasts, formed a dark pool in the woman's sucked-in abdomen, overflowed and stained crimson the flesh-colored silk thing that covered her thighs.

Dead. Vance Deen closed his eyes, swayed backward. Death was one thing; this manner of death was another. The woman was Mrs. Burns, Alden Goyette's housekeeper. A good woman. A charming, gray-haired, middle-aged matron, good in every sense of the word. And now this . . . .

Deen's eyes smouldered. He stiffened, lurched erect and stood with fists knotted.

"I told you," he said almost fiercely. "I told you something was wrong with this damned house!" For an instant he stood wide-legged, glaring savagely at the huge structure that rose bleak and sinister out of the fog. Then he stooped, gathered the mutilated form of Mrs. Burns in his arms and staggered toward the front of the building.

Lights had winked on in some of the structure's many windows. The 'front door opened even before Deen reached the end of the flagstone walk and began stiffly to ascend the steps. On the threshold stood Alden Goyette, tall and thin, staring with wide eyes at the thing in Deen's arms. In a quavering voice Goyette said: "What—what is it? That awful screaming . . . ."

Other men had been roused from those inner rooms, too. They crowded forward, staring, mumbling, as Deen carried his burden down the wide hall into a parlor. Stark, staring fear was in their eyes. Death was not new to them—they had walked hand in hand with it, all of them. But that had been years ago, when they had paced the stone corridors of the state prison. Now they were ordinary men, out of tune with things abnormal. Perhaps . . . .

Deen lowered his burden on a divan, turned slowly and jammed both hands against his hips. Grimly he peered from face to face, stared into the firm features of Ex-Warden Little, into the horrified countenance of Little's wife, and then, in turn, into the fear-filled faces of each of the seven men whose names were on the books of States Prison.

Every man was present. So, too, were the womenfolk, including the thin, nervous, nineteen-year-old Maribel Mac-Cullough, daughter of Lyon MacCullough, whose heavy arms encircled the girl and hid from her the gruesome shape on the divan. Present, too, was the dark, ascetic-faced Paul, Goyette's butler. No member of the household remained unaccounted for.

Only a few hours ago, these same people had been gathered about a dinner-table. Conversation had been brilliant; liquor had flowed freely. There had been tall tales of deep-sea fishing from Saul Resnik—tales which had excited the others to such an extent that immediately after dinner the motor launch had been sent back to Owl's Head on the mainland, for deep-sea tackle and live bait. The launch would not return now—not in this fog. . . .

Cold doubt assailed Deen's heart. No man was missing. Yet some man, some fiend, had less than fifteen minutes ago committed hideous murder. Some one of these men, now seemingly sane, had then been a mad monster. . . .

Deen aimed a stiff arm at the thing on the divan. "I saw the man who did this. I saw him come into this house.

"We must search the entire building," Alden Goyette said. "From top to bottom."

The others nodded. Goyette took a loaded revolver from a desk drawer, passed the gun to Byron Little and said: "Remain here with the women. You are best qualified to take care of them."

The rest found weapons, fearfully armed themselves with fireplace irons, improvised clubs, kitchen knives supplied by Paul, the butler. They separated. Mac-Cullough, with the butler, went through the kitchen and descended dark stairs into the cellar. Others climbed the winding staircase to the upper floor. Still others invaded closed rooms, probed shadowed niches, wall-retreats, closets.

Vance Deen, alone, stalked silently out of the house, became an indistinct shape gliding through gray fog. His thoughts went with him: acid thoughts that burned deep, brought a cold glint to his eyes.

Privacy Island, owned by Alden Goyette. To that island had come a group of men, some of them bringing their women-folk. Goyette had invited them. No other person had been on the island at the time of the launch's arrival. Deen himself, with Ruth, had explored the tiny paradise from end to end, before darkness and fog had set in.

There had been no prowling intruder, then. There could be none now. No man could hope to reach Goyette's fly-speck island through such a wall of fog as now smothered the black sea.

Yet Mrs. Burns lay dead, foully murdered, her near-naked body savagely mutilated by a human fiend. And the guests at Alden Goyette's isolated home were one-time criminals . . . .

CHAPTER TWO

Horror Chamber

DEEN circled the house slowly, kept close to the wall and strained his eyes to pierce the gray world that enveloped him. Occasional voices, muffled by walls and fog, came to him from the huge pile beside him. Lighted windows, haloed by swirling vapor, leered out.

Step by step, fingers clamped hard around a gun in his fist, Deen advanced, found himself returning after a nerve-racking eternity to the spot he had started from. Ahead glowed the parlor windows, outlined by lines of misted ocher encircling drawn blinds. In there, Ex-Warden Little was standing guard over the women.

A sullen roar blasted Deen out of his thoughts, sent him lunging forward, sucking breath. The roar came again: a staccato revolver bark, strangely hollow, empty. When it died, a yowling voice of triumph, harsh and vibrant, shrilled from the echoes.

Deen's hands whipped up, pawed the frame of the nearest window. Blood froze in his face as he heard sounds of terror from inside, shrieks from the throat of a woman, hoarse gurgling ejaculations from a man. Feet pounded the floor of the parlor; something hard, heavy, thumped the wall; furniture went over.

Deen heaved against the window, slammed it up. He heaved himself across the sill, freed one hand and leveled the revolver in his fist.

The muscles of his body went taut. In there, in the parlor, Ex-Warden Little had been hurled bodily against an upturned table, slammed with such savage strength that he lay now in a sprawled, moaning heap, crucified against the table's outjutting legs.

Little's wife, too, had been hurled aside; and Maribel MacCullough, daughter of the big Scotchman, was frantically fighting a locked door, trying to escape from the horror chamber.

It *was* a horror chamber. At the far end of it, near the divan that supported the mangled body of the slain housekeeper, two staggering bodies were locked together, furiously fighting. One was short, squat, the same squat murder-fiend who had hurtled through the fog, outside, less than half an hour ago. The other—and at sight of that terrified face, Deen's blood ran cold—the other was Vance Deen's promised wife.

The girl's brave struggles ended even as Deen heaved himself over the sill and dropped bent-legged into the room. An animal snarl hissed from her assailant's hooked mouth; cruel fingers fastened in the girl's throat, forced her back across the heel of the big divan. Bestial claws ripped and slashed at her clothing, tore it from her body, exposing the pale satin of smooth flesh.

Vance Deen hurtled forward, hurled out a cry that was a mad bull's bellow. The hunched shape stiffened, released the girl and spun to meet him.

No thought of quarter entered Deen's mind; his soul was too filled with other hideous visions. Lunging headlong, he jerked up the gun in his fist, pressed the trigger again and again. At that distance he could not miss. The slugs tore home, ate into the contorted body of the fiend in front of him.

But the man remained standing, remained for some inexplicable reason alive and snarling. With superhuman strength he flung himself forward, hurled himself like a great ape upon Deen's lunging body.

The gun jarred from Deen's fingers; hooked hands clawed at his throat, burned into flesh. Crushing legs encircled his middle, exerted savage pressure as his assailant raked him, gouged him, clung to him like a bloated leech.

Deen staggered, reeled backward, carried that squirming, snarling form with him. Sharp teeth dug into his cheek, met there through flesh that spurted blood. Again and again Deen's knotted fist drove upward, made pile-driver contact.

Then, abruptly, the encircling legs relaxed; the writhing body released its grip, slid down Deen's braced legs and thudded to the floor. There it lay still. Sobbing, for breath, Deen stepped away, put a hand to the ruptured flesh of his cheek and fought the sickness that welled inside him. With blurred eyes he stared down.

The man on the floor was dead. Across the room, voices were clamoring beyond the locked door; hard fists were pounding the panels. Deen stumbled forward, turned the key in the lock and dragged the door open. Then, with anxious eyes, blood pounding at his temples, he walked to the limp, unconscious form of Ruth Little.

The girl had been flung across the divan, had fainted when those bestial fingers had torn the clothing from her body and pawed the ivory softness of her exposed breasts, her slender throat. She lay now in a heap on the carpet, her head lolling against the moulding.

Deen picked her up, pressed his cheek

against her bare breast, sobbed his relief when the beat of her heart found its way through the pain of his face. Quietly he carried her to a chair and lowered her, then turned, stared around the room.

Other men were staring, too, with wide, unbelieving eyes. MacCullough, the big Scotchman, was soothing his sobbing, hysterical daughter; others were pouring brandy down the throat of Ex-Warden Little and attending to Little's wife. Alden Goyette and the rest were bent above the body of the fiend on the floor.

Deen paced forward, pushed his way into the circle. The face that gaped up at him, convulsed and hideous, was the face of a madman, its eyes white-rimmed, protruding like stuck-on buttons, its lips flecked with crimson foam. At least three death-dealing bullets had imbedded themselves in that twisted body; red blood flowed sluggishly from the wounds and puddled the floor at Deen's feet.

Mad. Every single thing about the dead man indicated madness. And yet only a very short while ago this same murdering fiend, this same snarling vulture, had been sane. Only a short while ago at a dinner table, this same madman had been merely a plump, jovial, intoxicated teller of tall stories.

The man on the floor was Saul Resnik.

VANCE DEEN said nothing. Assuring himself that the three women were properly cared for, he walked out of the room, made his way down the corridor and entered a small book-lined study. There he slumped in a chair before a fireplace where a gas-log glowed dully.

He wanted to think.

Think? There was more than one thing to think about! In the first place, something had gone wrong in that room of horror, at the moment of the fiend's attack The door had been locked; how, then, had the man forced entrance? Byron

Little had used a gun, yet had failed to hit the intruder at a range no greater than the width of the room—and Little was a sharpshooter par excellence, member of a dozen pistol and skeet clubs.

Deen scowled, stared into the fireplace All the small questions led into one monstrous one. What had caused Saul Resnik, a mild-mannered little mill-owner, to become a fiend incarnate, a devilish, sadistic maniac?

Footsteps invaded the study. Deen turned abruptly, nerves on edge, and stared. The man who came toward him was another of the ex-crimininals—a thick-shouldered, fat-hipped man with chin-shadows and tufted knobs of sandy-colored hair. He was, Deen remembered, a small-town pharmacist, Orville Bishop.

"Mr. Deen—"

Deen nodded wearily. "What is it, Bishop?"

"These guns." Bishop extended a pair of revolvers. "One is yours, I think. They were lying on the floor in the other room. I've taken the liberty of looking at them."

Deen scowled down at them, pocketed his own and balanced the other in his cupped hand. It was the gun Alden Goyette had taken from a desk drawer and given to Ex-Warden Little.

"Please examine that weapon," Bishop faltered. "I know very little about such things, but—"

Deen removed the clip, thumbed out the bullets. He caught a quick sharp breath, lowered his face over them. "Good God!" he whispered. Blanks—"

"Yes. Blanks." Bishop was breathing hard, rubbing moist palms together. "Warden Little doesn't know; I took the gun before he could ask for it. But he says he can't understand; he fired at the —the monster as it came into the room, but his shots had no effect. Then the thing locked the door on the inside and fell upon him like a mad beast.'

Deen dropped gun and bullets into his pocket, stood up. His lips were a tight line "Where's Goyette now?"

"He's in the dining-room. They're all in there; that is, all the men. The women have gone to their rooms."

Deen strode, tight-lipped, down the corridor, turned into the spacious dining-room. A glowing chandelier hung from the ceiling, revealing the gaunt and haggard faces of anxious men. Glasses and liquor containers stood in disarray on the polished mahogany.

Warden Little, his face streaked with strips of adhesive, one arm bandaged to the elbow, was saying grimly as Deen entered: "It can't be anything but coincidence. The man was mentally diseased, and he chose this particular time to go mad; that is all."

There were mumbled words of agreement, muttered exchanges of comments. Some of the men looked up as Dean paced forward; one said with apparent sincerity: "We have Deen to thank that something even more terrible didn't happen."

Deen said nothing. He fumbled with the blank cartridges in his pocket and glanced sideways, suspiciously, at Alden Goyette. The man seemed even more terrified than his guests. His thin, pale face was twitching, his hands working nervously. He was not drinking, Deen noticed. Most of the others were. Empty glasses, empty bottles gave evidence of the quantity of liquor consumed.

He poured himself a drink, raised it to his lips, then slowly lowered it without drinking. Saul Resnik, at the dinner table, had been the only man drunk, and Resnik had gone suddenly, inexplicably mad. Deen raised the glass again, sniffed it. There was no foreign odor.

He pushed forward, put a hand on Warden Little's arm and said quietly: "I'd like a word with you alone."

Little nodded. The others stared. Hall said, "If you ask me, I think we could all use some sleep. Talking about this thing will only make it worse. It's over and done with."

Nervous words. The whole room, Deen realized, was full of tension; the atmosphere was a taut steel wire, vibrating to every impulse. These men, Degnan, Bishop, Goyette, Hall, Lees, MacCullough, were no longer hardened criminals, immune to emotional strain. They were ordinary human beings, sick with horror.

HE TRAILED Ex-Warden Little from the room; the others followed, separated in the corridor. Silently, Deen went outside with the former official. They trudged down the flagstone walk toward the water's edge.

Gray vapor swirled around Deen, seeped through his light clothing and put clammy hands against his skin. He breathed deeply; it was like inhaling thick wet smoke. Little, pacing ahead, was a towering ghost-shape in gray gloom. Then the ghost-shape stopped, stared back at the haloed windows of the house and put a hand on Deen's arm.

"Well, Deen?"

"Do you," Deen said, "actually believe what you said back there—that Resnik's madness was mere coincidence?"

"No." The answer was positive.

"Look at these." Deen put the blank cartridges in Little's hand. "Those were in the gun Goyette gave you. This whole week-end party was Goyette's idea."

Little was stiff, silent as he turned one of the slugs btween thumb and forefinger. He swelled his chest with fog, raised his head slowly and met Deen's leveled gaze. "Thank you, Vance. This explains—"

He stopped talking, shifted his big body and looked toward the house. The front door had opened. On the threshold, silhouetted against the light within stood the thick-shouldered, big-headed form of Lyon MacCullough.

MacCullough's grunt, when he saw the men he was seeking, was audible even through the murk. The big man strode across the veranda, reached the steps. Behind him another shape, darker and smaller, detached itself from the doorway and trailed after him.

Deen held his breath, stared. Something about that second shape was sinister, suggestive of evil. The man was bent low, arms extended; he was creeping, not walking.

Too late, Deen thundered a warning as MacCullough hesitated on the veranda's edge and groped to descend the fog-hidden steps. The creeping shape shot forward, leaped like a monstrous cat. Full upon the Scotchman's broad back it landed, lashing an outflung arm around MacCullough's neck.

The impact carried MacCullough stumbling down the steps, hurled him in a sprawling heap on the walk. He struggled to hands and knees, fought blindly to free himself from the clawing shape that clung to him. Hoarse oaths bellowed from his big throat, cut through the fog as Deen lurched forward.

The oaths became a lurid scream then a deep gurgle of agony. And over and above MacCullough's racked voice came another sound, a vibrant peal of madman's laughter, rising in shrill crescendo. With uncanny quickness the man's assailant leaped erect, swayed on bent legs and launched himself in a shrieking attack upon Vance Deen, as the latter closed in.

Just once Deen saw the fiend's face, recognized it. The man's arm lashed up, swept down again in a savage arc, gripping a hooked weapon that streaked through the fog like a thin white flag. Behind Deen, Byron Little's towering bulk lumbered up the path, surged like a monster through the murk.

Hot, sharp pain stabbed Deen's arm, would have knifed his throat had he not rocked backward. He struck out savagely, felt his knuckles grind into lips and teeth. The madman's laugh ended, changed to a snarling spray of foam and spittle that hissed into Deen's face. Blindly, Deen warded the fiend off with one hand, groped with the other for the gun in his pocket.

Next moment he was down, hurled into Byron Little's huge legs by his assailant's furious forward leap. Little was bellowing above him, endeavoring to lunge ahead. With a throaty snarl, the mad killer darted back, cleared MacCullough's sprawled body in a flying leap and raced away into the fog.

Deen groped erect, clung to Little's thick frame and hung there, groaning. From a distance, miles away it seemed, a jangling cacophony of shrill laughter welled through gray emptiness. The voice of a man gone mad. . . .

Deen released his grip, swayed on spread legs and held himself up with an effort, then took a step forward, went to his knees beside the silent form of Lyon MacCullough. Ex-Warden Little, beside him, leaned over and peered down, abruptly caught his breath. A convulsive shudder ran through Deen's body.

MacCullough was dead. The same gleaming instrument that had slashed Deen's arm, missing his face by fractions of an inch, had torn the Scot's throat and head to bloody shreds. He lay now in a lake of his own blood, face down on the flagstones, his head nearly severed from its thick neck.

Deen swayed above him, felt his own temples pounding. His face turned ghastly white as sickness choked him. He heard words from Byron Little's lips, meaningless, incoherent words that seemed strangely out of place in this spot.

Once again, from a great distance, came a shrill peal of madman's mirth, eating its way faintly through the gray winding-sheet that covered Alden Goyette's island of death.

Deen stood up, said dully, heavily to the man beside him, "The fiend who did this was Degnan. Joseph Degnan. I saw his face, and it was the face of a maniac. Give me—a hand I'm—hurt."

CHAPTER THREE

Woman Gone Mad

THE group of haggard, gaunt-faced men sat like robots in Alden Goyette's parlor.

"The man was mad," Byron Little told them. "He murdered MacCullough and escaped. He's at large somewhere on this island—a prowling maniac seeking blood. He will surely strike again unless we strike first."

Silence followed the ex-warden's statement, tense, fear-laden silence. Then one of the men leaned forward, stared with bulging brown eyes. The man was Lazarus Lees, small, effeminate, with a round white soap-bubble of a face.

"I—I can't help thinking, Little." He hesitated; was trembling all over, licking his lips with a small, pointed tongue. "My God, do you suppose this horrible business isn't—isn't natural? We've all sinned against society. All of us—except you, of course. It was a long time ago—but this is the first time we've all been together since then. Do you suppose—"

Deen suppressed a shudder at the man's sincerity. Lazarus Lees meant what he was saying; the man had taken his religion seriously since his exodus from prison. He was the sort who climbed soap-boxes and raved to assembled strangers about the sins he had committed, telling them how he had seen the light and how

they too might find the path to peace . . .

"I—I'm not superstitious," Lees moaned. "It isn't that. But two of us have gone mad. *Mad!* And there was no *reason* for it, unless some mysterious outside force—"

"For God's sake, stop it!" Anthony Hall lunged up, faced the little man vehemently. But he stopped abruptly. "I —I'm sorry, Lees," he mumbled. "Upset, I guess." He slumped down again.

Orville Bishop said dully: "We've got to find Degnan, of course. But suppose this horrible curse strikes more of us? Suppose we *all* go mad! Suppose you—" he stared at Little— "and Deen and the rest of us should suddenly be obsessed with this awful desire to commit atrocities?"

Deen walked stiffly to the door, turned. "This is getting us nowhere. Degnan is out there, planning more murder."

"You're forgetting the women, Deen." Byron Little peered at him with strange calm. "Before we go after Degnan, the women must be protected."

"Well?"

"They must be locked in an upstairs room where they'll be safe. I'll stay in the house, to be sure. The rest of you can go out, search the island."

Deen narrowed his eyes, hesitated. Was there a taint of triumph of sinister meaning in Little's even-toned words? Had that hellish germ of madness found its way into his mind and begun to fester there?

Concealing his suspicions, he nodded wearily. "All right. Whatever you think best." He paced into the corridor, shoved a hand against the revolver in his pocket as he pushed open the front door. Behind him, in the passage, lay the slashed, bloody body of Lyon MacCullough, stretched out on the floor where he and Little had laid it . . . mute, horrible evidence of the strength and cunning of the mad killer who was somewhere out there in a dank terrain of fog.

On the veranda Deen waited for the others, saw when they came that they were all armed. He gave quiet instructions, stood and watched the gaunt-faced men as they separated and were gulped up in gray vapor. Voices, footsteps, were audible in the fog for a while; then silence settled down again, a thousand times more evil, more suggestive.

Men—man-hunters—out there in an unreal world of darkness, seeking to kill or capture a mad fiend who had once been their companion. Slowly, Deen descended the steps, prowled along the side of the house. Above him, lights glowed dully from upstairs windows. Behind one of those haloed oblongs would be three terrified women, cringing in fear in a locked room, where Byron Little had led them. And Little himself would be somewhere in those dimly-lighted passages, pacing relentlessly back and forth, on guard for sounds of intrusion. *Perhaps.*

Deen paced slowly toward the rear of the house, watching, listening. There was a rear entrance. Through it he could gain silent admission, keep check unobserved on Little's actions. Perhaps his suspicions were unfounded, but—

He stiffened, stared ahead into the fog and stepped abruptly backward. He flattened against the wall and hung there motionless. In that murky gray blanket something had moved. Now a ghost-shape, blurred by its winding sheet of swirling vapor, glided slowly out of darkness and approached across the wide lawn of Alden Goyett's house.

Deen watched, clenched his fists and bent forward from the waist, staring holes in the gloom.

THE shape came closer, took form. Sucked-in breath whistled against Deen's teeth. He recognized the twisted, evil features of Joseph Degnan, saw in those features the same unholy madness that had urged Degnan to slaughter Lyon MacCullough. A step at a time the man approached, mad eyes focused hungrily on the upstairs windows of the house.

One of those windows was open. Only a human fly could hope to scale the niched wall beneath and reach the aperture; yet Degnan advanced, arms curled, thick body hunched forward. His bloated tongue was out, licking his lips. His hair was a wet mop, stringing down.

Deen waited, slid a silent hand into his pocket and brought out the gun that lay there. Less than ten paces separated him from the advancing killer. In a moment Degnan would surely see him, despite the fog, despite the gloom of the niche that sheltered him. Then . . . .

Deen leveled his gun, took careful aim. At that range he could not miss; his curling trigger finger would send screaming lead into the fiend's legs, crippling him. Then the horror would be over and—

From the upstairs window came a sound that made Vance Deen forget his caution. Weirdly, shrilly, the sound sliced its way through fog and dark, stabbing the night with knifelike sharpness. Up there, a woman was screaming; the scream was a throat-tearing blast that endured for a dozen hellish seconds, then broke, became a hoarse voice pleading, sobbing.

Deen lunged forward, forgot the creeping shape before him. The shape whirled, stood on bent legs and rocked backward, facing him. From above came dull sounds of heavy bodies thrashing about, of furniture thudding, and again that vibrant shriek of mortal terror from the lips of a woman in agony.

Vance Deen jerked backward. He would have ignored the madman confronting him and raced blindly to the rear door of the house, rushed upstairs into the room where the horror was being enacted. But he had no chance.

With a hoarse snarl, Degnan hurtled toward him, arms outflung to drag him down. As if catapulted from a sling, the man's bent body whipped through space, aimed straight at its human target.

Deen lunged aside, snapped up his gun hand and squeezed the trigger. He had barely time for one shot. The slug sped six inches from the gun-muzzle and buried itself in Degnan's twisted bulk. Then, hurled backward, Deen staggered, tripped, went down with a wounded, snarling, clawing madman on top of him.

Like a h u n g e r - m a d cat, Degnan swarmed over him, fought with such terrible intensity that Deen found no opening for defense. The man employed feet, arms, teeth; his curled fingers were everywhere at once, gouging flesh, tearing Deen's clothes. Half naked, bloody in a score of places and sobbing for breath, Deen finally rolled over. He heaved himself up on pistoning arms and legs and tossed his assailant off.

It was his turn to leap then, as Degnan rolled clear, snarling, fighting empty air. The man was drooling, frothing at the mouth. His eyes were half out of his head, his twisted body soaked with blood where the bullet had ploughed through.

Deen leaped, locked both hands in the man's throat, straddled that heaving body. He made a fist of one hand, drew back and rammed the fist savagely into the man's drooling maw of mouth. Then, rocking backward, he swayed on his knees, gazed down at spurting blood and broken teeth, felt the twitching shape beneath him go limp.

Sounds of conflict were still issuing from the open window above.

Deen swayed erect, sucked air to steady himself and bent again to scoop up his revolver. Then he ran, staggered his way crookedly along the wall, found the rear

doorway and smashed through a dark kitchen. Blindly he raced up a flight of unlighted stairs to the upper level.

A door hung open ahead. Across the threshold, as Deen stumbled forward came a lithe, leaping figure, a girl's figure, laughing harshly and shrieking mad words that echoed and reechoed down the dim hall. She saw Deen, turned toward him with fantastic quickness and stopped shrieking, made low animal sounds in her throat. Then she saw the gun in his fist, backed away from him.

Whirling, she sped like a hunted deer down the hallway, vanished abruptly in deeper darkness, leaving Deen only a memory of her face. It was a face flecked with madness, smeared hideously with gleaming red blood! White-rimmed eyes bulged out of their sockets, red lips were drawn back to expose a red mouth, and reddened teeth!

That face, the last time Deen had looked into it, had been young, somewhat pretty and timidly charming. It had belonged to Lyon MacCullough's daughter, Maribel. . . .

D EEN stumbled forward, reached the open doorway and stood staring. The sight that met his wide eyes sent a roll of horror through him, shook his lean body from head to feet. He mumbled, released his grip on the door-frame and went in, went toward a shape that lay still and limp on a bed near the wall.

From the floor at the foot of the bed came a dull groaning, and the sound of a heavy body laboring to rise. Deen stopped, gaped down. The man on the floor was Ex-Warden Little.

The room itself was a shambles, a chamber of horrors. Table and chairs were shattered, upended; the glass on a dresser was splintered. Sheets on the bed were tangled, half trailing the floor, half covering a thing that lay with its head

buried in a gap between two bloody pil-
lows. In a corner, across the broken legs
of a chair, lay Ruth Little, head lolling,
hair dangling floorward, wide eyes gazing
sightlessly at the ceiling.

Deen lurched forward, certain that the
girl was dead. He suppressed the sob that
welled in his throat. Then he fumbled
with large green buttons, ran a trembling
hand inside the limp neck of her dress
and knew that he was mistaken. His fingers encountered warm soft flesh, probed
deeper into the gentle vale between satin-
smooth breasts, and were rewarded by a
throbbing from the heart beneath.

He straightened, eased the girl to the
floor and turned again toward the bed.
At the foot of it, Byron Little was on
hands and knees, choking, swaying, in
danger of falling again. Deen gripped
the man's armpits, hauled him erect and
helped him backward into a chair. Something sharp, jagged, had ripped Little's
face from eye to throat, down one cheek.
Blood ran sluggishly from the gash, formed a scarlet river down the man's neck and
into the ripped front of his shirt.

Little opened his eyes, stared at Deen
and said thickly: "My—my wife. My
daughter. Are they—"

"They're all right." Deen glanced at
the thing on the bed. "All right. What
happened?"

"I—don't know. I heard my wife
scream. I rushed in here, and that—that
girl attacked me."

Deen said, "Take it easy," and walked
to the bed, looked down at Byron Little's
wife. He swallowed hard, downed the
horror that surged up inside him. He had
lied, of course. The woman on the bed
was dead, terribly dead.

She had been an attractive woman,
younger by far in appearance than in fact.
She lay there now in a shredded tangle
of her own clothes, bloody bed-sheets cov-

ering only a small portion of her body.
The rest was naked, or so nearly naked
that the remaining shreds offered no
protection.

And something had made a ragged hell
of her shapely body. Gaping gashes ran
from her lolling breasts into the gentle
slope of her abdomen, vanished there
under a fold of torn garment. The woman's thighs, full-formed and rounded,
were punctured in a dozen places, as if
stabbed with a short, wide-bladed knife,
stabbed deeply and then slashed.

Deen stepped back, thought of the madness he had seen in the face of Maribel
MacCullough. He knew, without asking, who was responsible for the atrocities
inflicted upon the pitiful creature on the
bed. Dully, he reconstructed the horror.

The mad girl had fallen upon Little's
wife, hurling aside the woman's husband
and daughter who sought to intervene.
Then, free from restraint, the murderess
had played with her victim, played with
her terribly, hideously, as a cat might
have played with some screaming, helpless
rodent, seeking new ways of inflicting
agony. Deen stared again and closed his
eyes, shuddering. Only a woman could
have devised such savage ways of tortur-
ing another of her kind. No man would
have known such evil methods. . . .

He walked away, stumbling. Downstairs in the house, men's voices were audible, and footsteps. A moment later
Anthony Hall and Orville Bishop came
along the upstairs corridor, staring and
mumbling questions.

The questions were unanswered. Fearfully, the two men entered the room, staring about them as if sensing the horror
they would find. Deen said to them dully: "Help me get Ruth and her father
out of here. And be on guard. Somewhere in this house there's a woman gone
mad, waiting for another chance."

CHAPTER FOUR

Poison Pellets

BISHOP and Hall moved like robots, both of them white-faced and staring, as if afraid even to lift their feet from the floor. Obeying Deen's command, they went to Byron Little, helped the man to his feet and aided him to the door. Deen lifted the girl in his arms and followed.

He led the way then, strode down the corridor to the staircase that led below. Behind him, Hall and Bishop stumbled awkwardly, supporting the almost dead weight of the ex-warden between them. Little's feet dragged on the floor, made skidding, scratching sounds. The man was barely conscious, his bloody face a red gargoyle, his mouth screwed tight, stifling the agony that racked him.

A strange, slow procession. . . . And behind Bishop and Hall as they timidly trailed Deen down the winding staircase, a slim, shadowed figure glided from the darkness of a half-open doorway and followed.

On noiseless feet the shadowed form closed the gap, reached the head of the staircase before the slow procession had descended even to the half-way mark. Neither Bishop nor Hall looked back; had they done so, they would have gaped into a face evil with savage hunger, a nineteen-year-old face that once had been pretty but now was a leering mask of madness, made doubly hideous by the crimson smear of fresh blood that reddened those curled lips.

But they did not look back. Below them, Vance Deen was groping down the last few steps, carrying Ruth Little in his arms. Above, the pantherish form of the mad woman suddenly leaned forward, lunged into space. Something gleamed dully in the girl's outflung hand as she launched herself furiously upon the bent back of Anthony Hall.

Hall had no chance. With the fury of a leaping tigress, the girl fell upon her prey, landed squarely on Hall's back and buried her gleaming weapon in the flesh of his neck. The savage impact hurled him forward, rammed Bishop and Byron Little down the staircase.

Again and again the girl struck, driving home the murderous thing in her fist, swarming over the fallen body of her victim and smothering his convulsive movements. She clawed at him with hooked fingers, buried her teeth in bloody flesh. Hall's scream was a wail of torment, so violent, so vibrant that it endured only an instant, then became a hoarse, bubbling effort for breath.

Bishop and Little could not go to his aid; both were tangled in a heap at the bend of the staircase, flung there by the girl's onslaught. Vance Deen spun around. Leaving the unconscious girl at the foot of the stairs, he heaved himself up again, pawed the bannister as he lunged forward.

Maribel MacCullough saw him coming. Like an animal guarding its kill, she rocked backward, bared her teeth. Her curled fingers still gripped the weapon that had drunk deep of Hall's life-blood. She launched herself anew, hurled her slender body furiously upon Deen's ascending form.

Deen met the charge by bending under it, thrusting out a stiff shoulder. His arm and shoulder caught the girl's stomach, sent her whirling above him and crashed her against the wall. Grimly he leaped, whipped sideways to avoid the gleaming weapon that struck at him; his stabbing hand caught the flailing wrist and wrenched it. The weapon fell from agonized fingers.

But Lyon MacCullough's daughter was not done. Madness gave her the strength of a wounded jungle cat, transformed her into a scratching, clawing mistress of hell. Animal sounds burst from her writhing lips, chilled the blood in Deen's heart. Furiously the girl sought to break loose, used teeth, arms and feet as she fought for freedom.

Her own efforts ripped the thin dress that covered her squirming body, bared the whiteness of her flesh under Deen's relentless embrace. That flesh was hot, slippery; his clutching fingers dug deep, left red welts on the girl's heaving breasts. With an effort to protect his face and eyes from the stabbing fingers that raked him, Deen stooped low, thrust an arm between the girl's twisted legs and swung her from the floor.

Warm flesh slipped in his grip; his fingers dug deep into the girl's hard thighs, clung there. Savagely she flung both arms around his neck, clawed his hair, sought to fasten her teeth in his throat.

He stumbled backward, crashed into the wall. His mouth made words against the unwelcome pressure of her bare body: "You asked for it!" His knotted fist whipped up, made driving contact with the girl's jaw. She exhaled explosively and went limp in his embrace.

BELOW, on the staircase, Orville Bishop was on hands and knees, staring; Byron Little, unconscious again from his fall, lay limp against the wall.

Deen looked down at the girl in his arms, made an attempt to cover her partial nakedness. Slowly he descended, carried her along the lower corridor into the parlor, and dumped her in a straight-backed chair.

Unsteady on his feet, he stared around for something to tie her with, found nothing and, with a shrug, ripped the girl's own dress and twisted the cloth into ropes. When he had finished, she was bound

hand and foot, lashed securely to the chair that supported her.

Then, silently, Deen returned along the corridor, found Bishop struggling to shake Ex-Warden Little back to consciousness.

Deen said, "He's been through hell. Leave him alone," and gathered Ruth Little in his arms. He carried her into the small book-lined study at the end of the hall and turned on more lights. Striding back again, he climbed to the bend in the staircase, looked long at the contorted body of Anthony Hall, and backed slowly away from it. Near Hall's dead body lay the weapon that had murdered him: a pair of sharp-pointed, short-bladed manicure scissors, keen enough and slender enough to stab through even leather.

Deen picked them up, dropped them in his pocket without wiping the blood from them. Mumbling to Bishop, he hooked an arm under Byron Little's legs; he and Bishop carried the unconscious man into the study.

Then Deen slumped wearily into a chair. "There's nothing we can do, yet," he said dully. "Degnan is dead outside; Hall is dead. When the others come back, we'll get to the bottom of this." He pushed stiff fingers through his disheveled hair, wiped his face and neck with a cupped hand and stared at the blood that came away on his palm. "We'll get to the bottom, if someone else doesn't go mad first."

Bishop said in a whining voice: "Mother of God, I want to get away from this awful island, before I go mad!"

"You'll have to swim."

"But there must be some way! We could telephone or—"

"There's no 'phone," Deen growled, "and even if you could get word to the mainland, they wouldn't send out a boat. Not in this fog."

"But we can't stay here!" Bishop's wail

approached a shriek. "Three of us gone mad already! There's no telling who'll be next! It might be you, might be me!"

"It might be!"

"My God, Lees was right. Some horrible curse—"

Deen said curtly: "Shut up, will you?" He stood erect, walked to where Ruth Little lay on a red-leather divan. The girl was moaning, twitching with returning consciousness. He sat beside her and stroked the hair back from her high forehead, murmured in a low voice, "Easy, darling. Everything's all right."

She opened her eyes, looked at him and put trembling fingers on his arm. "Vance. Oh, God, that girl—"

"Easy. Tell me about it later."

She shuddered, rolled her head and stared around, then tried to sit up. "My mother—is she—"

"She's upstairs." He tried hard to sound convincing. "Asleep."

"And dad?"

He pointed. "He's asleep, too. He'll be all right."

"Oh, God, Vance! That awful creature—"

"What happened, Ruth?"

"I—I don't know. We were all together in the room and we talked for a while and then just sat around, waiting. And then—then Maribel got up without saying anything and went to the dressing-table and began picking things up and putting them down again. And—"

"And?"

"I—it was getting on my nerves, so I asked her to please sit down. And then she turned around and laughed. Oh, her face was awful, Vance! She had a pair of scissors in her hand and she just stood there, glaring at us and laughing like—like a mad thing. Then she hurled herself straight at mother and I tried to stop her. I—I don't know what happened then."

"What made her go mad?" Deen asked quietly.

"Oh, God, I don't know!"

"Something she ate, or drank?"

"No. Yes—yes, she did. But—"

"What was it?"

"But it couldn't have been that, Vance!" The girl's eyes were wide, her fingers clinging tightly to Deen's arm. "It was only just a sip of whisky. Mother gave it to her to steady her nerves, just after dad made us go into the room. Mother had a small flask; she always carries it. She—she doesn't think I know, and she doesn't want me to, because she's afraid I'll drink, too. But I've seen it often and—"

DEEN interrupted softly: "She gave Maribel some whisky?"

"Yes. Just—just a sip, when I was in the bathroom. She didn't want me to see."

Deen stiffened, said slowly: "She didn't want you to see." It was not a question; it was a spoken thought, tensing the muscles of his body. Again, almost inaudibly, he mouthed the words. *"She didn't want you to see."*

"Why, what do you mean?"

Voices in the corridor outside saved him the necessity of answering. He turned, peered at the doorway and said to Bishop: "You'd better go tell them where we are."

Bishop complied, and a moment later the members of the searching party came sluggishly into the room: weary, fog-drenched figures, gaunt-faced, haggard pilgrims from the gray ghost-world outside. Deen said quietly: "After Bishop has told you what happened, we'll get to the bottom of this, right here and now, before anyone else feels the urge to spill blood."

Bishop talked; the others listened, grew whiter and more haggard with each hystesical word. When it was over, Deen interrupted coldly: "Now, listen. In spite of Lees' superstition, the answer is this: Something in this damned house has the power to bring on madness; it's not an ethereal something, it's tangible." He turned his gaze on Goyette, stared holes in the man. "You own the place, Goyette. You arranged this little horror party. What is it?"

"I—I don't know. My God, I swear I don't know!"

"You knew enough to put blanks in the gun you gave to Little."

"No!" Goyette recoiled, gaped. "The gun was loaded!"

"With—blanks?" The question was a hoarse whisper.

"You know damned well."

"I—I didn't know. I swear to you, I didn't know!"

"All right," Deen said. "No one can prove anything, and blank cartridges don't drive people mad. What does?"

There was no answer. Paul, the butler, moved quietly to the door, said mechanically, "If I may be excused, I'll bring liquor. It is good for the nerves." He went out. The room was still silent, still tense as a smoldering volcano when he returned. Methodically he poured drinks, passed them around.

Deen sniffed the whisky, wet his lips with it and left it alone. He heard a coughing sound, turned and looked at Byron Little; the ex-warden was sitting up, shaking his head to clear it. Paul, the butler, refilled empty glasses and went the rounds a third time.

Near the doorway, Lazarus Lees shifted on uneasy feet, put an empty glass on an end-table and jabbed a hand into his coat pocket, hauling out a damp handkerchief. Something came with the handkerchief, dropped soundlessly to the thick carpet and rolled a few inches, came to rest behind a leg of the end-table. Deen

stared. Orville Bishop stared, too. No one else had seen. Lees used the handkerchief to mop a perspiring forehead, then stuffed it back again.

Deen stood up, paced slowly to the end-table and took a cigarette from an open box that lay there. He dropped the cigarette, stooped, picked it up and scooped up the other object with it. The object was a round metal box, thin and light and shaped like a pill-box. Holding it in a cupped hand while he put a match to the cigarette, Deen studied it, saw the word ASPIRIN stamped on the metal cover.

A moment later he walked unnoticed to a corner of the room, opened the box and dumped its contents into his hand. A dozen or more brown pellets, not aspirin tablets, rolled in his palm.

He shoved box and pellets into his pocket, glanced sideways at Lees. He saw that Lees suspected nothing, paced slowly toward the little man.

Halfway there something he glimpsed out of the corner of his eye caused him to stop short, jerk about and stare at Orville Bishop.

Bishop was standing stiff, rigid, in the center of the room. The man's face had gone white; his eyes were bulging with terror, his cheeks sucked in around thin bones. A shudder shook him, beginning at his feet and leaving no part of his plump body untouched.

He put a palsied hand to his throat, caught flabby flesh in his fingers. A hoarse outcry began deep in his fat neck, found its way upward and tocsined shrilly, wailingly from his gaping mouth.

Then, while the others stared in amazement, Bishop reeled backward, became a writhing, quivering madman, fighting something within him. Incoherent words bubbled from his lips, spewed out to fill the room.

"Hold me! My God, don't let me get like the others! I can feel it inside me!"

He whirled, lurched toward Lees and jabbed out a rigid arm, pointing into Lees' terrified face. "It was him! *Him!* He took something out of a little tin box and put it in his whisky, then changed glasses! I saw him! By God, I'll—"

Deen shot forward, leaped in front of Lees as Bishop lunged. The man was insane; raving madness filled his wide eyes, saliva drooled from his gaping mouth. He thrust out both hands to claw Deen aside.

Deen's fist arched back, forward again, crashed against the man's jaw. With a dull groan, Bishop stopped, swayed drunkenly and slumped to the floor, unconscious.

CHAPTER FIVE

A Woman's Scream

DEEN picked the man up, carried him to a chair and dumped him onto it. His fat body was still twitching. Deen peered down at him, said nothing. The others crowded around and stared.

Then Deen turned grimly, glared at the chair where Lazarus Lees had been sitting. The chair was empty. The door leading to the corridor was ajar; from the front of the house came the thud of another door banging shut.

"After him!" Alden Goyette croaked. "If he gets out in that fog, we'll never find him!"

Deen stayed where he was; the others surged past, choked the doorway. Bloodhounds, hungry for their escaping prey. Deen shrugged, listened to the pounding of heavy feet in the corridor and waited quietly, stiffly, until the rattle of diminishing voices had died away. Then he faced about and saw that Orville Bishop was regaining consciousness.

Ruth Little and her father had remained behind. Deen said to the girl:

"If you feel strong enough, help me tie this man up before he comes to."

Stripping the man's shirt, he made ropes of it. With Ruth's help, he dashed Bishop to the chair. He ran probing hands through the man's pockets, brought out cigarettes, billfold, a crumpled envelope, and tossed them on the table. When he had finished, he glanced at Byron Little and put a hand on the girl's arm. His voice was low, full of deadly sincerity.

"Listen, Ruth. Maybe this whole mess will be over when they catch Lees; maybe it won't. Take this." He put a revolver in the girl's hand. "I—I can't bear the thought of turning into the kind of beast these others have become. If you need this, use it. God knows who'll be next to go mad; it may be your father, maybe me. No matter *who* it is, use this to protect yourself."

Ruth took the gun silently. Deen walked to the door, stopping on the way to take from the table the envelope that had come from Bishop's pocket. It was addressed to Bishop from Alden Goyette. He pocketed it. He looked back to find Ex-Warden Little staring at him.

"Better lock this door after I'm gone," Deen said. "I'll be back as soon as Lees is caught."

He closed the door after him, strode down the corridor and stopped under a bracket lamp to look at the letter. Reading its scribbled contents, he stuffed it back again, scowled. He walked across the wide front veranda into a winding-sheet of gray fog that closed tenaciously about him, smothering him even before he had descended the veranda steps.

He stood listening then, but no sounds came out of the gloom. The fog hung milk-thick about him, clung to him as he walked the flagstone path. Somewhere out in that world of dampness, prowling ghost-shapes were frantically stalking the man who had seemingly brought horror upon them all.

Deen reached the pier, stopped there and realized that it might take him an eternity to find the man he sought. The island's shore line was a snake-track of steep cliffs and thick swamp, sinister with surf, evil with man-deep pits of salt-marsh. It possessed a thousand places for a hunted man to hide, to vanish.

Slowly, Deen followed the shore, listened to the incessant throb of savage water and heard the suck of his own feet in wet sand as he picked a cautious path away from the big house behind him. The house was already gone, gulped up in dense vapor; a strange sensation of loneliness, isolation, crept into Deen's heart, chilling him.

Moments passed before he heard voices, heavy footsteps. He stood tense, waiting. Gaunt shapes moved out of the fog and came toward him, grew larger and more distinct as they drew nearer. Two men—one of them dragging the other, and the dragged man whimpering, pleading with every forced step.

Deen called out, moved forward. Wide-eyed, he stared into the fog-drenched face of Paul, the butler, then shifted his gaze to the cringing shape in the butler's relentless grip. The captured man glared at him with blood-shot eyes, made a feeble effort to free himself.

"I didn't do it!" he cried. "God help me, I didn't put anything in Bishop's drink! Oh, God, believe me!"

"What's the use of lying, Lees?" Deen said.

"I'm not lying! Mother of God, I'm not responsible for all this horror! I—"

"Why did you run away?"

"I was 'fraid! You'd have killed me, all of you!"

Deen glanced at the scowling face of the butler, saw cold triumph stenciled there. He shoved a hand into his pocket,

brought out a small metal box and brown pellets that went with it. "You ever see these before, Lees?"

Lees gasped. "Yes, yes, they're mine! But they're not harmful. I didn't use them on anyone else!"

"What are they?"

"They—they're for indigestion. I have to take them because—"

Deen failed to hear the rest of it. Faintly through the fog had come a sound that stabbed into him, sapped the blood from his face: a sound so high, so tenuous, that distance could not stifle it.

Like the wail of a tortured cat it pierced the grim gray winding-sheet that concealed its source. But Vance Deen knew the source. The sound was a woman's scream of terror, and there was only one woman left conscious on Alden Goyette's island of hell. The woman he loved!

HE LUNGED about, raced blindly back the way he had come, leaving Lazarus Lees in the grip of the man who had captured him. Sucking damp vapor into his lungs, he ploughed through fog and darkness, growled a curse when he stumbled, prayed to a merciful God that he would reach the horror-house in time.

He had been away from the house more than ten minutes. It took him less than three to retrace the route, to charge up the flagstone path and heave his big body up the veranda steps. Twice during those hellish three minutes the scream had been repeated; now, as he lunged along the corridor toward the room where he had left Ruth Little, the huge house was silent as a tomb.

The room was empty. Choking back the fear within him, Deen rushed again into the corridor, stood swaying on the balls of his feet, groaning. The girl was gone. So, too, were Ex-Warden Little and the madman who had been bound there.

Gone *where?*

Deen lurched forward, strode down the corridor toward the rear of the house. A sound stabbed him, dragged him to an abrupt stop. For an instant the sound seemed to come from all directions, from walls, floor, ceiling; then he placed it, dropped on hands and knees and listened fearfully.

A low peal of laughter, vibrant with evil, penetrated the floor beneath him, tightened the cords of his throat with its hellish significance. He heaved himself erect again, ran headlong. The sound had come from the cellar, somewhere down in the black bowels of the building. There must be a stairway leading down from the kitchen.

He found it, jarred the door open and took the first stairs two at a time; then, realizing the necessity for caution, he caught himself. Toeing softly, he reached the concrete floor and stared ahead through darkness. At the far end of the room a thin streak of light stabbed under a closed door and mottled the floor.

Behind that door a low voice was speaking guttural words, words that echoed hollowly into the chamber where Deen snaked forward.

He stared around, shuddered. The cellar was a boundless expanse of blackness, filled with gargantuan shapes that mocked him with their bigness. A huge furnace loomed within reach; he groped toward it, pawed with his hands and found an iron poker. Gripping the bludgeon in both hands, he advanced toward the inner door, cursing himself for having handed his gun to Ruth Little.

Again that guttural voice was audible behind the barrier, sending forth throaty chuckling words that needled Deen's spine.

He put a hand on the door-latch, raised it slowly. With infinite caution he inched the door open, until the aperture was wide enough to admit his body. Then, rigid on the threshold, he stood staring.

The room was a game-room, warmly furnished, walled with antique wood. Twin lights, dangling above the green lawn of a billiard table, sprayed their glare over what lay there, and what stood there. Only for an instant did Deen shift his gaze to a third figure that lay sprawled in a corner; then, eyes narrowed, lips curled against clenched teeth, he crept forward.

The monster had not yet seen him, was unaware of his presence. Stripped to the waist, the man was hunched over the billiard table, over the inert form that lay there. Sweat gleamed on the naked torso; drenched hair hung in a sodden mop over the man's lowered face; but enough of that animal countenance was visible for Deen to label it.

The madman who leaned there above the thing on the table was Alden Goyette.

AND Goyette *was* mad, as mad as the others of the doomed group had been before him. Worms of hunger crawled in his bulging eyes; his bony chest swelled and deflated as if worked by a bellows. Sucking sounds emanated from his moving lips; he was mumbling to himself, chuckling, making so much noise that he failed to hear the whisper of Deen's approaching feet.

Then, as Deen reached the halfway mark, Goyette bent even farther forward, scooped up a billiard cue that lay across the end of the table. His big hands closed over it, snapped it in two; he tossed one piece aside, fingered the splintered end of the other and laughed with a vileness that spiked Deen's heart. Then, gloatingly, the madman ran exploring fingers over the girl who lay before him.

The girl was Ruth Little. Whether she was dead or unconscious, Vance Deen could not be sure. Every inch of her clothing had been removed and thrown to the floor. She lay face up, one arm draped limply across her stomach. Light from the twin lamps above, playing over her nude form, whitened the gentle curve of her throat, the soft, flawless mounds of her breasts.

Goyette's eager fingers, traveling slowly, searchingly over that nude body, missed nothing, lingered longingly on breasts and throat, probed every shadowed secret.

Vance Deen, creeping slowly forward, raised the iron poker in both hands and suppressed the snarl of fury that threatened to burst his lips. Another dozen steps and—

Goyette had stopped pawing. The man's face tightened, filled with bloodlust; his mouth curled into an ugly gash full of guttural noises. He hunched his big shoulders forward, clamped both hands on the butt end of the broken cue. Deliberately he poised the jagged end of his murder-weapon above the soft slope of the girl's abdomen.

One savage downward thrust of his corded arms, and the jagged stick would have impaled its target. But Vance Deen moved first.

With a bull-like roar that filled the whole room, Deen covered the last few yards in a headlong rush. Goyette, lunging on stiff legs, spun to face him, leaped sideways like a giant ape to avoid the iron poker. Savagely, Goyette stabbed out with the broken sword-stick.

The stick missed its mark. So, too, did the descending poker in Deen's fists. Next moment the two men were locked in savage, snarling combat, reelingly drunkenly away from the table that supported Ruth Little's stripped body.

Madness had endowed Alden Goyette's gangling body with superhuman strength. He wrenched himself free, stabbed a hand into his trousers pocket and jerked the hand loose again with his fingers curled around a gun—the same gun that Vance

Deen had given to the girl on the table.

Deen sucked breath, dove under the swinging weapon and buried his head deep in the man's stomach. His fist shot out, opened, clamped over the gun wrist and heaved it sideways. Savagely, while Goyette grunted for breath, he straightened inside the big man's embrace, drove his head with pile-driver force against the man's chin. Bones broke; Goyette spat teeth and blood, crumpled. His head slapped the concrete floor.

Deen rocked backward, leaned against the wall and stared down. The madman lay still.

CHAPTER SIX

The Man Who Was Sane

MINUTES passed before Deen moved again. Then he groped toward the billiard table, steered an unsteady course toward the nude form that lay there. He stared into the girl's face, felt warmth and relief surging through him at the touch of her hot breath as he bent above her. The girl's body was unmarked, untouched. She had fainted, was beginning now to moan her way back to consciousness.

Deen stooped, gathered her discarded clothing off the floor and covered her nakedness. He walked to the slumped form of Byron Little and shook the man until signs of life rewarded his efforts. Then he propped Little against the wall, stared at him and said: "Snap out of it. I want to know what happened."

Little gaped at him, fought to regain strength. "I—I can't remember everything—"

Impatiently Deen waited. Little sucked breath, groaned, said finally: "Ruth and I were waiting in the room where you left us. We heard footsteps in the hall, and Ruth went out to see who was coming. I—I heard a scuffle. Before I could reach her, Goyette had overpowered her and taken the gun away from her. Then—he pointed the gun at me."

"And brought you down here?"

"He ordered both of us to walk ahead of him, and made us come here. I tried to—to find a way to turn the tables, but he gave me no chance." Little glared at the battered shape on the floor and clenched his fists savagely. "As soon as we were down here, he turned on me like a wild man and clubbed me with the gun. That—that's all I know."

"You left Bishop in the study?" Deen asked.

"Yes."

"You sure?"

"Yes, yes. He was tied to the chair."

A worried expression crossed Deen's face. He said stiffly: "All right. Are you strong enough to—"

He stopped abruptly. From the doorway behind him a low, purring voice had interrupted him. "Yes, the good warden left Bishop in the study."

Deen turned slowly, so slowly that his feet barely moved on the floor. The doorway was filled with a large, big-boned shape, a shape that was topped by a leering gargoyle of a face. That face was not mad; it was merely vicious, loaded with terrible triumph. And beneath it, in an outthrust hand, lay a leveled, menacing revolver.

Orville Bishop said softly: "You see, I intend to finish this in my own way."

Deen's face was white, bloodless; hope died within him and left him staring with lifeless eyes. He found words, but the words died in his throat. Byron Little, standing rigid as wood, glared at the gun and licked dry lips.

Bishop came slowly forward, stopped at a safe distance. "Most likely," he said, "you know the whole truth by this time. If not, it will be a pleasure to inform you." He grinned, curled his leering mouth into a half-moon. "The entire affair was my idea; it was I who suggested it to Goyette." He raised eyebrows at Deen. "You probably know that, after reading the note you took from my pocket while I was feinging madness."

"I know enough," Deen growled, "to hang you!"

"But I don't intend to hang." Bishop's grin faded, became a savage snarl as he leveled his gaze at Byron Little. "For years I've been waiting for a chance like this. It was Little who kept me behind bars for eight long years. Eight years! The best years of my life he took away from me! And I swore to Almighty God that I'd have revenge. I swore I'd make Byron Little suffer and make all his loved ones suffer as I did, and worse!"

Savage fury filled Bishop's face as he came a step closer, aiming his gun at Little's tense body. "And I had another good reason for bringing these men together. They're all worth money—*money!*—the thing I never had a chance to earn. They're all insured—in a fraternal organization that *I* induced them to join! Who controls that insurance? *I do!* I can make their money mine, all of it, and no one will suspect me or even think that I'm concerned with it!"

HE LICKED his lips, leered hungrily. Then his anger fadded, he grinned again. "You want to know how I drove men mad, don't you? Well, then, I did it with a drug, a gentle little drug that I manufactured myself—a blend of lycoctonum and a corrosive sublimate of my own making. It wouldn't have killed them; it merely turned them into bloody beasts and made them kill one another! Yes, it is a very lovely drug. It works only for a short while, but that was quite long enough for my purpose."

"How did you give it?" Deen demanded, playing for time.

Bishop's voice was a chanting sing-song

as he answered, "You can wonder about that in hell." He stroked the gun with affectionate fingers, raised it an inch higher and stared at Deen over the top of it. "I thought my drug would do this job for me, but somehow things didn't go as smoothly as I'd hoped. Now—"

His finger curled in the trigger-guard. Deen, facing annihilation, staked everything on a desperate chance. He forced a slow smile to his lips, shrugged his shoulders and said quietly: "The joke's on you, Bishop. That particular gun is loaded with your own blank cartridges."

Bishop stiffened, turned pale. His hands tightened on the revolver; he looked down at it.

Next moment Deen's knotted fist had sent him staggering backward, slammed him against the wall. Before the man could straighten, regain his balance, Deen was at his throat.

Bishop struggled fiercely. His big hands raked Deen's face, tore flesh, ripped clothing; he made hideous sounds in his throat, growled like an animal deprived of its hard-won prey. But Deen for the moment was a fighting madman without mercy. He used his fists to make pulp of the man's face. He pounded him to the floor, and there clubbed him into a moaning, whimpering heap.

Even before Ex-Warden Little could come to Deen's assistance, the combat was finished. Deen backed away, picked up his own gun from the floor and covered Bishop with it.

"You're through, Bishop," he said.

The soul had gone out of Bishop's body. He stared with enormous eyes, made whispering sounds with his bloody lips. Then his eyes closed; he said mechanically, in a voice barely audible: "I——I'm through. I've failed."

"And somewhere in this house that damned drug of yours is hidden. Where is it?"

"I—I won't tell you." Bishop's refusal was a last grim defiance. "Find it yourself. If you find it accidentally, God help you!"

"Where is it?"

"Find it!"

Deen stood above the man's contorted body, stared down. "You're going back to see prison bars again, Bishop. Iron bars that stare back at you day and night, night and day, hemming you in, making a caged animal of you. For years and years those bars will be staring at you, until you go mad from looking at them. Iron bars—"

"God in heaven, stop it!"

"Iron bars, Bishop." Deen bit the words out. "Or else a long slow walk to a room where they strap you in a big chair and—"

Bishop's face became a writhing mask, choked with terror. He strained upward, clawed at Deen's legs.

"I'll tell you! I'll tell!"

"We're waiting."

"Let—let me have a cigarette and I'll tell you." With the words Bishops thrust a trembling hand into a pocket of his coat. But he found Deen's fingers clamped hard on his wrist when he tried to pull the hand out again. Deen pulled it for him, expecting to find a gun gripped in it. But the hand came out clutching a crumpled pack of cigarettes, nothing more.

Bishop stuck one in his mouth, took a light from the sputtering match that Deen thrust forward. He sucked hard, gulped the smoke, said in a whining voice: "I—I'll tell you. The drug was in powder form and I put it everywhere. It's in the drinking water and in some of the whisky and—and everywhere I could think of."

Smoke curled around his chalk-colored face, came in twin gray shafts from his nostrils as he mumbled the words. Blood had surged into his neck, reddened his throat. His whole body was twitching on the floor.

"You yourself—" He stared at Deen, spoke slowly, so slowly that moments passed while Deen waited— "You yourself almost took enough to make a raving madman of you, when you smoked one of the cigarettes in the study. You took the wrong cigarette out of the box. If you'd taken the one next to it—"

His voice rose to a piercing shriek. "If you'd taken one of these that I'm smoking now—one that contains a double amount of—"

With a mad lunge he leaped erect, hurled himself. Madness was in his eyes, in his screaming mouth. Madness gave him the strength of two men, drove him forward in a desperate effort to reach Deen's throat with his outflung hands.

Vance Deen had no time to use the gun. He dropped it, caught his assailant's lunging body in both arms and with a mighty sobbing effort heaved the man clear of the floor. In midair Bishop hung like a squirming rodent, screaming, wriggling, clawing blindly at the rigid arms that held him.

Then, with all the strength in his shoulders, Deen slammed the man down, hurled him to the concrete floor with such force that the room trembled to the impact, the billiard table jumped on its heavy legs.

Bishop groped to his hands and knees, swayed there, and collapsed with a bubbling groan, spitting life-blood. He did not move again.

DEEN stepped slowly backward. Ruth Little was sobbing. Byron Little looked down, wet his lips and broke the silence by saying heavily: "I have seen many men go to their deaths for crimes committed. This is the first time I have ever considered it a privilege to—to be a witness."

Deen said nothing. Silently he gathered Ruth Little in his arms and led the way out of the horror chamber, slowly climbed the stairs that led to the main portion of the house. In the front parlor, Lazarus Lees was sitting very still and stiff in an overstuffed chair; Paul, the butler, was leaning wearily against a table.

Paul gaped at Deen, said anxiously: "I hurried back here as quick as I could, but you were gone. The place was empty."

Deen nodded, knew that no sound from the torture chamber in the cellar had invaded this part of the huge house. He stood Ruth Little on her feet and put an arm around her, glanced down into her pale face.

To Byron Little he said quietly: "If you don't mind, Ruth and I would like to take a walk out there in the fog, where it's cold and — clean — and —" He shrugged. A slight pressure of the girl's hand, as he steered her to the door, told him that she understood.

Next Month—

ANOTHER SPINE-TINGLING HUGH B. CAVE NOVELETTE

Out August 24th!

THE BLACK CHAPEL

AND now that you have finished the first issue of TERROR TALES, we meet together in The Black Chapel to talk of the sinister things that were and the sinister things that will be. We trust that in these tales you have just read, terror has stalked beside you to thrill you and chill you. For in them you have glimpsed the dark and hidden things that move beneath the surface of seeming reality—and your blood has pounded more swiftly at what you saw.

Nor is it strange that you have wanted to look. Always, man has. The caveman trembled at the darkening sky and the thunder. He ran in terror from the weird and hideous beasts about him, shuddered at the myriad strange sights he saw and the sounds he heard! Yet always he groped to find the truth that lay behind them.

The men of the Mediterranean, more civilized, met to hold fantastic conclave over dark mysteries, and followed fiendish rites. In Medieval times, when life bubbled over the brim in its fullness, man did things that now seem unbelievable. In scores of dark chambers he bent above smoking crucibles wherein were brewed strange—some say devilish —mixtures. In hundreds of dungeons he watched his victims writhe in cunningly fashioned torture machines. And on a thousand desolate hilltops he wallowed in the wild orgies of the Witches' Sabbath.

Now, some of these things are gone

—though other things more fearful, perhaps, have come to take their place. For still man strives to pierce the dark unknown. And we, being human, would wish to know of it.

You have seen much in the first issue of TERROR TALES; in the issues that are to come you will see more. You will find tales of horror and fiendish devil's traffic, of lust and blood-hunger and dark thoughts that dwell in the bottom of men's minds. Men who know these things—men who are masters at the art of eerie tales—will bring you stories that will make your heart pound madly in your breast; that will root you helpless to your chair and send the cold fingers of dread to play along your spine.

We warn you that there is no weakling's fare in store for you. Can you stand it? If you can, we are prepared to welcome you each month as a true initiate into the dark and devious ceremonial of The Black Chapel!